KATHRYN NOLAN

Entangled Publishing, LLC
644 Shrewsbury Commons Ave., STE 181
Shrewsbury, PA 17361
rights@entangledpublishing.com

Amara is an imprint of Entangled Publishing, LLC.
Visit our website at www.entangledpublishing.com.

Edited by Lydia Sharp
Cover original illustration and design by Elizabeth Turner Stokes
Edge design by Elizabeth Turner Stokes
Edge image by ptgregus/Shutterstock
Interior design by Britt Marczak

Paperback ISBN 978-1-64937-849-1
Ebook ISBN 978-1-64937-817-0

Manufactured in the United States of America
First Edition July 2025
10 9 8 7 6 5 4 3 2 1

For all the Priscillas and Adelines that came before us. For every single name we'll never know. A tiny revolution, each and every one.

Thrill of the Chase is an exciting and adventurous sapphic romance with a happy ending. However, the story includes elements that might not be suitable for all readers. Parent death, family abandonment, homophobia, panic attacks, and severe anxiety are mentioned in character backstories. Perilous situations and physical injuries are shown on the page. Readers who may be sensitive to these elements, please take note.

Chapter One

Harper

Eleven days left to find the mysterious Monty Montana and write the article that will save my career, no pressure!

Barb's Pawn Shop sat in front of me like a squat brown toad. The lightbulbs circling the sign blinked an odd pattern in a kind of desperate Morse code. It was my sixth day on the road—or fifth…seventh? Truthfully, I was more fast-food wrappers than human being at this point.

And fully convinced the treasure hunter I'd been chasing was nothing more than a ghost story.

Twilight painted the foothills surrounding the city of Santa Fe a rosy indigo. Though that shimmering magic didn't extend to where I now stood, in the middle of a forlorn parking lot, surrounded by shops in various stages of disrepair. So I tilted my rental car's side mirror to check my lipstick one last time, fixing a minuscule smear. Tightened my bun, smoothed a stray wrinkle from my navy-blue trousers.

Then I gathered up what felt like the very last of my energy and strode inside.

Long, dusty rows of furniture and boxes stretched out in front of me. Two sets of cluttered staircases led to the second floor, and tiny handwritten signs dangled from the shelves. I followed the sounds of a TV, rounding a corner until I came upon a woman behind a waist-high counter, surrounded by pure chaos. A baseball hat sat atop her long, graying hair, and she wore a Hawaiian shirt in a color I could only describe as *hot tangerine*.

"Can I help you?" she asked, eyes glued to the flickering screen. Her voice was rough, her lined skin ruddy and sunburned around the elbows.

I offered up my friendliest smile. "My name is Harper Hendrix, and I'm trying to track down the whereabouts of a local treasure hunter. I was hoping you could point me in the right direction. You're Nadine, right? The owner here?"

She stiffened. Dragged her gaze to mine with a slow reluctance. "That's me. Don't know anything about a treasure hunter, though. This is a pawn shop. You got something you wanna offload? I'm your gal. That's about all I can tell you."

I stepped closer, laying a hand on the filmy countertop, and tapped my nails against the glass. "Do you know Loretta-Mae Montana? She usually goes by the nickname Monty."

Nadine shrugged and fixed her eyes back on the TV screen.

"So you *don't* know a treasure hunter named Monty Montana?"

Another shrug. "I don't know shit, lady. Now, do you have something to sell me or what?"

I tipped forward, just slightly. "That's strange, because I could have *sworn* you're the same Nadine that I've been talking to on the website X Marks the Spot."

She frowned, turning. "Couldn't say. Though I *can* say that this conversation is starting to get creepy. Are you stalkin' me or something?"

"Nothing untoward, I assure you," I said cheerfully. "In your public bio on the site, this pawn shop is listed as your place of business, with a note encouraging people to visit." I arched an eyebrow. "Now does *that* ring a bell? Or is there another Nadine, at another Barb's Pawn Shop in Santa Fe, that I'm unaware of?"

She sat back in her chair and notched the brim of her baseball cap up with a single finger. "Maybe it does, maybe it doesn't. Though you're standing here with nothing to sell me. So I'd love to know if you and me are gonna have a problem?"

I dipped my fingers into my bag and brushed the edges of my father's latest memoir. But it felt too early to use it to sway her, so I grabbed my pocket-size notebook instead. Flipping through the pages, I pretended to scan my handwriting.

"There's no problem at all," I said. "I'm simply looking for Monty, and I believe you know where to find her."

"I don't know who the hell that is."

"Yet you're bragging about knowing her on X Marks the Spot." I tapped a page, glancing up at Nadine to flash a sweet smile. "We spoke earlier this week. I wanted to ask some questions about a missing fortune here in Santa Fe that you've been discussing in the forums. Something called...the Blackburn Diamonds?"

Nadine managed a hearty scoff, but I didn't miss the way her gaze darted to the back of the store.

"Some people in that same forum were gossiping, claiming that Monty and her wife were the last people to make a serious play for the Blackburn Diamonds," I continued. "That's when *you* chimed in, saying you'd sold an antique locket to Monty around the same time. A locket that turned out to be a vital clue."

There was another frantic dart of her eyes, and the space between my shoulder blades prickled with awareness. "Is everything all right? Is there someone back there?"

Nadine drummed her fingers against the top of the TV. "Listen, lady—"

"Harper Hendrix," I corrected brightly.

"Are you a cop?"

I reared back. "A...*what*?"

"Are. You. A. Cop?" she bit out. "Because legally, you gotta tell me."

"No, not even close. Wait, do I *look* like a—"

But she was on the move before I could finish that sentence, rounding the counter and brushing past me so deliberately that I stumbled.

"I gotta...gotta check on something," she called over her shoulder, taking the staircase to the left, two steps at a time. "Be right back."

Eyes narrowed, I watched her reach the top and disappear onto the second floor.

"I still have questions, though," I yelled in response. "Nadine?"

The ceiling creaked overhead, then came the sound of a metallic whine.

Like a door being wrenched open.

"Oh, for fuck's sake," I muttered under my breath, grabbing my bag. I climbed the staircase after her, reaching a musty-smelling room filled with sheet-covered furniture. And saw the door marked EMERGENCY EXIT about to close. I raced across the room, then managed to slip through the remaining opening and crashed to a halt outside against a wrought-iron fire escape.

Chest heaving from the sprint, I leaned as far past the grating as I could, and spied Nadine as she rushed across the store's parking lot.

But when I spun back around to re-open the door behind me, it wouldn't budge.

No way back inside.

I swept the hair off my neck and fixed my bun. Inhaled. Exhaled. Then I reassessed how high up I was—and how in the hell Nadine had managed to make it down. Scowling at the distant asphalt, I swung one leg over and felt with my dangling foot until my heel connected with the edge of the grate below. With two more steadying breaths, I carefully climbed my way down and landed on the first-floor fire escape. Leaped down the final few stairs, into the parking lot, and ran toward Nadine, who had one hand on her car door, shaking her head at my approach.

"Nope," she was saying. "I'm not talkin' to you, Hannah."

"It's Harper." I bent over at the waist, trying to catch my breath. "And I'm not a cop, I'm a reporter for the *New York Review*—"

"You're a *reporter*?" She huffed out a sarcastic laugh. "That's even worse. Why can't you all just leave Monty alone? She's been through enough."

I narrowed my eyes, head cocked. "Why? What happened to her?"

"You think I'm stupid?"

"Not at all. And I'm not trying to give Monty a hard time. I'm only out here looking for her because I want to tell her story. From what I've gathered, she's lived a pretty incredible life." I raised my palms. "That's the truth, I swear."

What I neglected to add, of course, was that nailing this interview was the best opportunity I had to prove to my editor that I deserved the promotion I wanted more than anything else in the world.

Well, almost anything else. Doing the one thing my dad

couldn't do was just as enticing. More than the extra cherry on top. A whole fucking bushel of fruit.

So I *needed* to find this treasure hunter, the one who'd simply vanished into thin air like mist evaporating at dawn. And the sullen woman in front of me was the last verified person who'd interacted with her.

Nadine pressed her lips into a thin line. But she didn't climb into her car, merely rocked back on her heels as I finally reached her.

"Did you really sell that locket to Monty?" I asked. "Or were you just…I don't know, trying to ride her coattails to drum up some extra business? You wouldn't be the first person to do so."

Color rose in her cheeks, and a small thrill of satisfaction shot through me. I slipped a hand back into my bag and clutched the book. Ready to use it as soon as I had an opening.

"I'm not trying to ride anyone's goddamn coattails," she said forcefully. "I sold it to her. Picked it up from a local a couple of towns over. Later she told me it ended up being a pretty important clue about the missing diamonds."

"So where is she now?"

"Monty's out of the game," she said flatly. "She's been out. Off the grid, too."

I feigned a smile even as a surge of anxiety thrummed through me. "Then is there any risk in telling me where she's hiding?"

She crossed her arms and leveled me with a cocky glare.

Still smiling, I revealed the trick I'd had up my sleeve: a shiny hardcover titled *On Heroism: One Reporter's Journey Into Hell…and Back*. The middle-aged white man on the cover looked just serious enough for the literary crowd. And just rakish enough for his massive, adoring fan base.

Notably, this massive fan base included the sunburned woman standing in front of me. It hadn't taken me long to search her profile and discover she was an extremely vocal member of one of my father's many online groups.

Nadine inhaled sharply at the sight of the book. She moved to snatch it, but I held it just out of reach.

"That's Bruce Sullivan's latest memoir," she said.

"Sure is."

"But it's not due out for two more days." Her eyes flew to mine. "Why do *you* have a copy?"

I nodded toward the photo on the front. "Because he's my dad. I always get early copies."

"Bullshit." Her head tilted, like she was studying me. "Prove it."

I was already scrolling through my phone for a recent picture. "I was born Harper Sullivan, but we no longer share the same last name. Look…here he is with me and my sister at my college graduation."

A bright recognition dawned across her face. "Holy shit. You're *Harper*. From all of his stories. He talks about you and your sister all the time."

"I'm surprised he remembered us," I muttered.

"What was that?"

"Always lovely to meet a fan," I corrected. "Speaking of, if you love his work so much, why did you laugh when I said I was a reporter, too?"

She shrugged. "That's different. He's a *real journalist*. He went to war and stuff. No offense." Then her eyebrows pinched together beneath the brim of her ball cap. "I am sorry about what happened to your mom. It sounded awful."

I blinked, shocked at this sliver of compassion from a near

stranger. "Oh, uh...thank you. For saying that."

Clearing my throat, I waved the book in front of me. "Listen, this is an early copy of Bruce's newest work. A *signed* copy. And it's all yours...in exchange for a bit of information, of course."

The expression on her face was as hungry as it was prudent. Sighing, I flipped open to the page with my dad's signature: *Here's to the everyday heroes...like you*, he'd inscribed, followed by those confident loops in his name. Per his publicist, these were special copies he'd wanted to send, just for me and my sister. But when we did a bit of research in his online groups, we discovered that his "everyday heroes like you" line was standard across the board.

Nadine rocked back on her heels again. "What's he like, your dad?"

Forgetful. Irresponsible. Dismissive.

"He's the best," I lied. "And this is his best memoir yet, so it's all yours if you'd like it."

She made a move to grab it again.

"Not so fast. We had a deal, you and me. Where's Monty? And if you don't know, send me to the person who does." I held her gaze, refusing to back down. "Or give me the dirt on those missing diamonds everyone's been talking about."

She made me wait for it, I'd give her that. Glancing over her shoulder like she was worried someone was watching us. Removing her hat and raking her fingers through her hair. When I sighed and made a move to leave, she said, "Hold your damn horses."

I paused, book in hand.

"There's an antique salvage shop a couple miles past the city limits," she admitted. "It's called The Wreckage. Eve Bardot works there, and she's the only person I know with a real connection to Monty. She's kinda your best bet."

Hope sang through my limbs as I passed the book to Nadine, who then cradled it to her chest like a newborn kitten.

"Thank you for the information," I said. "This is so very helpful."

"Yeah, well, you didn't hear it from me."

"I can keep a secret," I said with a wink.

She took a step back. "Good luck with Eve. You'll have an easier time squeezing blood from a fuckin' stone than getting much from her."

I began walking toward my car, pausing to toss a wide smile back at Nadine. "I'm not too worried about that. I'm extremely persistent."

Chapter Two

Eve

Wreck Your Heart Out

The antique bar was like something out of one of my dreams. It was detailed in gold filigree and gorgeous, with the kind of Art Deco starburst design that made my heart spin and cartwheel. Using my teeth, I tugged off my work glove and checked every seam, disappointed when nothing sprang loose at my touch. No hidden compartments filled with love letters, stolen away to be read a hundred years later.

I kept every single one that I found, though. On display in the shop, a tidy stack of secrets from the past—scribbled recipes on receipts, phone numbers gone obsolete, waterlogged photos, and creased postcards.

I loved keeping these little notes. Loved the reminder that whoever had written *"Call Jack about the pecans"* on the back of an envelope and left it in the drawer of an armoire had been a person. That even in their anonymity they wouldn't be forgotten.

The bar had come from today's haul at The Plaza, a dilapidated historic hotel just outside Santa Fe. Cleo, my co-owner at The Wreckage, walked a slow, appreciative circle around it, whistling under her breath. She was a tall Black woman with plum-colored glasses, medium-brown skin, and a constellation of gold jewelry curving up both ears.

"Besides some cleaning," she said, "maybe a few touch-ups on the mirror, she's practically in mint condition. Someone took good care of her."

I eyed the chips and scratches in the wood, all the cracks along the razor-sharp edges of the starburst. "And she's still got some personality left, too. This was The Plaza's main bar, right?"

"It was, from the early 1920s through the forties. It survived Prohibition." Cleo paused to push a few stray curls back behind her ear. "One of the guys on the demo team told me the hotel was rumored to be a speakeasy...and that it catered to a distinct clientele."

When I arched an eyebrow in question, she said: "The Southwest's very vibrant queer population."

"Is that so," I murmured, splaying my hand across the top. My mind filled eagerly with all the empty spaces and missing moments of this bar—the smoky light, the lilting jazz. The metallic clink of martini glasses and the heavy pours of whiskey.

All that was said, the whispered secrets and desires.

And all that wasn't—the coded glances, the furtive touches when no one was looking. Pretty women, dripping with pearls, searching for a forbidden love in this dangerous land of endless violence.

"Damn. Maybe we don't sell this beauty at all," I said, flashing a grin. "She'd be right at home here at The Wreckage. We're pretty fucking queer and vibrant, too."

"It's not a bad idea," Cleo mused, nodding. "We could host community happy hours. Bring in some cute bartenders from the restaurant scene." She wrinkled her nose. "Although…are there any cute bartenders left in Santa Fe who haven't had their hearts broken by you?"

My grin widened, turned cocky. "Not my fault people can't stop falling in love with me."

"You should come with a warning label, Eve."

"Now where's the fun in that?"

She snorted, slapping a work glove against my arm. "Stop being a menace and help me move the bar into the workshop."

We bent together and lifted, moving carefully as we eased beneath the garage door and back into our large, drafty workshop.

Cleo and I had met in a beginner's woodworking class, shortly after I'd moved to Santa Fe. We'd bonded instantly. Cleo was professionally restless, a welder and contractor feeling frustrated with the red tape and bureaucracy that came with her job. And I was a recent PhD dropout, a historian with a passion for old and beautiful things—and a career I'd just burned to the ground.

We started salvaging antiques together on the weekends, our obsession growing in tandem until we realized the best way to combine our unique skill sets.

And we opened The Wreckage a year later.

The front half was a storefront, with our finished items on display and catalogs of what we were working on. The workspace in back, where Cleo and I gently placed the mahogany bar, was where the artistry happened: restoring, painting touch-ups, complete reconstructions.

I pushed to stand, pulling off my gloves and shoving them into the pockets of my navy-blue coveralls.

Cleo was already hauling out her tools, wearing an expression of jubilant concentration.

Laughing softly, I nudged my shoulder with hers. "Do you need any of my help for this? If not, I was going to tackle the rest of this month's invoices."

"Go get after it," she said with a smile. "Also, I almost forgot, but a reporter's been calling you all morning. I'm guessing it's about what we salvaged today. The Plaza's pretty high profile."

"You take it," I said, sauntering in the direction of the office. "You're better with the press than I am."

Cleo furrowed her brow. "You sure? They asked for you specifically."

"Absolutely. I don't fuck with reporters."

I moved back through our quiet shop, beneath the dangling antique lamps, the bins of reclaimed subway tile, the gilded mirrors and refurbished desks. The neon sign at the front, hanging above our doors, read WRECK YOUR HEART OUT. It was candy-apple red, pulsed with a gentle hum, and was the very first thing we'd purchased together when we opened.

In the office, I scooped up my phone from the desk. No missed calls. No new messages.

So I dialed my aunt Monty's number for the third time that day. There was a reason why I never trusted reporters—and it was absolutely because of what they'd done to Monty and her wife, Ruby Ortega, all those years ago. Circling them like sharks scenting blood in the water, more compelled by a news deadline than anything resembling compassion. The way the press had stalked them, camping out on their front yard. All the homophobic tabloid headlines, the taunts about her marriage, her "gay lifestyle," the casual destruction of her privacy.

How quickly my aunt had lost her humanity, nothing more to them than a human-interest story to be read quickly and tossed in the trash.

Reporters were a direct threat to Monty's hard-earned peace. I hadn't been around back then to protect her from them, but I'd do it now in a heartbeat.

Her phone rang and rang on the other end of the line, and when her robotic voicemail message came on, I couldn't even say I was surprised.

"Monty, it's me again." I sighed. "I know you love your off-the-grid routine, but this is getting beyond ridiculous. I'm really worried about you. Can you call me? Please?"

I hung up before any more vulnerability could creep into my tone, just as a heavy dragging sound caught my attention. I tipped my head, listening, but could only hear rustling. Maybe a muttered curse. I walked back into the shop, scanning for signs of customers—

And that was where I saw the source of the noise, a woman in the middle of our antique book section, balanced on the highest rung of the rolling ladder.

Her fingers danced along the dusty spines with a languid reverence. The hazy afternoon sun filtered in through the stained glass in our windows, painting her in muted multicolor.

Perched like that, she appeared...enchanted. A handful of pencils winged out from the top of her high bun. She had pale skin and dark brunette hair swept back from her neck, though a few stray hairs lay at the nape. And when her profile slowly came into view, I noticed her square-rimmed glasses. Her front teeth biting into her full bottom lip.

Her lipstick was a rich carmine—the sharp color like a bloody, fiery heart.

Awareness shivered across my skin.

I propped my shoulder against the bookshelf. "Can I help you find anything?"

She gasped, the motion shifting the ladder back. I grabbed the bottom to stabilize it, and she sagged forward with relief. Then peered down at me with pink cheeks and dark blue eyes.

A smile spread across her face. Sweet, a little tentative. Behind her glasses, our gazes met. Held. It could have been from that same afternoon sun, but I swore her cheeks darkened a shade.

Whoever this stranger was, she was pretty to the point of distraction.

She let out a breathy sigh. "I don't know who you are, but you just saved my life. I feel a thank-you is in order."

My response was a leisurely grin. "No thanks necessary. I didn't mean to scare you, was just shocked to see a customer up on that ladder. Usually I'm the only one brave enough to climb it."

She peered out over the store. "I couldn't let a chance go by to live out my *Beauty and the Beast* fantasies. A bookish girl can dream, can't she?"

"Should I bring out our dancing candlesticks? Or would that be overkill?"

A single brow winged up. "Oh, I would be *delighted* by a musical number right now."

She descended the rungs, revealing pointed boots beneath trousers that cinched high around her waist. A sleeveless silk top buttoned all the way to her neck. Our eyes connected again when she reached the floor.

My stomach did a neat little flip.

I gripped the back of my neck and indicated the space around us. "What brings you into our salvage shop?"

Instead of answering, she extended a hand and said, "Harper Hendrix."

My fingers slid across her soft palm and brushed the inside of her wrist. Her grip was surprisingly firm. Another burst of awareness shot forth from where we touched.

"Eve Bardot. I'm one of the owners here." I released her hand, slipping both of mine casually into the back pockets of my coveralls. "Are you looking for anything specific?"

Harper seemed to hesitate, as if unsure. A tiny alarm sounded in the back of my head, but it was probably just a side effect of my Monty worries.

She adjusted her glasses, wandering farther down the aisle. "Just browsing. It's my first time in an antique salvage shop, and I had no idea everything in here would be so—"

"Really fucking old?"

She bent at the waist to examine a typewriter. "I was going to say *magical*. Don't you agree?"

Beneath the sweep of her dark lashes, Harper's eyes were the color of an impending storm, a sapphire flecked with gray. Freckles dusted the bridge of her nose. And I hadn't noticed the tiny golden hoop in her septum earlier.

"I do," I said. "This place is brimming with magic."

A taut energy hung in the space between our bodies. Those red lips curved up, her eyes flashing playfully.

"Sooo…how much nineteenth-century erotica do you think was written on this?" she asked, pointing at the typewriter.

I laughed, surprised. "What do you think's inside those books you were browsing?"

"My, how *scandalous*. Peddling vintage smut under the guise of being an innocent antiques dealer."

"Sorry if I gave you that impression."

She clicked her tongue. "This isn't a warehouse filled with antique erotica?"

"No, I meant..." I kept my gaze locked on hers. "I've never been that innocent."

Another graceful arch of her brow. "My apologies for being so boldly presumptuous."

Harper spun in a half circle, meandering forward while her fingers fidgeted with the pencils stuck in her hair. I followed as if we were leashed together, pulled along by the sway of her hips.

"Do you ever find anything interesting hidden inside any of the antiques?"

"All kinds of things," I admitted, thinking about our new bar. "You'd be surprised at what random bits of personal history end up stored inside the pieces we come across. I once found a love letter stuck in the book jacket of a poetry collection by Audre Lorde."

Harper's face brightened. "She's one of my favorite writers."

"Same." My stomach did that slow, deliberate *flip* again. "I got in trouble in high school for writing an op-ed in our school newspaper, calling out my English teachers for not including her in their discussion of modern American poets."

"That's a disgrace," she said. "What was their reasoning?"

"Too niche."

Which I'd learned, after years of existing within my parents' elite and insular academic community, was code for *too disruptive, too angry, too Black, too queer.* An insult tucked neatly inside their pretentious literary criticism.

Harper hummed beneath her breath and continued walking. "What made you get involved in architectural salvage?"

I gave a half smile. "Proud PhD dropout. I was studying history and completely burned out. But I never lost my obsession with it." I cocked my chin toward the items surrounding us. "Now I just direct that passion to restoring forgotten artifacts."

"That's so interesting." She traced the shape of her bottom lip, pulling all my focus to the slide of her finger along that deep scarlet color. "It's almost like modern-day treasure hunting."

I stilled. The alarm in my head was back, louder. "You could say that."

She turned to face me. "Do you do a lot of treasure hunting? I hear it's quite popular in the Southwest."

Unease flared through the center of my chest. "Not really. Why?"

"I'm a reporter from New York," she said lightly, as if those words weren't a kick to my gut. "And currently on deadline, though that's my usual state of being. It's why I'm in Santa Fe."

Her tone was sweet, polite. Her body language friendly, eyes warm.

But that feeling of unease tripled in size, growing unruly and ugly. "What are you investigating?"

"I'm profiling a well-known treasure hunter named Monty Montana. Or I'm supposed to be." Harper's head tilted to the side. "She's famously hard to find, and I'm at my wits' end. I've spent the past few weeks wading through internet discourse, and apparently some people are attempting a hunt for this local urban legend. The Blackburn Diamonds. The last person who made a public attempt to find those diamonds was Monty. I've been hoping she'll come out of hiding and try again—"

Cleo walked past us, carrying a few cans of paint. But she stopped at Harper's words.

"Sorry, are you here about Monty?" Cleo shot me a concerned look. "What happened? Is she okay?"

Harper swiveled her head back to face me, that friendly smile turning smug. "Wouldn't you know...that's exactly why I'm here. Where is she, Eve?"

My stomach pitched to the floor as a nervous fear for my aunt flooded my body.

Followed by anger at the reporter in front of me.

Every bit of flirtatious interest I'd had in this woman vanished beneath my irritation. I turned on my heel, stalking back to the cash register, eager to ignore her so she would get the hell out.

Eager to warn Monty that people were looking for her again. Though...maybe Harper Hendrix wasn't the first reporter to come out here. Maybe Monty had been forced to disappear recently for this exact reason. Which made me even angrier.

I reached beneath the cash register to haul out a stray pile of paperwork, needing to give my hands something to do.

Harper appeared almost instantly, leaning across the glass table and propping her chin in her hands. "You know Monty Montana, don't you?"

I kept my eyes down, fingers busy. "Yep."

"Then can you tell me why every person I talk to acts as if this woman is a national secret they would die to protect? The story I'm working on about Monty isn't even *remotely* nefarious, and neither am I."

I scoffed under my breath. "I'm not buying this little act of yours. Unfortunately, I've seen it before."

"It's not an act. It's my job," she argued. "And whatever you need me to do to prove my intentions are pure, I'll do it. Say the word."

Frustration finally got the better of me. My gaze rose, tangled with hers, and I just barely managed to ignore her parted red lips, the flash of teeth.

"I'll save you some time. Monty is my aunt, my dad's younger sister. She legally changed her last name decades ago."

Harper's blue eyes widened behind her glasses.

"She's difficult to track down *on purpose*. The people in this town will always protect her from reporters, regardless of their intentions. She's been burned too many times by journalists making the same claims who then invade her privacy and write something insulting afterward."

A heavy silence lingered. Harper's nostrils flared. "But that's not me, *obviously*. I'm not the enemy here. I'm actually trying to help."

"Any reporter looking for Monty *is* the enemy. Now get out."

Her eyebrows twitched together. "Are you being serious?"

"I'd never joke about something like this."

After a moment, her spine straightened, shoulders rolling back. "You're underestimating how persistent I can be, Eve."

I smirked in response. "And you're overestimating how much I care."

She made a soft, strangled sound of annoyance. "You haven't seen the last of me," she said, then whirled around and marched out of the store.

I tore my eyes away from those swaying hips and the nape of her neck, bare and vulnerable. I didn't fuck with reporters, and I certainly didn't *flirt* with them.

No matter how lovely.

I did, however, need to find Monty—and fast.

Before reporters like Harper could ruin her life for the second time.

Chapter Three

Harper

Ten days left to find Monty Montana, who is, like, the Mt. Everest of treasure hunters

The next morning, I sipped a strong cup of bitter coffee in the front seat of my car and glared out at The Wreckage. My sleep the night before had been more restless than restful, my body too keyed up from the day's bizarre events to truly settle.

Exhausted or not, Eve would be in for a rude awakening when she realized just how determined I was to find Monty and write this story. I'd spent the better part of those sleepless hours rehashing every frustrating detail of our interaction yesterday.

Her coy, flirtatious energy, just this side of cocky. Her confident walk, practically a swagger. That lazy half grin of hers, all sultry heat.

Even her hair felt dangerously alluring—dark as midnight, shaved close on both sides with a riot of wavy curls on the top. A single lock had fallen carelessly across her forehead, like she was the wicked rake in a historical romance.

My fingers had itched to sweep it back.

I took another sip and sharpened my glare out the window.

The salvage shop's front door opened, revealing a person I didn't recognize. Probably just a customer, but I couldn't risk being wrong. I ducked my head beneath the steering wheel like the world's clumsiest detective on a stakeout. Coffee spilled down the inside of my wrist, dripping onto the stack of notes I'd balanced in my lap. Cursing, I tried to mop it up with the fast-food napkins I'd collected from my past week on the road, chasing the ghost of Monty Montana through what felt like every town in New Mexico.

My phone buzzed with a text from Greg, my editor, that just said, *update??!?!?*

I was used to Greg's inane use of superfluous punctuation by now, but the sight of it still sent my butterfly-filled stomach pitching about like a ship on stormy seas.

Greg had been my editor for the past three years. What he lacked in humor he more than made up for by having a giant stick up his ass. After debating a few different replies, I went with politely begging for an act of editorial mercy: *I'm making decent headway, though an extension would be helpful. There are signs Monty might be gearing up to search for the missing Blackburn Diamonds—a popular urban legend and famous mystery in this region. But it's also on many verified lists as being one of the last truly hidden treasures in the U.S. Would make a great extra story angle!*

His immediate response: *No extension. I need the story in ten days.*

"Goddammit," I whispered, tossing my phone across the seat. Half my research time in Santa Fe wasted, and what did I have to show for it? The magazine had already booked my return flight home.

At this rate, I'd be writing up most of my article on the plane. Without an interview, I only had a skeletal outline to work from so far, plus a hasty summary of Monty's accomplishments. I'd attempted to write last night but only managed to type out: *"a story about a treasure hunter infamous for her air of mystery is actually super fucking boring if she refuses to divulge her secrets even though I am actually quite nice and only trying to help!!!"*

I flinched again when my phone rang, but my anxiety turned to delight when I saw who was video-calling me. I propped the phone on my dashboard and swiped to answer it.

My sister Daphne's sleepy face appeared, chin propped on her hand. She was standing in the dimly lit kitchen at the coffee shop where she worked, wearing large gold earrings that dangled in her messy hair. The apartment we shared in Brooklyn was just around the corner, a small but sunshine-y spot we'd filled with too many books and just enough plants.

"Morning," Daphne said through a yawn. "You look like shit."

I tugged down the mirror, frowning at the dark bags beneath my eyes, all the wisps of hair that had already escaped my meticulous bun. "Cut me some slack," I grumbled. "I'm a reporter on deadline. On the road, no less. Can't a girl get a little unconditional love from her only sibling?"

Daphne lowered her voice, and I was all too aware of the very real concern in her eyes. "I can tell this job is getting to you, Harp. I'm worried about you."

"Don't be," I said breezily. "I'm booked and busy. Happy and healthy."

She pursed her lips. "You're exhausted and permanently stressed out. You haven't taken a weekend off in years. In fact, this Monty story is the first time I've seen you actually intrigued by an assignment in a long time."

"You know why, though," I said, fighting the urge to fidget. "Dad said—"

"Not just because of Dad," she interrupted. "I think you like this Monty person. I think this story is *fun*. When was the last time you let yourself be inspired, like when we were kids?"

"I hate to break it to you, but Monty is very MIA," I shot back. "Not sure I can be inspired by someone who refuses to be found."

Daphne grinned, tapping the screen the way she usually tapped the tip of my nose. "You're being deliberately obtuse."

"And you're being...being deliberately, um...*reasonable*," I stammered out.

Daphne laughed, but I realized she'd caught me in a *tiny bit* of a lie.

The name *Monty Montana* had rattled around in the dustiest corners of my brain ever since my father had first brought her up at a dinner party, saying her name with just enough disappointed yearning to pique my interest. But it wasn't until Greg happened to dangle her story in front of me a few weeks later, like I was a lion being fed at the zoo, that I'd let myself dig into her extraordinary backstory.

Twenty-five years ago, she very famously discovered the buried remains of *La Venganza*, a Spanish warship, at the bottom of the ocean off the coast of Florida.

Even the quickest internet search returned the photograph she was well-known for. A local reporter had snapped a picture of Monty and her wife, Ruby, as they'd walked onto a beach near Key West, both still in their wet suits and scuba gear. A crowd had gathered, following rumors that the expedition team had finally uncovered something.

In the photo, Monty's goggles are shoved up into her hair, and she's holding a piece of the ship's hull above her head. It's a pose of pure, unadulterated victory. Her grin is broad. Boisterous. But she's not even gazing at the artifact she'd spent two years searching for.

In the picture, she's gazing down at Ruby. Who, in turn, has been captured mid-laugh. Both of them proud and outspoken queer women in the notoriously homophobic nineties. Both of them brazenly in love.

I had never, not once, embarked on the kind of wild and windswept adventure these women had. Had never, *not even once*, had a romantic partner—of any gender—gaze at me with such ardent devotion.

The first time I'd seen that picture, my skin had heated with a delirious mixture of want and envy. And something defiant had taken root in my heart, delicate and audacious in equal measure.

It was so starkly different from the way I felt about my everyday life that it terrified me.

Movement in front of The Wreckage had my gaze snapping to the squealing metal door, currently being pushed open by the woman dominating my thoughts. Eve sauntered into the bright morning sunlight, glimmering above the asphalt. She wore a pair of ripped-up jeans and a white tank top, revealing strong shoulders and toned arms almost fully covered in tattoos. Her aviator sunglasses refracted the light, and her effortless smile was directed at a delivery person holding a large box.

My mouth went dry.

"Speaking of, uh...of fun," I said to my sister, "I just spotted my hot lead—my *warm* lead, I mean. For the story."

"Sure you did," Daphne drawled. "Go get that hot lead, Harp. Call me later?"

I rushed to grab my bag, keys, and notepad. "Love you, miss you, don't get into any trouble."

I jumped out of the car, forcing my body to slow down as I approached Eve, the best lead I had in a story that still felt too flimsy to sink my teeth into.

But I had way too much riding on this—professionally *and* personally—to let a little thing like "instant distrust" get in the way of seeing it through.

"Good morning, Eve," I said pleasantly, extending my hand. "Harper. Harper Hendrix? We met yesterday regarding the location of your aunt?"

Eve's expression was inscrutable behind those aviators, though I knew they hid wide, dark eyes and high cheekbones. Her expressive mouth was pressed into a thin line, and that same unruly curl tempted me to lean in close.

Eve Bardot's beauty was as compelling as a knifepoint— sharp. Distracting. The kind of woman who tempts and charms before smashing your heart beneath her boot heel.

In response, I straightened my spine and held my hand out even farther.

She ignored it.

"I remember you, Hendrix," she said smoothly.

"Then you'll surely remember my persistence."

She turned away immediately, leaving me to swelter in the sun. "And you'll surely remember that I'm not saying shit."

Then she slammed the door in my face.

Undeterred, I yanked it back open and followed the surly salvager inside her shop. My gaze skipped to the register to find her leaning against it, arms crossed over her chest, all lean muscle and loose confidence. A red handkerchief dangled from the side of her jean pocket, and her tattooed fingers flexed where they gripped her biceps.

"You're wasting your time, Hendrix," she said.

I raised my chin. "It's Harper, actually."

"I know what your damn name is."

My lips parted on a shaky breath. "Well, in that case—" I took a few wary steps forward, like I was approaching a feral cat. "Why don't you let me be the judge of my own time and whether or not I'm wasting it?"

Eve remained silent.

So I reached into my bag and revealed the historical photograph I'd printed this morning, sliding it across the register with my finger. "I've spent a lot of time on this online treasure-hunting forum called X Marks the Spot. I learned from the folks there that Nadine, at Barb's Pawn Shop, sold this locket to your aunt about six years ago. And the rumors surrounding the couple pictured in the locket are pretty epic."

Eve's shoulders rippled with restrained movement. "I cannot repeat this enough. But I really, truly, do not care."

"Do you know who this couple is?" I asked.

"Nope."

"You haven't even looked at the picture," I chided.

A muscle ticked in her jaw. She glared down at the locket and repeated: "Nope."

She was lying. She had to be.

"The pictures in the locket are of William Blackburn and his wife, Priscilla," I said. "William was an oil baron from New York City during the Gilded Age. Filthy rich, politically influential. On April 7th, 1900, his vast collection of diamonds was stolen and carried off in a large metal box.

It was a huge news story at the time. Especially since the diamonds vanished on the same day that Priscilla *also* went missing."

Eve's lips twitched into a smirk. "Can we speed this up? I've got a busy day."

My back molars ground together, but I forced a pleasant tone to match my smile. "Priscilla was never heard from again, and the diamonds were never found. The urban legend is that she fled an unhappy marriage, took the jewels to pay her way out west, through Santa Fe. Because *this* locket, with *these* photos, was discovered in a small town just outside here, leading many to believe Priscilla was ultimately killed by thieves while traveling through."

Eve's fingers tightened again, just slightly.

"Five years ago, your aunt and her wife made a very public attempt at finding the missing Blackburn Diamonds—and failed. And now I'm here in Santa Fe, trying to find Monty, and the local forums are suddenly *filled* with rumors that multiple groups of treasure hunters are making a big, splashy play for the diamonds. Late last night, some guy named Jensen and his crew did a massive dig at a nearby state park."

Eve's eyebrows knit together in a flash of genuine surprise. Though she smoothed her expression over just as quickly, cocking her head to the side like she was sizing me up. "Let me get this straight, Hendrix. You think *my aunt* is out there in the foothills, trying to find a bunch of diamonds that don't exist? It's an old wives' tale, always has been. Nothin' but a campfire story kids tell each other in the summertime."

"Interesting," I countered. "Because I've got the strangest feeling that if I follow those diamonds, they'll lead me right to Monty. Call it gut instinct from years of being a reporter."

Her dark eyes flashed with defiance. She stepped a few inches closer, her elbow sliding across the top of the register, body angling toward mine. I heroically ignored the low flutter in my belly that appeared at her nearness.

"I'm not gonna tell you again. Leave it alone, Hendrix," she said, voice husky at the edges.

"Why?"

"Can't tell ya why. Just drop it."

Eve pushed past me, heading back toward the front of the shop. But I was hot on her heels, and we reached the closed front door at the same time. Desperate, I slid in front of her, forcing her to stop. My shoulders pressed into the wood, and barely six inches separated the two of us. Closer even than before, because now I could smell her, like a sun-dappled hiking trail beneath fragrant cedar trees.

Or, somewhat less poetically, Eve smelled like a hot lady lumberjack, and I was deeply annoyed at my body's immediate reaction to her.

She cocked a haughty eyebrow. "You really are persistent, aren't you?"

"I'm sorry, but a bunch of vague statements demanding that I drop this story because of *mystery reasons* has the opposite effect on my motivations," I said archly. "I'm not here seeking your permission, Eve. I'm here seeking information I can use."

Her gaze fell to my lips for all of a second before flying to mine with a scowl. "You know this is why everyone protects Monty from reporters. You don't give a shit about her or what she wants. You don't even care about what *I* want."

"Why would I care about what *you* want? I literally just met you."

"A meeting I already fully regret," she muttered.

Irritation zipped along my spine. I lifted my chin, all too aware that somehow another inch had disappeared from the space between our bodies. Eve's thick, black eyeliner was smudged from the heat, giving her a just-woken-up look that was much too tempting given how pissed I was.

"I want this story... I *need* this story," I said slowly. Deliberately. "And nothing will stop me from succeeding."

Eve scoffed in response. "Don't think I won't stop you, Hendrix. You might as well pack your bags up and head home now."

My thoughts darted through my brain like ping-pong balls on a caffeine bender. The truth was, I didn't doubt this woman's ability to block my every move—after all, I was the one who'd shown my hand too early.

But then one of those ping-pong balls bounced off an idea so absurd I almost laughed. I shrugged, aiming for nonchalance. "Guess I'll just have to find the Blackburn Diamonds myself and force Monty out of hiding...that is, if she isn't already out there looking."

Eve reared back, lips quirked up in a mocking smile. "What the hell do you know about treasure hunting?"

My eyes narrowed in suspicion. "And what do you? Per our conversation yesterday, it doesn't seem like it's much of an interest of yours."

"It's not."

"So why do you care?"

"I literally could not care less."

Our gazes locked together, neither one backing down. Finally, I said: "Cool, well...guess I'll be seeing you around, then?"

Her attention had fallen to my mouth again, the long column of her throat working on a swallow. "I highly doubt it."

Biting back one last burst of frustration, I spun around and stalked outside. "Next time you see me, I'll be positively *swimming* in buried treasure."

"Well, don't come back here in a week, crying when you can't find a damn thing," she snapped. "Monty included."

"Thanks for your concern," I said airily. "But you'll be the one crying when I find those diamonds before anyone else does."

Eve's answering laughter was tinged with arrogance. "I'd like to see you try, Hendrix."

Chapter Four

Eve

Hotter Lois Lane

My headlights bounced off the metal sign posted at the trailhead, glowing ominously in the dark: PLEASE STAY ON THE TRAIL AND BE AWARE OF SHEER DROP-OFFS. On any other day, this was the kind of warning that thrilled me. Moving to Santa Fe with Monty all those years ago had activated every memory of the kid I'd once been—a dirt-stained menace, all skinned knees and endless curiosity for the world around me.

New Mexico's expansive beauty and bright blue skies had unlocked that deep, unquenchable curiosity again, had unlocked the person I'd been before my parents forced me into a tiny box made up entirely of other people's expectations.

But I wasn't here for a leisurely night hike.

I was here because I was freaking the fuck out.

After Harper stormed off yesterday, I'd frantically scanned the same forums she'd been boasting about, searching for the surprising news about Jensen's team that had sent an unpleasant shockwave through my bones. Every word out of her lush, berry-red mouth might have been aggravating, but—as I learned within minutes—she hadn't been lying.

I didn't know Jensen well, but he'd run in the same treasure-hunting circles as Monty back in the day. And I'd had no *idea* he was going after the diamonds. Which meant the hunt for the Blackburn Diamonds was officially *on*, and I'd existed on the outskirts of the local community long enough to know that people would soon be crossing state lines to get here.

I still didn't know where Monty was, but she sure as hell needed to know this extremely alarming news.

I put my car in park and flicked on the overhead light, snatching up the map of Monty's I'd brought along tonight for reassurance. Half a mile in on the trail was a scribbled red circle indicating a potential location of the diamonds. Scrawled over it, in her trademark blocky letters, was the word **BUST**.

And a journal entry from the week they'd spent here digging: **SEVEN DAYS OF HARD WORK WITH NOTHIN' TO SHOW FOR IT. DOESN'T HELP THAT RUBY AND I ARGUED FOR MOST OF IT. IT'S JUST THAT PRISCILLA BLACKBURN'S BEEN RENTING A ROOM IN MY HEART FOR DAMN NEAR HALF MY LIFE—BUT NOW EVERY TIME I THINK WE'VE FOUND HER, WE'RE COMIN' UP EMPTY.**

My chest ached at this rare glimpse of her pessimism, but I didn't doubt that hard work she'd mentioned.

It was why I'd hauled myself all the way out here, to see the dig in person, hoping to glean some tidbit of information I was clearly missing. There was just *no way* Jensen had uncovered something after Monty and Ruby had so expertly torn this place apart.

Right?

My phone buzzed with an incoming call. I propped it between my ear and shoulder while my eyes stayed glued to the map.

"How's it going at the shop?" I asked Cleo, by way of a greeting.

"Splendidly," she replied. "Now why don't you follow my advice from earlier and hang with me here, instead of traipsing around cougar country in the dark?"

"No can do," I said, refolding the map and shoving it back into my pack. "I need to figure out what Monty and Ruby might have missed." I peered through the windshield, out into the night, and thought I saw movement off to the side. "Cougars are the least of my worries."

"Maybe Hot Lois Lane could help you," Cleo said.

"Uhhh *who*?"

"Harper Hendrix? The reporter babe with the glasses?"

"But Lois Lane was hot," I said without thinking.

"Right, so like...*hotter*. Hotter Lois Lane."

A warm flush worked its way down the entire length of my body. A traitorous response if there ever was one, but I hadn't been able to shake our interaction from yesterday, the look of Harper pressed up against the door in front of me. Defiant and a little mouthy, her storm-blue eyes blazing with irritation.

And much, *much* too pretty. She'd shown up to challenge me with glossy lips and a pencil skirt that clung to her curvy hips. When she'd slid away to leave, I'd almost given in to the wild, desperate urge to grab her wrist. Pull her back. Breathe her in. Yank down that perfect bun and bury my face in all that dark hair.

"Ahhh, *I* see," I managed to say. "You've got a crush on the woman hell-bent on fucking with me right now."

"More like *you* have a crush," Cleo teased. "I was there when you met. Watched you trip all over yourself, trying to flirt with her."

"I'm committed to providing excellent customer service." Shutting off my car, I swung the door open to stand. "Oh, *fuck me*."

"What, what happened?" Cleo asked.

The movement I'd seen had unfurled fully in the dark, becoming the outline of a person with a high bun and a bunch of what I already knew to be pencils flaring out, looking eerily similar to the metallic starburst in the middle of that mahogany bar we'd rescued.

My stomach dropped. "Hotter Lois Lane is here," I hissed. "How in the hell—"

"*Oooh* boy, have fun," Cleo said. "I'll be here late if you want to swing by and tell me how your date went."

"This is the farthest thing from a... Hello? *Cleo?*"

With an annoyed grumble in my throat, I shut the car door and prowled along the dirt path toward my current tormentor, clicking on my flashlight. Harper stood by a tree, now slightly more visible, and I had the distinct pleasure of seeing the exact moment when she realized it was me. Her eyes widened, then narrowed sharply behind her glasses, her gaze sweeping me from head to toe.

"Fancy seeing you here, Hendrix," I drawled. "I thought the next time I saw you, you were gonna be, what was it...*swimming* in buried treasure?"

Two spots of red appeared on her cheeks. She wore an oversize, long-sleeve T-shirt over black bike shorts and a pair of hiking sandals that looked like they'd never been worn before today. I valiantly ignored the look of her thighs in those shorts, as well as the delicate dip of her collarbone.

"Oh, *ha ha*," she scoffed. "I obviously didn't mean I'd be recovering the treasure a mere twenty-four hours later."

I shrugged. "Sure sounded like you did."

She waved her hand between us, indicating my flashlight and pack. "For someone who literally couldn't care less, you certainly look like you're about to embark on a treasure hunt."

I forced a smile. "Maybe I like night hiking."

"At this creepy desert murder spot?"

I waved the flashlight up toward the sky. "This is one of the best places to see the Milky Way outside of Santa Fe. Probably wouldn't hurt to look up at the stars every once in a while, you know? Not everything's about the job."

She blinked, and for a moment I almost thought she looked hurt. "Must be nice not to have to worry about something as insignificant as paying your bills."

"The opposite, actually," I said, with more emotion than I intended. "I worry about everything. Constantly. But the stars help."

This time I couldn't decipher her expression at all—confused, maybe? Whatever it was, it didn't last. Instead, she lifted her chin and said, "Why are you out here tonight?"

"Hendrix," I started, then sighed, already shaking my head.

"Why are you out here?" Harper repeated, stepping closer to me in the dark. It was the worst time to notice that her lips were free of makeup, and something about the vulnerability of her bare skin sent a shiver down my spine.

She cocked her head to the side when I didn't answer. "Okay, I'll go first. I'm here because this is where that guy Jensen talked about digging for the diamonds, and I wanted to see it for myself, try to understand his reasoning. He's ignored all of my messages and won't return my calls, so I figured I'd go straight to the source." Her gaze swept the length of my body for a second time, but it felt more dismissive than anything else. "But if I'd known you were going to follow me, I wouldn't have come. Technically, you're my competition."

My lips twitched. "I live here, could walk the entirety of this park in my sleep if I had to. If *anyone* followed me to this extremely specific location"—I leaned in another inch—"it's you."

Harper shot me a scowl, then pushed past me on the trail, her shoulder brushing my arm as she stomped off. "As if I would. Don't flatter yourself, Eve," she called back. "No need to follow me again, by the way. I'm good."

"Except you're going the wrong way."

I heard her sandals stop abruptly on the dirt. When she flounced back to my side, she said, in a tone dripping with sarcasm, "Guess we're going night hiking, then."

"Guess we are."

I raked a hand through my hair and set off down the trail, suddenly anxious to get this over and done with. As fun as it was, briefly—*very* briefly—to rile up the woman next to me, she'd backed me into a corner and knew it. Time was of the essence here, and while having her inadvertently tag along was an annoying distraction, at most she'd be seeing a big, empty hole filled with nothing and lacking any of the vital historical context to understand it.

It was every other secret I was keeping from Harper that felt much too precious to divulge.

I made quick time on the trail, with Harper right behind me. Owls hooted in the distance, and the sound of bat's wings rustled as they darted over our heads. My flashlight beam bounced off thick roots and rocks, occasionally blending with slivers of silvery moonlight.

At the fifth fork, I turned left and followed a worn footpath down a steep incline covered in scraggly bush. Harper scrabbled behind me, sending tiny stones skittering past us. At the entrance to the site, I slid a leg over a jagged boulder. Then peered down into the deep pit I already suspected would be there. There were lanterns strewn about, a few still shedding feeble light. Which meant they were probably coming back in the morning.

I heard the hitch in Harper's breath. Felt her body heat when she crouched down next to me. "They weren't lying," she whispered. "Do you think they found them?"

"I think they're fucking idiots," I said, though my stomach still clenched at the possibility. "As you can see, they're not exactly experts in subtlety."

A line formed between her eyebrows. "Then why do it?"

"Honestly?" I leaned back on the rock, uneasy. "I don't know."

This kind of carelessness was concerning. They clearly hadn't recovered anything. We would have heard by now. But why else would they be acting this confidently?

Unless Monty and Ruby *had* missed something here.

When I turned my head, Harper's face was much too close to mine in the darkness. My stomach flipped over, and I heard her swallow, watched her eyelashes flutter.

"Eve," she whispered, her voice stripped of argument, "you're going after the diamonds, too, aren't you? That's why you're here tonight."

I sent her a look. "You already know that I am."

I expected her to gloat, to launch right back into another circular argument with me. Instead, she said simply: "Then take me with you."

I cocked an eyebrow. "What happened to being competitors?"

"This could be an *amazing* story," she said, her eyes bright behind her glasses. "It could be about you and Monty, your relationship, about second chances and coming out of hiding and—"

"Not a chance in hell." I swung my other leg around and slid down to the flat dirt surrounding the pit. "This is literally all that you're getting from me, Hendrix. This night hike through a 'creepy desert murder spot' is your one freebie. Enjoy it while it lasts."

I toed at one of the lamps, directing my flashlight farther into the hole. Followed the curve up, toward a small cave that matched both my memory and the map description. Harper tumbled down behind me a second later, and I didn't have to turn around to know she was pissed.

"I'm not your enemy here," she pressed. "I could be your partner. It's a genuine offer."

I walked a slow circle around the pit, trying my best to ignore Harper and concentrate on what I was missing. But she was much too angry and much too beautiful, and it was like trying to ignore the sun.

"Except I have no legitimate reason to trust your intentions and absolutely nothing to gain from you telling a story about me, my family, *or* the missing fortune. It's all professional benefit for you, invasion of privacy for me." I pointed the flashlight in her direction, pinning her to the spot. "Not to mention that anything you write about me would just point a giant red arrow in the sky, saying 'hey look here' to anyone with a shovel and a metal detector."

She propped her hands on her hips and shrugged. "After everything that happened to Monty, after *La Venganza*, doesn't… doesn't your aunt want to tell her side of the story?"

My throat tightened, and it was suddenly hard to hold her gaze. "The media is responsible for what happened to her. Reporters, Hendrix. Just like you. So the answer is *no*."

She released a noisy breath, tapping her foot against the ground. "Then I guess…I guess we're going to stay competitors."

I kicked a rock into the pit, listened to it bounce against the side. "Sure. Whatever. If you think you've got the skills to solve a mystery that I've been working on for years."

Harper perked up at that, as obvious as a hawk scenting a mouse on the wind. I snapped my mouth shut. *This* was why I need to stop indulging whatever this newfound urge was to bait and bicker with this woman.

The longer I did it, the easier it was to admit things that I shouldn't.

A twig snapped sharply from above our heads, followed by the sound of boots crunching on the trail, some muffled voices. It had to be Jensen and his crew—back already?

Harper went rigid next to me.

Then she snagged my wrist, ducked her head, and yanked me into the small cave.

Chapter Five

Eve

Night Hiking

I was so stunned I didn't even have time to resist. Suddenly Harper and I were huddled together in a cool, dark space, our hips pressed together, the bare skin of her arm warm against mine. The shower of electric sparks this elicited had me dazed and lightheaded.

That and the distinct smell of her this close, rising above the scents of stone and moss surrounding us—something sweet and citrusy, like a summertime memory.

"Dragging me into a cave against my will isn't a good look coming from the person talking about creepy desert murder spots," I muttered. "What are we doing here? And why?"

I could just make out the shape of her face in the shadows. She pressed a finger to her lips. "Someone's coming. So please, kindly, shut the fuck up. You're making it hard to spy."

"You mean...eavesdrop?"

"Gathering information in a more convenient and accessible way than using formal channels."

My eyebrows flew up. "Sorry but don't journalists have a set of ethics they have to follow?"

Harper was frowning down at the rows of ants crawling by her feet. "Uh...yes?"

"So is this ethical?"

"We'll never know, will we?" she whispered. "Because you're talking too much."

The sound of boots grew louder. Figures appeared by the pit—the man in the tan jacket and cowboy hat was Jensen, but I didn't recognize anyone else. Jensen held a small leather journal that he kept slapping against his thigh. Two others unpacked metal detectors and a few other tools.

"What do they know that I don't?" I murmured, without thinking. Harper's reaction was to press her hand over my mouth with a haughty, "*Shhhh.*"

I pushed her hand away. "What's your problem?"

"You're my problem, Eve," she argued, except she said it in a whisper. Directly against my ear, the barest hint of her lips on my skin. My limbs went taut, every nerve ending hovering between frustration and desire.

"Yeah, you're my problem, too," I whispered back. "And I'll remind you that you came into *my* store, threatened the privacy of *my* family member, showed up at *my* trail head without permission—"

"You can't own a trail head. You can't own *nature*," she hissed. "How arrogant do you have to be to think—"

"—fucking up plans I already had in place before you even *got here*—"

"—that you're the only one that gets to look for buried treasure? When *everyone else*—"

A craggy-looking face appeared in the mouth of the cave,

startling us both. I fell back on my palms, and my thumb slid across the top of her hand. Accidentally. She snatched it away like I'd burned her, then glared at me.

"Hiya, Eve," Jensen rasped. "We interruptin' somethin' or...?"

I sent him a weak smile. "Howdy. Fancy running into you here, Jensen. Are you also out on a...on a night hike?"

He dropped his hands to his knees. "You and I both know why we're here. And I should mention that we could hear the two of you arguing even back on the trail."

Told you, Harper mouthed at me.

You're infuriating, I mouthed back. Then I crawled out of the cave with the remaining dregs of my dignity, pausing only to knock the dust from my clothing. Jensen tipped his hat in greeting. He was a ruddy-cheeked white man about Monty's age, never without a cigarette in hand. He dragged on one now, blowing smoke out the side of his mouth as I waved hello to the other people gathered around.

Harper managed to crawl out from the cave with the grace of a dancer, hair still perfect and a professional smile aimed at Jensen. "Harper Hendrix, I'm the reporter who's been leaving you voicemails."

Jensen's gruff expression didn't change. "And I'm the guy who's been deletin' 'em."

I tipped my head down at the metal detectors on the ground. "You're being pretty public about all of this."

"Maybe we have information that you don't. And who says this is the only spot where we've been digging? You've been out of the loop, Eve. Monty, too. Not my fault you're behind."

I crossed my arms over my chest and hoped I didn't look as shocked as I felt. "Monty declared this location a bust. Pretty famously."

Jensen exhaled another long stream of smoke. "A bust is a bust 'til it ain't. You know that."

I did know that. Another shiver of worry rose up my spine.

"Besides, Monty would do the same thing if the timing was right. And she has. Maybe it's someone else's turn to strike gold for once. I got a wife and family to support, too."

The bitterness woven through his tone wasn't that surprising. He'd held a grudge against my aunt ever since she and her crew uncovered *La Venganza* before he had.

I raised an eyebrow. "And maybe it's not all about you, Jensen. This shit isn't personal."

His expression hardened even further. "Never said it was."

I bit back what I really wanted to say. That the Blackburn Diamonds *were* personal to Monty, to both of us. But that wasn't my story to tell, especially in front of a reporter.

"Do you happen to know where Monty is?" Harper asked him eagerly.

He dropped his cigarette into the dirt and stubbed it out with his foot. "Haven't spoken to her in years. Even if I had, she'd never tell me where she was. That's a lady that doesn't want to be found."

Harper's shoulders fell, her smile fracturing at the edges. Jensen walked away from us without a goodbye, muttering quietly with his crew standing around the pit.

Whatever he was relaying had them eyeing the two of us with obvious suspicion and more than a little hostility. Taking the hint, I climbed back up the trail and set off toward my car, and Harper was unusually silent as she followed me. My mind whirled with conflicting information, torn between writing it all off and taking Jensen at his word.

This would be a lot easier if Monty returned any of my calls.

When I reached the empty parking lot, I opened my passenger-side door and cocked my head at Harper. "Get in. I'll take you to wherever your car's parked."

She shot me a cagey look.

"Just because we're pissed at each other doesn't mean I'm gonna force you to walk alone in the dark."

Steeling her spine, she brushed past me and slid inside. We drove in terse silence over the bumpy road until I spotted her car and parked. I glanced over at her, noticed her fidgeting with her seat belt.

"That man, Jensen…" she said slowly. "He's your competition for the diamonds now, too, isn't he?"

I swallowed hard. "Looks like he is."

Harper twisted around in her seat to face me. "Eve, I'm out here for the next nine days regardless. Partner up with me," she offered again. *Persistent.* "I've got a team of researchers and fact-checkers at my disposal. Let me write this story, and I'll make it all available to you. It's a win-win."

It was tempting. But… The day that Monty showed me Priscilla's locket was seared into my memory—the sharp, crackling fire, the sound of ice in her glass of whiskey, the rustling tissue paper. How carefully she revealed the locket's secrets to me.

How protective she was of this unique bit of fortune. How protective I felt about it, almost immediately. Monty valued this piece of our family history more highly than any buried treasure.

"I can't do that," I said softly. "And I can't tell you why."

Her face darkened. "Don't say 'can't' when you mean 'won't.'"

I turned fully, draping my left arm across the steering wheel. We were, once again, stuck in a cramped space together while arguing. And I wondered what she'd do if I leaned across the console, hooked a finger in the top of her shirt, and dragged her mouth to mine? Pulled her onto my lap, dove my hands into all that hair, let her passionate anger consume me?

Like she'd said, she was only here for nine more days anyway. It was my favorite kind of relationship, really—one with an expiration date.

But Harper was already on the move, rifling through her bag with one hand and pushing open the car door with the other. "Never mind, forget I offered. Good luck on your own, Eve." She paused in standing up, peering back at me with an imperious air. "You're definitely going to need it."

"More likely *you* will." My attraction to Harper swung back hard to annoyance. "I'm the expert here, Hendrix. You're just some stranger who blew into town with a deadline. And the sheer volume of information you *don't know* about this situation is laughable."

Her response was to slam the door shut and stalk off toward her own car, frustration rolling off her body in giant waves. As soon as she was safely inside with the engine running, I peeled out of the lot and back onto the street.

I checked once in my rearview mirror for trailing headlights but found none. The empty road stretched long ahead of me while a narrow band of the Milky Way glimmered above.

I'd always assumed I'd have more time to find the Blackburn Diamonds. Assumed I'd gather together a team with Monty, figure out how she and Ruby had missed it all those years ago.

But everything was different now, with Harper here, and Jensen's crew was a legitimate threat. If I couldn't find my aunt—which was looking more and more likely—then I was out here treasure hunting all on my own. I'd scoffed when Harper told me, "Good luck."

But I needed all the luck I could get.

Anxiety scorched through me like a lightning bolt, the feeling so familiar it threatened to yank me back to some of my worst memories. Every passive-aggressive comment from my family I'd always tried to ignore. All the tiny resentments, the little cuts that added up to make me feel less than and lonely.

I was 1,800 miles away from them, driving a vintage Ford Mustang beneath the sparkling, celestial heavens, and they could *still* manage to hurt me. To them, I was just a daydreamer with no ambition. Lazy, unfocused, and unrefined. Aggressively average at best. And in a family of such uptight, image-obsessed overachievers, nothing was worse than being considered *average*.

If I was going to prove myself to my family, I needed to find those diamonds and reclaim Priscilla Blackburn's story, once and for all.

All while staying one step ahead of a very pretty, very persistent, thorn in my side.

Chapter Six

Harper

Nine days left to find Monty Montana, write this article, and also, apparently, find buried treasure??

The ghost town of Devil's Kiln was just half an hour from Santa Fe. The low shape of the foothills grew menacing as the sun dropped, all the shades of brown and red turning sapphire in the twilight. The adobe houses with wooden doors slowly disappeared, until I was driving down an empty highway. My headlights traced the curving yellow lines as I wound past strange rock formations and fields of scraggly brush.

I passed a wooden sign that read GHOST TOURS OF DEVIL'S KILN — NEXT RIGHT (IF YOU DARE!).

My hands tightened on the steering wheel as my stomach dropped. There was no getting around the fact that I needed to meet this next contact.

I just hated admitting—to myself *and* others—that I was almost thirty years old and still afraid of ghosts. Even obvious tourist attractions like the one I was about to drive into. It didn't matter if the vibes were, "It's all fake, we're just here to make money." It was a fear I couldn't shake. In daylight or not, in sunny weather or thunderstorms, alone or with friends.

My mom had loved scary movies of every flavor, and the night before she died, Daphne and I had watched some ghostly flick with her that had given me actual nightmares. I'd tossed and turned for hours, but had felt too embarrassed—at the ripe old age of fifteen—to run into my parents' bedroom.

It wouldn't have mattered anyway, since she passed away in her sleep from an undiagnosed heart condition. The ambulance was already on its way by the time Daphne and I had stumbled out of bed that morning and wondered why Dad was standing in the hallway with an expression of such anguish my blood had run cold.

Years of grief therapy helped me understand my emotional association between my mother's early death and the spirits that haunt us from beyond the grave. It didn't take much analysis to get it, but sharing this fear with anyone besides Daphne made me feel fragile and much too sensitive, like some Victorian widow fainting during a seance.

I turned right and drove slowly around the potholes dotting the road. I might have felt a little more emotionally resilient if I'd slept last night, instead of doing what I'd actually done. Which was conducting imaginary arguments with Eve Bardot in my head, making sure I won every time.

You're just some stranger who blew into town with a deadline. And the sheer volume of information you don't know about this situation is laughable.

My phone rang, and I sent it to my car speakers. My fact checker's voice crackled through.

"Hey, it's Kristi," she said. "How's life on the road?"

I forced a wide smile, then remembered she couldn't see me. "When I get back to Brooklyn, I'm never leaving my apartment again."

"Rough, huh?"

I passed a sign that said WARNING: GHOST CROSSING and immediately hit a pothole. "Just different," I said through gritted teeth. "Much less routine than I would prefer."

"It's been anarchy with the office supplies since you've been gone," she said. "The Post-it notes aren't stored by color, and the pen supply has gone rogue."

I shook my head. "Fucking monsters."

Kristi laughed, but she was one of just a few staff members who appreciated my intense and lifelong dedication to staying organized. But nothing quieted the chaos in my brain like the sight of a clean desk and a to-do list with every item neatly checked off.

Which made this treasure-hunting-themed work trip especially hellish.

"I've been poking around any other records of residence for Loretta-Mae Montana, and nothing's popping up. Just her house in Taos you already visited."

"And the neighbors told me it's being rented out," I murmured.

"That tracks, but I'll keep looking," she said. "And I've been gathering extra background information on William and Priscilla Blackburn. You know, before she disappeared with the diamonds, he was despised by the public. Wealthy men in that era were often torn apart in the newspapers and political cartoons, and William was no exception. Especially since he wasn't a fan of workers' rights *or* their safety."

My tires crunched over gravel as I approached the parking lot. "So what happened after his wife disappeared?"

"His public persona improved. Her disappearance was such a high-profile story at that time. A grieving husband, a pretty wife with secrets, scandalous marital rumors." Kristi's fingers clacked on her mechanical keyboard in the background. "Priscilla was portrayed as the villain, of course, and William the victim. He even got a few political appointments in the years after."

I slowed the car to a stop beneath a dimly lit streetlight, turning over this new information. "He sounds horrible, but I can't say I'm surprised that he came out of it on top."

"You haven't heard the worst of it," she continued. "I got sucked down a Reddit rabbit hole today about Priscilla Blackburn. There's a long-standing theory that she never left *or* stole the diamonds but was murdered by William because he found out she was cheating on him. The 'missing diamonds' angle was nothing but a cover-up."

I was already shaking my head before she even finished. "That would mean every treasure hunter I've been talking to out here has been chasing a dead end for decades."

"Don't you think that's slightly more realistic than believing this woman *actually* pulled off a diamond heist, then disappeared without a trace?"

Reaching across the console, I pulled out my notebook, flipping open to what I'd scribbled after several conversations I'd had today. "I get the reasoning, I do," I admitted. "But it doesn't explain the existence of Priscilla's locket, allegedly recovered in this area. Plus there are people I spoke to on X Marks the Spot today who showed me old newspaper clippings, eyewitness accounts of seeing Priscilla Blackburn get off the train in Haven's Bluff, a small town about an hour north of here. The same town where they found her locket."

"Hmmmm," Kristi hummed under her breath. "Not to be all 'fact-check-y' about this, but they could easily be fakes. Same as the locket. Can you send them to me for verification?"

"Already on the way," I said, with more confidence than I felt. I was a trained journalist. I already knew there were major holes in this story.

Didn't stop me from wincing in disappointment at everything she poked at. Seeking out this missing fortune was only supposed to be my way of finding Monty, of strategically hunting the treasure hunter. But I was starting to grow unprofessionally attached to the idea of Priscilla Blackburn stealing from her shitty husband and making a break for it.

The kind of professional error my father just *loved* to point out in my work when he spotted it.

"I also learned that the general store in Haven's Bluff kept a log of visitors to help identify people looking for family members who'd traveled through on the railroad. Local historians found the preserved logs from 1900... A few weeks after Priscilla disappeared, her name shows up on that sheet," I said, a newly learned detail that gave me goose bumps when I'd read it this morning.

"Send me images of the logs, too...*but...*"

"*Kristi.*" I laughed, letting my head fall back against the seat. "Don't say it."

"Something like that is easily forged, Harper," she said, a teasing warmth in her voice. "And I know you know that."

I stared out past the asphalt I was parked on, into a wide field, pale and misty in the moonlight. Thought about that famous picture of Monty, posing victoriously with her wife. Thought about Priscilla, dreaming at night about her great escape to the West.

A shiver passed through me, more from anticipation than fear this time. Whatever defiant little seeds were taking root in my heart had responded to these new clues today, unfurling at the notion of Priscilla, out here, fleeing down the train platform toward her freedom.

Basically the exact opposite of the neat and tidy to-do lists I used to keep control of my life back home.

"There's something about this story, Kristi," I murmured. "It's different. I can feel it in my gut."

A long pause, then she said: "I get it. Send whatever you've got, and I'll see what I can verify. Even if that means spending the next few days on true crime Reddit threads."

"We don't deserve you," I said with a smile before hanging up. Then I stashed my phone and notebook in my bag and stepped out into the swirling mist. My contact for tonight, Waylon Boyle, was the local who'd pawned Priscilla's locket to Nadine. She'd kept that information from me originally, but luckily I had a few extra autographed items from my father to use as an additional bribe.

Waylon was *also* the most sought-after ghost tour operator in the area and had a lifelong love for Devil's Kiln specifically. Per his instructions, he was waiting for me in the last building on the left.

"Guess I'll just wander through this ghost town filled with hungry and vengeful spirits all on my own," I muttered to myself, straightening my glasses and shoving a pen through my bun.

Then I carefully made my way down the narrow, dusty street. The mist swirled around my ankles the farther I walked, past boarded-up buildings that sat silent as a graveyard. There was a car parked at the far end of the street, and I assumed it was probably Waylon's.

Until I got closer and realized it was a cherry-red, 1967 Ford Mustang, looking seductively lethal beneath the moonlight.

As did the woman stretched out across the hood, gazing up at the stars with her back propped against the windshield. She wore Doc Martens with slouchy black pants and a cropped muscle tank, revealing her lean stomach and the very edges of a floral tattoo climbing up her rib cage.

My body went up in flames, torn between shocked irritation and a staggering lust. I didn't spend *all* of last night playing out imaginary arguments with Eve Bardot.

I actually spent a good amount of that time thinking about kissing her. Just shutting her up by fusing my mouth to hers, seeing if this undeniable—if infuriating—attraction I'd felt was reciprocated.

It certainly *felt* reciprocated in my fantasies, which occurred exclusively on that rolling ladder back at The Wreckage. Broad enough that Eve could lift me onto one of the rungs with her hand between my legs and her snarky mouth at my ear, whispering encouragement as her fingers worked and worked and—

"No fucking way you're here, too."

Eve's husky voice snapped me out of it, just in time for me to realize she was now sauntering toward me with a scowl. "Did you really follow me this time, Hendrix?"

I responded with a glare of my own. "Contrary to what you might think, I do have a job to do here, Eve. An article to write and diamonds to find." I brushed past her, stalking toward where I was supposed to meet my contact. "You're not the main character in this story."

Eve caught up to me easily. Where my muscles had gone taut, she'd already relaxed into her loping swagger. "Hard for me to think differently when you keep showing up and immediately picking a fight or trying to best me."

A blush burned my cheeks, and I was grateful for the moody darkness. "You were a potential lead. And then a possible opportunity. Now? You're nothing but an obstacle." I flashed her a mocking smile. "Sorry to be the bearer of bad news."

Something edgy danced in her eyes, almost playful. "Then stop following me."

"*I'm* here to meet Waylon Boyle," I said archly. "So can we please—"

Eve stopped in her tracks. "That's why I'm here, too."

"You've got to be kidding me."

She held out her phone, which showed the same text confirmation from Waylon that I'd gotten, for the exact same day and time. I gazed down at it, stunned, until she dropped it back into her pocket and raised an eyebrow. "Looks like we're night hiking together—again."

My lips twitched, and I pressed them tight, moving past her again down the path. A bat burst from one of the saloon doors, startling me, and I fell back with my hand on my chest.

Ghosts aren't real, ghosts aren't real, ghosts aren't—

"You okay?" Eve asked softly, dark brows drawn together with what looked like real concern.

"Yeah, just…just jumpy," I managed. "And I'm sure this man only made an administrative error. I'll wait outside while you meet with him. At least we won't have to see each other much longer."

A slightly awkward silence lingered after that, and I wondered if I'd been too harsh. Though I didn't need to spend time I didn't have caring about a complete stranger I'd never hear from—or see—again, especially once I was on my flight back to New York.

"I don't get it," Eve finally said. "Why does this matter to you so much?"

I sent her a sideways glance. "Because I want this story. I... genuinely think your aunt is interesting. Inspiring, even."

She rubbed a hand across the back of her head. "But that's not your only reason, right?"

"Sure is," I lied.

I could feel the weight of her eyes on my profile. "No, I don't think that's it. You're getting something from this. Something additional."

I reached up and fussed with my bun. "So what if I am?"

As if I'd let slip the personal reason buried within the professional—my father's aggravating ego and my own petty quest. The memory of that dinner party with my father as crisp as the night air around us. He'd spent the entire time using *me* to make himself feel superior to the colleagues sitting next to us.

And what I didn't say then, what I *never said* about the great Bruce Sullivan, was how lucky he was to have had a teenage daughter like me who never complained. Who accepted the role of being responsible after Mom died and he left Daphne and me, essentially on our own, while he was off earning Pulitzers. All the birthdays and holidays, the school lunches and field trips falling on my shoulders.

I was fifteen, bowled over by grief, carved out by the immensity of it, but I still got my ten-year-old sister to the school bus stop on time.

"Monty Montana, the one who got away," he'd said wistfully that night. *"I always did assume I'd be the one to bag that interview after she went into hiding. It was such a shame, you know, what happened to her. But if I couldn't find her, no one will."*

"My guess is you're getting a bonus or an extra fancy byline," Eve said, yanking me back to the present moment. "Maybe a promotion, a bigger office. You've got *workaholic* written all over you, Hendrix."

When I peeked over at her with curiosity, she shrugged a shoulder. Let loose a hint of the grin that had charmed me on the day we met. "It takes one to know one."

"You, a workaholic? No way."

"Former," she admitted. "An extreme case, actually."

I slid my hands into my trouser pockets. Squared my shoulders back. "I don't know why everyone in my life right now is convinced I work too hard," I said, hoping I didn't sound too petulant. "A career is important to me. So is stability, building a life for me and my sister where we don't have to worry if anything…" I swallowed. "You know, if anything bad happens."

"But are you happy?" she asked.

The simplest question in the world and suddenly every nerve ending in my body was shrieking into fight-or-flight mode. This would have been a great time for Waylon to show up and save me from having to answer. But I had no such luck. "Why do you care if I'm happy?"

She laughed softly under her breath. "That's right, I forgot. I'm nothing but an obstacle to you. My bad."

"You've been pissed at me since the moment we met," I shot back. "Why drop the act now? You can't possibly think I'll divulge some crucial diamond information after bickering with you for the past three days."

"Do you ever wonder if everyone in your life thinks you work too hard because of that giant stick up your ass?" she asked. Taunted, really. And when I whirled on her, her eyes blazed with annoyance again.

"Anyone ever tell *you* that your arrogance is immensely off-putting?"

Her eyes deliberately traveled the length of my body, sending a searing heat all the way to my toes. "Is it arrogance? Or do I just have you already figured out? Because I'd have to be an idiot not to notice every telltale sign that the only thing you care about in this world is climbing some bullshit career ladder that's never gonna make you *actually* happy."

I reared back in total surprise. "And you are...what, the person who's transcended capitalism? Figured out a way to bypass having to earn a living so you can feel smugly superior? Thank you *so much* for imparting these breadcrumbs of wisdom, Eve. Whatever would we do without you?"

Both of us were breathing heavily now. Both of us, from the look of Eve's flushed cheeks, legitimately pissed. If there was a time for me to kiss the hell out of my aggravating competition to make her finally shut up...it would be now.

And I almost did, too—my upper body curling toward her, Eve's eyes glued hungrily to my mouth, her hands already raising, as if to cup my face.

But then came a mechanical-sounding *whoosh* to our right, and a screeching phantom flew right into us.

Chapter Seven

Eve

Ghost Stories

There was a blur of movement. Harper screamed. I pulled her against me, where she trembled as I wrapped my arms around her. Half my brain was trying to figure out what had crashed into us—something long and drape-y that hung from a clothesline like a creepy scarecrow.

The other half was reveling in how soft Harper's skin was.

I was a few inches taller, so my nose pressed into her hair, which smelled like a combination of oranges and sunshine that seemed entirely out of place in this abandoned ghost town. Her fingers clutched at my top. Her face was pressed to the front of my neck.

A bizarre and confusing warmth hummed through my chest at her nearness, frying every coherent thought. When she raised her head to look at me, her eyes were wide and luminous in the moonlight.

The temptation to strip her bare and taste every single inch of her ached like a sunburn. Harper Hendrix was as irritating to me as she was intriguing. A new compulsion I couldn't shake.

Wasn't entirely sure I wanted to.

"Eve?" she whispered, lips parted.

I blinked. Attempted to swallow and couldn't. Attempted to speak.

Couldn't.

She squeezed her eyes shut again. "I'm too afraid to look. Can you just tell me if the creature dangling ominously next to us is a ghostly demon, hell-bent on eating me? And I know I sound like I'm joking, and I partially am, but I'm also being deeply, deeply serious, and I know I'm babbling, and it's the worst look, but I'm terrified of ghosts? And I know they're not real, or maybe they are, but it doesn't really matter because I've been this way since I was fifteen and I can't help it?"

Grateful for a task, I cupped the back of her neck and peered over at the thing. Which—now that I was no longer stunned stupid by the smell of Harper's hair—I could easily see was nothing dangerous.

I pressed my mouth to the top of her head. "It's just a Halloween prop. The kind of thing you'd see in a haunted house. It's safe to look, no demons in sight."

Harper went rigid in my arms. Sensing her discomfort, I pulled back an inch, and she sprang away from me. She straightened her shoulders, sniffed once, and tucked a loose tendril behind her ear.

I jammed both hands into my back pockets and shrugged. "So, yeah, you're good. We're good."

Her throat worked. She cast a sideways glance at the thing and visibly shuddered.

"Are you okay?" I asked, concerned.

She flushed, smiling nervously. "Sorry for…you know, leaping into your arms, then word vomiting my intrusive thoughts all over you. I was mostly kidding about, uh, the ghost stuff. After constantly bickering with each other, I thought sharing my childhood traumas could bring a breath of fresh air to our competition."

Silence lingered in the wake of her words, her flush deepening with every second. A surprising burst of empathy yanked at me, given that mere minutes earlier I'd been accusing her of being an uptight workaholic. But I knew what it was like to be desperately, nakedly vulnerable in front of someone who only ever made you feel embarrassed for it.

"Keeping things fresh is smart," I said, flashing a grin I hoped was comforting. "I wouldn't want our arguments growing stale, you know?"

A tiny, grateful smile appeared on her face, a response that felt truly earned.

It caused a corresponding flutter, low in my belly.

"And no apology needed," I added, keeping my tone light. "I've always been afraid of spiders, would rather be dunked in a sea of sharks than spot one skittering across my bathtub. My family used to…" I hesitated. "Well, they're all academics, most of them professors. Ivy League. They used to lecture me whenever I came running into a room, away from whatever insect that had frightened me. Fear's just an emotion, easily rationalized. Easily conquered. Or so they used to tell me."

Harper tipped her head to the side. "They said that to you as a *child*?"

"It sure didn't help. I'm still deathly afraid of 'em," I admitted.

Harper chewed on her bottom lip. "But the opposite is true. Our fear is…it's biological, it's how we evolved. I sometimes forget…"

She trailed off, then shook her head.

"Anyway, it's not important," she said quickly. "My mom died suddenly when I was fifteen. I've had this lingering and very irrational fear of ghosts and scary-movie-type things ever since."

My brow furrowed, chest aching. "That is important. Very important. Is it hard to talk about? We can go back to bickering if that's easier."

Her face shifted open. So different from the variety of guarded expressions she'd worn during each one of our encounters thus far.

But then came the sound of a door swinging open, heavy boots on a porch. We turned toward it in unison.

A burly white man with a shaved head stood framed in the doorway of the only building with lights on. "Are you two Harper and Eve? I'm sorry about the ghoul hittin' ya, my mistake. I'm not really a contraption kind of guy, but sometimes the tourists like it."

I remained frozen in place, totally forgetting the very reason why I was here tonight. Harper, however, was startled into action, instantly bright and professional.

She strode forward with her hand outstretched. "You must be Waylon Boyle. I'm Harper Hendrix with the *New York Review*. We spoke on the phone earlier today?"

Waylon shook her hand, then nodded toward me. "You're Monty's niece, aren't you?"

"Yep, I'm Eve," I said with a nod in return.

Jensen's confidence at the dig site had rattled me. Had sent me poring back over Monty's old notes and former leads with a fine-tooth comb, searching for what they might have missed.

I knew Monty and Ruby had interviewed him about the locket, years ago, but I never found a summary of what they'd learned, just a faded scrap of Monty's notes that said **WAYLON IS DEFINITELY LYING.**

"Come in, both of you," Waylon grumbled. "I had a last-minute group book this afternoon, so I'm squeezing you two in together. Hope that's not inconvenient."

"Not at all," Harper said cheerfully.

We followed him into his crowded office. Posters on the wall advertised the more ghastly elements of the town, plus a few framed newspaper articles about his tour business. Boxes full of files lay haphazardly around the space, and in front of his desk were two rusted over lawn chairs, turned cracked and pale.

Harper eyed them both, somewhat quizzically, but managed to sink down on one gracefully, crossing one leg over the other.

I stayed standing, propping my right shoulder against a bookcase. Waylon dropped into his own chair on the other side of the desk with a tired sigh. He was probably in his early sixties, and faded tattoos spilled over every cuff and collar.

He narrowed his eyes at Harper. "You're the one who's been calling, yeah?"

"I'm doing research for a story on the Blackburn Diamonds," she said, "and Nadine at Barb's Pawn Shop pointed me in your direction."

"And you?" he asked, turning my way.

I shot him a look. "I think you know why I'm here."

He huffed out a laugh, picking up a glass of what looked like whiskey. "Every damn treasure hunter in the tri-county area's been out here this week, all asking me about that locket I sold to Nadine. Are you two working together?"

"Absolutely not," I said, just as Harper replied, "I'm *trying* to convince her we should."

Which reminded me that any new information he gave us tonight would be heard not only by me, but also by the very persistent reporter I was desperately trying to stay one step ahead of.

At least until ten minutes ago, when I was—happily—protecting her from ghosts.

Bemused, he swirled his whiskey and took a sip. "Well, whatever you two are, you've got competition. A lot of it, and well-funded by the looks of it."

My stomach twisted into knots.

"Did you know the locket was Priscilla Blackburn's when you sold it to Nadine?" I asked.

He cleared his throat, swiping at a clump of dust on his desk. "My great-great-great-uncle Harry Boyle owned the Haven's Bluff general store, about an hour north of here."

Harper perked up at this information, scribbling something down in her notebook.

"My family's always been into genealogy, had all this research done," Waylon continued. "My uncle Harry never married, never had kids, but seemed like the unofficial mayor of Haven's Bluff. A typical Western mining town, though a bit bohemian for its day. That general store is now a state historical landmark."

Waylon pointed at a framed picture on the wall. "He lived in an apartment on the second floor of the shop, and in the attic, he had all these old records stored, along with a bunch of pictures. And that locket."

Harper glanced up from her notes. "It's one of the reasons why people believe she made it all the way out here, right?"

"Sure is," he said. "Eventually it was just one of those things, y'know, passed down on my father's side, with a note attached that read *William and Priscilla*. Wasn't hard for us to piece it together from there. Her disappearance is still one of those unsolved mysteries people love to theorize about."

I tipped forward. "Waylon. Was there *anything* in those old papers indicating who gave Harry that locket? Or how it came to be in his possession?"

Priscilla. Say it was Priscilla.

It'd been my and Monty's secret theory all along—that the diamonds were buried somewhere between Santa Fe and Haven's Bluff because Priscilla Blackburn and Harry Boyle knew each other. That this area was chosen on purpose.

Though my conviction was partially based on evidence, and partially on pure, foolish hope.

If Monty were here, she'd say, *That's what treasure hunting is, kid.*

Waylon held my gaze. "I wish I knew. Everyone's always asking, but I don't know shit about where it came from or why he kept it and never sold it. I ain't got a clue."

He busied himself with tidying a stack of papers on his desk. Harper and I made tenuous eye contact, and I wondered if she was thinking the same thing I was.

Waylon was lying.

"So what do you think happened?" Harper asked. "I'm sure you've thought about it."

He propped his elbows on the desk. "Yeah, I've got a theory. I come from a long, proud line of thieves and scammers. Harry was probably the first."

Disappointment flickered across Harper's face, matching my own.

"*If* Priscilla Blackburn made it all the way out here without getting caught—or killed—it would have been a miracle. Either she made it here and Harry stole it from her? Or Harry took it off of whoever originally stole it. Hell, he could have won it in a poker game for all we know. But if you want my theory...the locket's a red herring, not an actual clue."

"But what about her name written in that log at the general store?" Harper asked. "The eyewitness accounts in the paper?"

Waylon rubbed a hand across his bald head. "A lot of people think that stuff was forged or made up. Priscilla was on the run from a rich and powerful man. Why would she do anything to give away her location?"

Another wave of disappointment crashed through me at Waylon's casual dismissal of a story that had captivated my imagination for most of my adult life.

It was unnerving, having so many paths continue to come up empty. My most persistent late-night anxiety wasn't that someone else would find the diamonds before we did.

It was that the real reason Ruby and Monty hadn't succeeded the first time was because the diamonds never existed in the first place. That they really were just an old campfire story.

Harper tapped her pen against the side of her notebook. "Then maybe coming here was intentional. Maybe your uncle Harry was Priscilla's contact out here. He could have helped her on her journey."

I sent her a covert look, surprised that she'd come round to my and Monty's favorite theory through instinct alone.

"Why do you say that?" Waylon asked.

"I can't know without proof, obviously," Harper said. "But given the time period, she would have needed a solid plan to steal her husband's fortune and not get caught. And she would have needed help to do so, which is why I was wondering if your uncle was an accomplice."

"Huh," Waylon said, twisting his glass of whiskey back and forth. "That's an interesting idea."

"Think about it," Harper said, growing more excited. "She was a white woman in the 1900s, married to an oil baron. Her freedom was limited, yes, but she had *way* more privilege than most. She was risking that privilege, risking her reputation, her safety, her future. She'd broken the *law* and by all accounts fled, alone, into a part of the country that still relied on vigilante justice."

Waylon arched an eyebrow. "What's your point?"

"That this was a last resort for her. That Priscilla Blackburn had to have an extremely valid reason to do what she did, given what she left behind."

I shifted on my feet, suddenly restless, thinking of all I'd been keeping from Harper.

"William could have been abusive, certainly," Harper continued. "But maybe she fell in love with someone else. Someone she wasn't supposed to."

"Like who?" I asked.

She peered over at me with cheeks gone pink. "What if… what if she'd fallen in love with another woman?"

Chapter Eight

Eve

Feckless Daydreamers with No Goals or Ambition

What if she'd fallen in love with another woman?

Waylon averted his gaze, re-tidying the papers he'd just fixed a few minutes ago. Meanwhile, I was yanked back to the day Monty had first showed me Priscilla's locket.

My most prized possession, she'd said, her fingers trembling uncharacteristically as she'd passed it to me. *We could have uncovered the rarest jewels from that Spanish warship we found, and none of it would ever matter as much as this does to me.*

She'd looked at me then, slightly cocky in her cowboy hat, her gray braid reflecting the orange hue from the fireplace. *This is our legacy, Evie. Yours and mine. No family of ours can ever take it from us.*

I cleared my throat, raking a hand through my hair when Harper glanced over at me again, curiously. But then Waylon was rising from his chair and grabbing a hat and flashlight. "Look, that's nice of you to think, Miss Hendrix. But there's no evidence of any of that. It's pure conjecture at this point, which, to be honest, is all the Blackburn Diamonds have ever been."

Harper jumped to her feet, her smile tight at the edges. "I do have more questions. I'm sure with some time we can unravel this mystery. You've already been so helpful."

Waylon moved past us to open the door, letting in the cool night air. "Probably, but I'm just not interested. And I don't know anything else." He clicked on his flashlight, turning his round face ghoulish. "Now if you don't mind, I've got tourists to scare."

I swallowed a frustrated sigh. "Thanks for giving us your time. It was nice to see you."

"You'll give my regards to Monty?" he asked.

If she ever calls me back.

"Sure thing," I said with a nod.

Behind me, Harper was passing along about fifteen different ways to keep in touch with her. By the time she and I were walking back down the narrow street, bursts of headlights from the parking lot were already appearing.

"I think Waylon's hiding something," Harper said softly.

I opened my mouth to agree, then snapped it shut. We weren't working together.

"I'll keep on him. He'll talk eventually."

I cut my eyes to her profile. "You heard him back there. He already shared all he knows, and it's not much. I wouldn't waste your time."

I freed my keys, lengthening my stride as we neared the Mustang.

"I don't have time to waste either way," she murmured. "I fly back to Brooklyn in a week, and if I can't get him to trust me in person, I doubt he'll do it over the phone."

We reached my car, and I leaned back against the driver's

side door. I'd parked next to a crumbling saloon, the swinging doors still attached, and what sounded like an entire family of bats living inside. The clouds parted, revealing a three-quarters moon like a blossoming gardenia, floating above our heads.

"And you really think you're gonna find the diamonds before then?" I asked, though I still didn't believe she'd come even close.

True to form, Harper raised her chin. "I'll find the diamonds or Monty, whichever comes first."

Hesitantly, as if concerned I would bite, she leaned back next to me, though at least a foot separated our bodies. Her suspicions back at Waylon's office had me studying her in a new light. And I noticed, for the first time, the weary lines around her mouth when she wasn't smiling. The purple circles beneath her eyes.

"Why did you mention you thought Priscilla might have run off with another woman?" I asked.

Harper released a tired-sounding breath. "Do you know who the journalist Bruce Sullivan is?"

"Of course. Why?"

"That's my dad."

I sent her a look of pure surprise. "Are you being for real?"

She pressed her lips into a thin line. "We don't share the same last name. I legally changed it to my mother's maiden name when I graduated from high school. He's a very talented writer. He's not that great of a dad."

I shifted on my feet. "I've got some experience with parents who aren't that great."

Her eyes softened. "I'm sorry to hear that, Eve."

"It's nothing. Really," I said. "What does your dad have to do with Priscilla?"

She was quiet for a moment, staring out at the abandoned field that surrounded us. "My dad always taught me that interviewing people means stripping away our assumptions. We enter every situation with our own internal biases, our own personal histories and experiences. And if we're not careful, those biases can lead us to ask the wrong questions. Which, of course, is *exactly* what I did with Waylon."

My entire body tightened with an unexplained anticipation.

"I could have pressed him more, tried another angle to get him to reveal whatever it is he's lying about." She turned her body until she was facing me. The energy between us shifted with her movement, regaining the same heady buzz from earlier. "Technically, I'm out here to write a story about Monty, but over the past couple days I've grown so captivated by Priscilla's life. She risked everything to do what she did. And all these online amateur sleuths love to paint her as some opportunistic *femme fatale*. But I think…"

Harper went quiet again. I didn't interrupt, all too aware that a few missing pieces were about to snap into place. Answers to a burning question I'd had from the first moment I'd seen Harper balanced on top of that rolling ladder, her fingers tracing the spine of each book with devotion.

Her eyes slid to mine. "I think Priscilla Blackburn was queer."

My stomach flipped over about a dozen times.

"Something about her just calls to me. I can't even fully explain it. I certainly wouldn't share this feeling with my editor. Or, worse, my dad."

"They wouldn't trust your professional instincts on this?" I asked carefully.

Harper laughed bitterly. "He would call it confirmation bias, not instinct."

Then she looked up at me, almost wary. A little uncertain. It provoked an immediate impulse to soothe, to make it easier for her to say what I suspected she needed to.

"I get being called to it," I said slowly. "I'm bi. And there are just some things that *feel* queer to me. Some stories and people and narratives that resonate with me at this soul-deep level."

Harper's eyes lit up, the barest hint of a smile in the curve of her lips. "I'm bi, too." She reached up, touched her nose self-consciously. "In case you, um...missed my septum ring."

I held her gaze for a long second. "I noticed it."

Stopped myself from saying, *Because I noticed you.*

When she spoke again, her voice shook slightly. "All of that is to say, it's why I'm worried that none of this is instinct at all. Only seeing myself in the lives of unhappy women throughout history."

Guilt whispered through me. If there was a perfect time to reveal my secrets, it would be now.

"I do the same thing, though," I admitted. "I spent years, essentially living in various campus libraries, searching for myself in every story that wasn't told. Searching for...for queerness, for transness, for gender non-conformity. For all the ways people built community outside of the status quo. For the people who fought back, who defied every law. Every time I stumbled upon someone like us, hidden in the back pages, it felt like discovering a tiny revolution."

Harper was nodding. "Yes, that's it. That's exactly how I feel about Priscilla. Professionally speaking, this is the worst time for a story to get this personal. Except here I am, fervently hoping I'll discover some indisputable clue that tells me who she really was. That tells me she was, in her own way...a revolution."

I was suddenly very aware of how alone we were in this parking lot. Of the long shadows, the slick stillness, the cluster of freckles beneath Harper's left eye I hadn't noticed before.

Harper gnawed at her bottom lip, her gaze darting across my face. "I wasn't going to say anything earlier. It didn't feel right, in between arguments, to offer up an apology you might not even want. But I...I know what happened to Monty and Ruby after they found *La Venganza*, what you were referring to on the day that we met. I'm appalled, and I'm truly sorry."

My face went hot at the quick subject change, followed by a familiar spike of betrayal.

"It felt like everyone in the world was trying to be the photographer that captured the moment Monty Montana struck gold again," I said bitterly. "But that media frenzy never captured the true spirit of why Monty and Ruby went after that ship in the first place, which was more about the joy of discovery, of intrigue, the true spirit of adventure. Everything they found, all the jewels and valuables, they returned to the Bahamian people."

"I didn't know that," Harper said softly. "Why?"

"The Spanish crew of *La Venganza* had stolen it from them in the first place," I said wryly. "Monty and Ruby returned it to its rightful owners."

I passed a hand through my hair, tugging at the curls. "But all the hate mail, all the attention, it wasn't the same for Monty and Ruby after that. They went into hiding, and it strained their marriage. Everything got even worse when Monty became obsessed with the Blackburn Diamonds and sunk thousands of dollars into research, travel, hired local historians. It was a huge gamble, but Monty swore it was worth the risk."

Harper pushed up her glasses with the palm of her hand. "And that's why they're separated now?"

My stomach twisted at the memories. "Monty won't talk about her with me. She's secretive and a bit paranoid on a good day. Talking about messy relationship feelings has never been on the menu for her."

A slow understanding dawned on Harper's face, and she took a step away from me. "You're never going to let me interview her, are you? Even if…even if I earned your trust? Or hers?"

"You're a reporter, Hendrix. The media ruined Monty's life. How could I expose her to something like that ever again?"

She was nodding with a look of complete disappointment on her face. "What the press did to your aunt is unforgivable. It's the ugliest side of my industry, one I take no pride in. But I'm not like that, Eve. Doesn't your aunt deserve a chance to tell her own story?"

My eyes narrowed. "You've already admitted that you'll do anything to get this scoop, all just to hit some deadline. How can I trust that once you got back to New York you'd keep your word?"

Her blue eyes flashed. "That's not fair."

"We're total strangers," I said, eyebrow cocked. "I have no reason to believe you and no reason to fight fair."

"But I thought…" She stopped, looking hurt, then I watched her plaster what seemed to be a very fake smile on her face. "You know what? It doesn't matter. You're right, Eve. We don't owe each other a damn thing."

And then she strode away, leaving me alone in the mist and the moonlight with an echo of thwarted longing in my chest. All of it reminding me, yet again, what my parents' abandonment had taught me, in ways both big and small.

It was always better to leave them before they left you.

A sudden weariness flooded my body, but there was no time to rest. Not if I was going to stay one step ahead—at least—of Jensen's crew, and whoever else was already out there searching. And definitely not if I was going to keep pace with Harper's tenacity.

My family believed Monty and me to be feckless daydreamers with no goals or ambition. I'd already quit my doctoral program, the worst possible sin for a pair of reputation-obsessed professors. Monty had already tried to find the diamonds once and failed.

What would it say about us if they were found now, by Jensen or Harper or anyone else?

I couldn't let that happen.

Which meant the chase was officially back on and I needed to start preparing.

Immediately.

Chapter Nine

Eve

Harper Hendrix is Extremely Determined

I was balanced at the top of a ladder, removing the bolts surrounding two antique light fixtures. A pair of screws dropped into my open palm. Shoving the drill into my tool belt, I gently lowered the light—a set of teardrop-shaped bulbs, sea-green beneath the grime.

We were back at the same hotel demo site where we'd retrieved the starburst bar, but my restless mind was a thousand miles away, planning for a treasure hunt I still desperately hoped I'd be doing with my aunt.

And trying not to get caught up in yet another erotic fantasy starring the very pretty, very persistent reporter I needed to stay away from. She'd been a constant presence in my head ever since she'd walked away from me last night. Something about all that dark, gorgeous hair of hers, perfectly controlled in that bun. The way it exposed the nape of her neck, her ears, every tender place I'd press my mouth to, my tongue. My teeth.

I wanted to see that hair undone and unruly, falling in glorious waves that I gathered up in my hands. Wanted to tug her head back and see that delicate throat exposed, to see her vulnerable and open. Needy.

"You're thinking about Hotter Lois Lane again, aren't you?" Cleo said, effectively snapping me out of it.

I pulled down the bandana covering my nose and mouth and pretended to scowl. "I was *actually* pondering the effects of the Great Depression on the Art Deco movement, thank you very much."

Cleo snorted. "So...super-horny thoughts, then?"

Laughing, I made my way down the ladder and draped an arm around a middle rung, unable to stay composed around my best friend. I'd filled her in last night on my conversation with Harper outside of Waylon's office but hadn't realized how confused I'd still feel about her come the next day.

Not about my physical attraction to her, which was obvious. But about her candor.

"I...I just don't know what to think, Cleo," I admitted. "About any of it. The media has only ever been untrustworthy when it comes to Monty. Something to fear, to avoid at any cost. But last night, Harper, she was..."

Cleo gently took the light fixtures from my hand. "It sounds like our intrepid reporter might be a little more complex than you first assumed."

I frowned. "More than that, even. She was...she was sincere. Expressed regret over what happened to Monty years ago and I believed her. Thinks my aunt deserves a chance to tell her own story, which I don't disagree with."

"Harper's bi. I'm sure her regret *was* sincere," Cleo said. "And look, I love your aunt, and I love how protective you are of her. But I would also hate to see her hide away forever, you know? Maybe Harper really does want to help."

I gripped the back of my neck as my thoughts roiled. "How do I know if I can trust Harper's intentions, though? It's a big ask, and it's not just me it affects."

Cleo sent me a knowing look. "You can't fully know, at least not all at once. What does your gut say?"

"I'm not fucking sure." My face flushed. "But I do know that I...I can't stop thinking about her."

Cleo stared at me for a moment before pulling me in for a long hug I hadn't known I'd needed. "Don't worry, babe. This is a first for you, but I *think* you've got it bad for Harper."

I held her close until I heard my phone vibrating on the table. "I can't *have it bad*," I said, walking over to scoop it up. "I need to be running in the opposite direction every time I see her."

Then I saw who was calling me. "Wait, holy shit." Shoving open the side door, I stepped out onto the hot asphalt. "*Monty?*"

"Hiya, Evie. How's it goin', kid?"

My head fell back against the warm brick, part relief, part aggravation. "I was just about to issue a missing person's report on your behalf, you know."

My aunt barked out a laugh. "Why the hell would you do that? I ain't fucking missing."

"Because I haven't heard from you in over a *month*. The least you can do is not disappear completely on me. You're the only blood relative I have left."

"That's not true," she chided. "I'm just the only blood relative you *like*."

Monty was the black sheep of the family before I was, and they viewed us both with a mix of thinly veiled disgust and pity. But she'd been my idol from the moment I met her at the age of ten—watching in fascination as she kicked her dirty boots onto my mother's pristine white tablecloth after dinner, asking if she could smoke her cigar inside.

And Monty had been there on my worst day, waking up in a hospital bed after another unrelenting panic attack had sent me to the emergency room. Barely three months into my doctoral program and I was drowning in anxiety with no end in sight. Just wave after crushing wave, holding me down.

When I'd opened my eyes that morning, Monty was in the chair next to my bed, her frayed cowboy hat low. At the sound of my stirring, she'd pushed the brim up with a single finger and shot me a devilish grin. "Whaddya say, kid? You wanna go back to that stuffy Ivy League school of yours? Or do you want to come home to Santa Fe with me and Ruby?"

The choice to flee out west had been easy in the end. And it wasn't like I'd *really* expected my parents and brothers to fight for me to stay. But it didn't stop how painful it was when they let me go without saying a goddamn word.

"I'd like you more if you returned my calls," I said. "A simple text message would suffice. *Don't worry, I'm alive and haven't been kidnapped, etc.*"

Monty laughed. "But isn't that the kind of thing a person who's been kidnapped would say?"

Through the phone I heard what sounded like cars speeding by on the highway.

"So where are you, then?" I asked.

"Not home, if that's what you're wondering. Been on a little road trip to clear my head. Camping, fishing, the usual."

I pinched the bridge of my nose. "Monty, you have to tell me these things. A month is a long time. I've been freaked out and worried about you."

"Hey, uh…" A pause, and I heard what sounded like a truck

rumbling by. "Did I hear you say on one of your voicemails that Jensen's going after the diamonds?"

"So you were getting my messages," I said, sounding hurt. Feeling hurt.

"Come on, now. You can't be mad at me for acting like I always do. Now what's going on with Jensen?"

I sent my gaze back up to the bright blue sky. I'd called Monty again after speaking with him the other night and probably sounded as panicked as I felt. "He told me to tell you it wasn't personal. He already dug up that spot you and Ruby discovered out by the Sun Mountain trail head."

A bust is a bust 'til it ain't.

"And Waylon Boyle told me everyone's been out there, asking him about the locket."

"You've been chatting with Waylon?" she asked, sounding genuinely surprised.

"Well...yeah," I said slowly. "We've gotta get a move on, Monty. I'm trying to do as much of the legwork as I can now, but if you come back into town, we can take off. I've got a bad feeling, a *real* bad feeling that the rug's about to be yanked out from under our feet. Jensen was way too confident. It was unnerving."

I heard her sigh. "Jensen's always been a bit of an asshole. I never met a treasure hunter with so little love for the spirit of the thing. But we can't do it now, even if he's out there, making a fuss."

"I know you always wanted to wait for Ruby, but we might be out of options."

"The world's full of options, and we've got plenty of time," she said. "Trust me on this. I know how scary it is when you feel like the heat is on, but just because some people are lookin' doesn't mean they're close to finding anything. You know what I mean? They can look all they want."

My aunt's focused and assertive confidence was one of the things I loved most about her. Except in times like this, when I wanted to reach through the phone and shake her until she stopped giving me obtuse fucking answers.

"Besides, didn't you say there's some reporter out here, looking for me?" she added. "Probably not the best time to show my face, huh?"

"Her name's Harper. She wants to give you a chance to tell your own story," I said. "Like a profile. For the *New York Review*, so it'd be fancy."

"Yeah, I'm not even remotely interested," she said with a chuckle. "Don't like reporters. Never have, never will."

"Harper Hendrix is extremely...determined," I said. "I don't know how much longer I can hold her off."

Then I swallowed a half-formed thought—*what if you heard her out?*

"Well, if I come home, it'll make it that much easier for her to find me, won't it?" she teased in her usual singsong-y voice. "She'll lose interest eventually. They all do."

I rubbed my forehead, staring down at my scuffed work boots. "Monty...*I* need you to come home. I need...I need my aunt, the person I thought I was always gonna do this with. I'm not trying to be a hard-ass, but we gotta go for it now."

There was silence on the other end, nothing but the sound of passing cars. My whole body ached with missing her.

"Evie...I'll explain when I can, I promise, but I can't come back just yet. And please don't do anything rash."

"A bit hypocritical, don't you think? You left your niece for a whole month and didn't say a word. And this isn't even the first time you've done something like this."

"It is hypocritical. I'm not fightin' you on that one," she replied. "But you weren't here when me and Ruby went for the diamonds last time. It took us years of planning, raising the funds, then the actual hunt itself was almost a year long. Even if I came home right now, we couldn't just up and go. I'm sure if you asked Jensen, he'd tell ya he'd been planning this behind the scenes for a lot longer than you probably realize."

I knew all of this and yet disappointment sat heavy and bitter on my tongue. Harper's words yesterday had unlocked something in me, all the reasons why Priscilla Blackburn mattered to me that *weren't* about proving myself to my family.

Here I am, fervently hoping I'll discover some indisputable clue that tells me who she really was. That tells me she was, in her own way...a revolution.

I didn't realize how fervently I'd been hoping until this very moment, hearing Monty shoot it down without hesitation.

"I don't want to do this without you," I said slowly, "but I might be forced to. If you won't come home, if I get news that I need to act fast... Monty, I'm gonna go for it."

She sighed, sounding irritated. "Kid...I'm asking you not to." Behind her there was some scuffled commotion, a person distantly calling her name. "Oh, uh...listen, Evie, I gotta go. Just wait, okay? I'll explain everything that I can, when I can. Trust me."

And she hung up.

In so many ways, loving Monty was like loving a feral cat. An affectionate one, but still untamed and prone to wandering.

Didn't mean it didn't hurt, being kept out of her life like this. Especially when she knew all of my secrets, had seen me at my lowest.

Especially when it meant what I'd been fearing was now a confirmed reality. I'd be going after the Blackburn Diamonds all on my own.

Chapter Ten

Harper

Six days left to find buried treasure and stay one step ahead of an infuriatingly gorgeous salvager

Every single sound at the diner grated on my already jumpy nerves. The orders being called, the tiny bell over the door, the clang of pots and pans in the kitchen.

The Pantry was a lively and bustling spot—a tan building with a teal retro sign. Locals streamed in, bringing blasts of warm summer air and the scent of sunscreen. Through the windows, the sky was that same dazzling blue, so clear I could see the foothills in the distance.

My anxiety wasn't the popular diner's fault. Or the lovely, balmy weather's.

It was the message I'd just received from my editor, Greg. A terse "calling in ten" that sent my heart galloping in my chest. I'd worked on the article last night—sleepless and bleary-eyed— and had managed to write: *"My only solid connection to the elusive Monty Montana is an infuriatingly gorgeous salvager who I desperately want to make out with. But, spoiler alert, she believes me to be no better than a slimy tabloid reporter and is now destroying all of my hopes and dreams."*

A server with hot-pink hair poured me another cup of coffee with a sympathetic smile. I returned the gesture, then rubbed my throbbing temples, tired and wired and nervous.

I couldn't stop thinking about Eve. Her hand on the back of my neck. Firm and protective, the way she naturally angled me away from what had caused my fear.

The fact that I was fairly certain she'd dropped her nose into my hair and smelled it, a deep inhale I'd felt against her chest.

This had haunted me all night long—the evidence of Eve Bardot's desire.

Therefore, quality sleep had eluded me yet again.

I'd suspected Eve was queer but now knew for sure. Knew that she was bi, just like me, which never ceased to make my little bisexual heart glow with that unique pleasure of feeling seen.

And she found herself poring through historical texts for the same reasons I was suddenly so obsessed with Priscilla Blackburn.

All of it added a confounding layer to an attraction I assumed was shallow, if captivating. It wasn't like I had plans of sticking around New Mexico, which meant Eve would only ever be a sexy fantasy at best. She had *messy* written all over her, and the very last thing I needed right now was some complicating hookup that would only distract from the extremely important reasons I was out here.

Greg called at that exact moment, sending my pulse into overdrive.

"Good morning from New Mexico," I said brightly. "It's so gorgeous here. You should see the way the—"

"I have an email from you here with your updates on the

Monty Montana story," he interjected. "Which so far looks like a whole lot of nothing. Unless there's been some kind of mistake?"

My lungs seized up. "No mistake. Did you see my lengthy summary on Priscilla Blackburn and the missing diamonds?"

"You mean a dead woman from over a hundred years ago and an urban legend that's proved impossible to verify? It's got nothing to do with the reason why we sent you out there. Which was to convince Monty Montana to give her first interview in thirty years."

I held my tongue. Admitting that I still didn't know where she was didn't feel like the smartest move.

"I know she's famous for being hard to find," he added. "But you said you were ready for a challenge, Harper, and you know what's on the line. Don't make me regret giving this to you."

Greg hung up before I could reply, leaving me sitting in an empty booth and blinking back tears of frustration. As covertly as possible, I swiped at my eyes and dropped my phone into my bag, every inch of my body burning with embarrassment.

I had plenty of friends from school who never understood why I wouldn't ride my father's pristine reputation all the way to the top of an industry that worshiped him like a deity. Or why I'd clawed my way through unpaid internships and shitty assistant jobs when Dad had been bragging for *years* that he could get me a top gig at the top media outlets with a single phone call.

But I knew better than to trust a man who chose his career over being there for his grieving children.

Pulling out my recorder and notebook, I slid a pencil from my bun and took one last sip of coffee. The bell over the door rung, and I glanced up, expecting to see my appointment.

Instead, Eve strolled in.

"Oh, for *fuck's sake*," I whispered.

The pink-haired server approached her, and Eve slowly removed her aviators, flashing her charming smile. Whatever Eve said had the server blushing and looking nervous. And when Eve finally turned and spotted me, her body seemed loose, shoulders relaxed.

Then she slid right into my red vinyl booth, sitting directly next to me.

I gaped at her. "I'm sorry, did I *invite* you to sit here? I've got an interview any second now, and I'd love for you to be as far away from it as possible."

She hooked a tattooed arm around the back of the seat. Doing so brought her knee against mine, sending a shock of sensation through me. Drawing my eyes to the dip of her collarbone, the column of her throat, the shape of her breasts in her tight black top.

"Hendrix? My face is up here."

When I wrenched my eyes back to hers, one end of her mouth was tipped up and there was a slight arch to her brow. I turned away from her—my body burning from embarrassment yet again—and flipped open my notebook. "Like I was saying, I'm busy. Please leave."

"I know you are," she said. "Why do you think I'm here?"

My stomach plummeted. "Did Waylon call you, too?"

She picked up the menu for a casual perusal. "I wanted to follow up on our conversation from the other night. Something wasn't sitting right. And when I did, he was surprised. Said he'd just called you and was on his way here. I didn't want you getting any vital information before me."

"Right," I said flatly. "You've forced your way into this conversation because I'm just some stranger. As you said before, there's no reason for you to fight fair."

She snorted. "Don't pretend like you've been playing fair this whole time, either, Hendrix."

I couldn't help the sharp disappointment I felt at how quickly we'd descended back into our sniping. Foolish of me to think we were getting somewhere after our more serious conversation in Devil's Kiln.

Foolish of me to wish that just because we shared an identity, had something *real* in common, our dynamic might shift.

"I hope it's okay...I brought you an oat-milk latte, Eve."

The voice of our server startled us apart, and this time I noticed their name tag—which read *Ember (they/them)*—and the sweet, almost knowing look they sent the both of us.

Eve recovered easily, shoving her curls back and raising the mug to her lips. "Thanks, Em. It's nice to see you. Everything good?"

"Everything's great." Their smile widened. "I, uh...hope to see you around sometime."

"Same here."

As soon as they left, I cocked an eyebrow in Eve's direction. "They like you."

She sipped her drink. "We used to date."

I am not jealous I am not jealous I am not—

"So you're not...still dating?" I asked. Aiming for nonchalance and probably sounding desperate.

Eve shook her head. "Em's awesome, but I only do casual, and they wanted something more serious."

I added "only do casual" to my list of why the woman sitting next to me was fantasy-only, not reality.

"Ah, I see," I said. "You broke their heart."

Eve sputtered out a laugh, looking surprised. "I just told you it was casual. No hearts involved. But I know how you're automatically biased to assume I'm the problem in any situation, so it makes a certain kind of sense."

Now it was my turn to smirk. "Really? You've got 'heartbreaker' written all over you."

"I could say the same about you."

My eyebrows flew up. "*Me*? Absolutely not."

Her answering grin was all confidence. "In my experience, it's always the nice ones. You never seem 'em coming."

I wasn't sure if Eve calling me *nice* was a compliment or an insult, but that smile was pure flirtation. My pulse skipped a beat. My stomach hollowed. I distracted myself by sipping my now-lukewarm coffee and then saying, "Every romantic relationship I've ever had ended amicably and respectfully. I highly doubt I broke anyone's heart."

"Has anyone ever broken yours?" she asked, more sincerely than I expected.

I frowned, mulling it over like a scientist examining lab results. In the midst of building my career and working non-stop, I tended toward partnerships that were easy and stable, requiring minimal effort. After the chaos of my childhood, I found a deep safety in already knowing the outcome so I could prepare ahead of time. Passionate affairs or weekend flings incited an out-of-control feeling I avoided like the plague.

But that didn't mean my long-term relationships had been that passionate, either.

Eve shook her head and said, "If you have to think about it, my guess is *no*. That shit hurts. You'd remember it."

"That's presumptuous."

She lifted a shoulder. "Well...have you?"

I sat back a little, fussing with the menu. "I'm sure I have. It's not like I ended these relationships and felt *nothing*. I'm not a sociopath. I was certainly sad and...and disappointed. But then I just moved on, no hard feelings."

She studied me for a moment. "You've always been the one to end things?"

I nodded, suddenly nervous.

Eve raised her mug to her lips and peered at me as she sipped. "So you *are* the heartbreaker. I was right. You probably left a trail of bisexual chaos all throughout Brooklyn, didn't you?"

I ducked my head, hiding the smile that threatened to fly across my face. "The exact opposite, I'm sure. I despise chaos."

"You flew halfway across the country to find Monty, and now you're tacking *dig up buried treasure* onto your to-do list. That's pretty chaotic, Hendrix."

"Yes, well..." I fiddled with my earring, feeling her eyes on me. "That's... You have an extremely unrealistic idea of my romantic prowess. And really, this conversation was about *you*."

"That's right. Apparently 'heartbreaker' is written all over me. But you've given no evidence to your point." Eve leaned back, running a hand through her curls and looking like she'd model for a magazine called *Sultry Lady Mechanics*. It was the rakish tilt of her mouth, the white tank, her narrow hips in those jeans, the way she studied me like a beloved painting.

"You know, your..." I swallowed. "Dashing good looks or whatever. Don't pretend you don't know the effect you have on people."

A blush appeared on her cheeks. My pulse tripled at the sight of it.

"No hearts involved when it comes to me," she finally said. "I'm just regular hot. Not heartbreaker hot."

"How charming," I said, rolling my eyes.

"Just telling the truth."

"But if hearts aren't ever involved, how do you know how badly it hurts?" I protested.

She grimaced in response, then hid it. "A lot of people can break your heart, not just romantically. At least that's been the case for me."

I pictured my mom on that last night, how she'd kissed the top of my head five times, said, "See you in the morning, lovebug," then shut off my bedroom lights. The finality of it, how I'd spent months after that trapped in magical thinking, wishing I'd only asked her to stay for one more minute. Then one minute more.

"I know how that feels," I said softly. "It hurts just as badly. I'm sorry that happened to you."

Our eyes caught, and held, and this time something warmer passed between us. I wanted to ask *who* and *how*, to crack open a door to the secrets beneath Eve's confident exterior. Though even as I wished that to be the case, I knew how dangerous it could be. To push past the scorching heat of my attraction to all that was hidden beneath, every need and vulnerability.

Eve's brow furrowed, like she was trying to puzzle me out.

But Waylon chose that exact moment to push open the door, raising a hand in greeting and then sliding into our booth, across the table.

And all that tender, tenuous warmth between us went icy cold.

Chapter Eleven

Harper

Still six days to go, and we are definitely NOT a package deal

"**F**or two people who aren't working together, you sure keep arriving as a packaged deal," Waylon said, rubbing the top of his bald head.

"Yeah, well, she's quite insistent," Eve said.

I was mid-scowl when Ember returned with a cup of coffee for Waylon.

"Whatever you say." He knocked a packet of sugar into his mug. "I'm just glad you agreed to see me again, Miss Hendrix. I, uh...didn't feel right after you left the other night. Eve can probably tell you that it's hard to trust in the treasure-hunting business."

"There are incredibly high financial and personal stakes involved," I said. "Your hesitation to speak on the matter is understandable."

"Some of us are more hesitant than others," he grumbled. "But that's beside the point. Listen...what you said about Priscilla falling in love with someone she wasn't supposed to… It got me thinking. About this nagging feelin' I always had. It never made much sense to me, her running away like that, knowing the diamonds made her such an easy target."

Waylon reached into his pocket and pulled out his wallet, placing a creased photo onto the table. It was clearly taken on his wedding day. He looked especially boyish in a suit with a disheveled tie. The person next to him, also in a suit, was a shorter Black man with a wide smile and a salt-and-pepper beard.

There was a corresponding twinge in my belly at the sight of this. A sensation I associated with ideas that were earthy and magical. A sensation I'd been feeling ever since I'd arrived here in New Mexico.

"This is my sweet husband, Ned. We were married five years ago, but we've been together for twenty. He's…" Waylon cleared his throat. "He's everything to me."

Picking up the picture, I swiped my thumb between their matching euphoric expressions. "He's a real dreamboat, isn't he?"

"Always has been," he said with a smile. Then he handed me a second photo, this one much older, forcing Eve to squeeze in close to peek over my shoulder. I squinted at the blurry image: two white men stood stiffly next to one another in dark vests, a tie, and large-brimmed hats. They were unsmiling, faces stoic.

"Who is this?" Eve asked.

"Harry Boyle, my uncle. The man who had Priscilla's locket hidden in his attic," Waylon said. "This is from a newspaper article in 1903. Behind him is the general store. The man standing next to him is his business partner, Eugene. Per all that genealogy research my mom paid for, Harry and Eugene owned the shop together. Harry lived in the attic apartment until he died."

Waylon rubbed the top of his head again. "And, uh…Eugene also lived there with him."

Beneath the table, Eve nudged my knee with her own.

I brought the picture close, considered the respectable space between their bodies. It was about as opposite from Ned and Waylon's wedding picture as physically possible.

A feeling of pure tenderness gripped my throat. Was this how they disguised their romantic relationship? Business partners rooming together out of practicality and not love?

"I always felt a strong connection to Harry," Waylon continued. "It sounds weird, I know. He's a distant relative at best. Been dead for over a century. But he's stayed part of our family lore 'cause of him owning that store in Haven's Bluff. Growing up, I always heard people describe him as a bit funny."

My eyes flew to Waylon's.

"You know," he said. "Different. Strange."

"Deviant?" Eve asked gently.

His eyes crinkled at the sides. "One of those permanent bachelor types."

Eve gave a lazy smile. "Hendrix and I are a couple of permanent bachelor types ourselves."

His shoulders relaxed down an inch. "Always relieved to know that I'm among friends." He reached out, carefully took the picture of Harry and Eugene back. "I just hope they were happy. As happy as they could be at the time."

My throat still ached, crowded with bittersweet emotion. It was the contrast between the abundant joy in that wedding picture—and the howling misery I felt when I looked at Harry and Eugene. Because we had no way of truly knowing if their love stayed protected, if their safety remained intact.

"I was tellin' the truth before," Waylon said. "I really don't know how he came to have that locket. But I couldn't stop thinking about your theory, Harper. That he and Priscilla knew each other, that he helped her escape. How they would have known each other, though, is beyond me."

"*If* Harry was involved in her escape, maybe the locket wasn't stolen at all," I said, my mouth bunched to the side. "Maybe it was a gift."

Eve made a soft sound of protest. "Why did you pawn the locket? Why not keep it, search for the diamonds yourself?"

The smile Waylon offered us was almost sheepish. "It felt wrong to me, messing around with a story that was probably a tragedy. Didn't want that kind of energy in my life. I kinda assumed that Priscilla was killed in the end, either by her husband or some vigilantes. But if you're right, and she and Harry helped each other, well…that would be one hell of a story, wouldn't it?"

I swallowed hard. "It really would."

He nodded. "I'll send you that genealogy report. It's pretty dry stuff, but there might be something in there that I missed. And you've got my permission to tell Harry and Eugene's story, if you want. Me and Ned haven't had much trouble out here. And my parents loved him, lived long enough to celebrate at our wedding."

Waylon smiled warmly at the memory. "But it's not perfect, and a lot of these folks think gay people were invented in the 1980s. Might do 'em some good to learn that we've been here all along, yeah?"

That twinge of inspiration inside me blossomed like a field of delicate wildflowers in early spring. I felt the soft brush of these new blooms everywhere, from the top of my head to the tips of my toes.

There was a story there, demanding to be told. About Monty

and Ruby, Harry and Eugene, Priscilla's desperate flight out West. Pieces were clearly missing, and I still didn't know what thread tied them all together, but I couldn't ignore what was happening inside my body. A feeling I hadn't experienced in *years*—and now that I realized it'd been missing, painted a truly bleak picture of what I'd been writing and reporting on all these years.

But that could change, couldn't it?

Waylon tossed us a friendly wave from over his shoulder as he left. I twisted at the waist, suddenly full of motivation, only to find myself blocked in the booth by Eve. There was a line between her brows, and she looked uncharacteristically nervous.

"What is it?" I asked. "Because I need to go. This changes—"

"Monty called me yesterday," she interrupted. "She told me she doesn't want to speak to you and doesn't want you coming to find her, either."

I reared back, stunned. "Monty...called you? You know where she is?"

"I don't. She won't tell me. She disappears a lot. On purpose. This is one of those times."

"But..." My mind raced, catching up to the finality of what she said. "You told her about me? Did you tell her what my intention is? That I'm different from the others?"

Eve traced her thumb along her lower lip. "Are you different?"

My shoulders sagged. I knew I looked visibly deflated but couldn't find the energy to care. The way I wanted this story defied rational explanation—the promotion, my dad's boasting, the magical sense I had that *this was it* somehow.

I wanted it the way a deep-sea diver greets the air after breaching the ocean's surface: ferociously, hungrily. As if I would die without it.

"I wish you hadn't done that, Eve," I said sadly. "I really wish you'd let me be the one to broach the topic with her, because I *do* care about her and the integrity of this story, whether you believe me or not."

She gave me a look of pure exasperation. "I'm sorry it's not gonna work out for you. But I can't let you spin out on a wild goose chase any longer. She said no, *and* she told me herself that she's not hunting the diamonds. It's over. Just accept it."

I was already shaking my head, trying to push past her in the booth.

"Hendrix—"

"*Please* move," I said sharply, glaring at her. She held my glare, nostrils flaring, but then reluctantly shifted up and out of the seat. I brushed past her, out the door and into the bright sunlight, and knew without even looking she was right behind me.

"I had to tell you. I saw what Waylon's story was doing to you," she was saying. "Saw it inspire you, and I get it, I do. You know me well enough by now to know how much I relate to what he said. Harry and Eugene…they were their own tiny revolution, and I had no idea. I don't even think Monty knows this."

I whirled around so fast Eve crashed into me. I caught her by the elbows, but she was still talking.

"I'm doing the right thing here," she protested.

"And I had a lot riding on this, Eve. Professionally *and* personally," I snapped. "Save your apologies. You're not sorry. This is the outcome you wanted from the beginning."

She crossed her arms. "So what *was* your professional reward for getting Monty to talk, huh? A bonus? A promotion?"

I dropped my eyes to the sidewalk. "A promotion, a big one. Not that it matters. That's off the table now."

"Got it. So you *don't* care about my aunt," she said bitterly.

My gaze jumped back to hers. "It's possible to hold two conflicting truths at once. I care deeply about your aunt and what the media has done to her. And I *also* have a sister that relies on me, who's relied on me ever since our mom died and my shitty, famous dad left us to fend for ourselves so he could go be a fake hero. Wanting stability in my life doesn't make me a bad person, Eve."

Eve's dark eyes softened, and she leaned in closer. "The reason that my aunt goes off the grid regularly is *because* of what happened to her after they found *La Venganza*. They camped out on her front yard. Followed her to the store and when she ran errands. Late night talk show hosts turned her queerness into a joke, turned her *life* into a joke. There are so many times when I just wish..."

Eve trailed off, and I found myself stunned by the barely restrained anguish in her voice. I'd seen her pissed off, seen her frustrated. Seen her flirtatious, even.

Not this. A protective instinct rose in me, to pull her close and keep her safe from every bad feeling.

"Eve...if I could go back in time and change it, I would," I pleaded. "You don't have to trust me or even like me, but please believe me when I say that. I'd undo every awful thing the media did to her. She didn't deserve it. No one deserves it."

Her eyes darted across my face, searching. "But you can't change what happened. And you're still here."

My stomach clenched so hard I worried I might dry heave. "I'm...I'm still here, yes. And I can't quit. Not yet."

She shoved her hands into her pockets and nodded. "Thought so."

"Eve, don't—" I started.

But she'd already turned on her heel and was walking back down the sidewalk, away from me.

• • •

A summer storm was rolling in across the foothills, turning the morning sky a bruised-looking purple. It was just past dawn, and I sat huddled and miserable on my motel's tiny balcony, watching the clouds.

I tugged the blanket tighter around my shoulders. A strong gust of wind whipped past, releasing my hair from its tie. I made a pitiful attempt to gather the thick strands into some semblance of order but was too tired to make any real effort.

I had five days before my flight back to New York and all the motivation I'd ever need to write the story that had evaded my best efforts to capture it. But Monty didn't want to talk to me. Using the Blackburn Diamonds to get to her was apparently a bust.

And all I'd succeeded in doing yesterday was making Eve trust and like me even *less* than she had before.

I picked up the picture of Monty and Ruby that I'd printed out, the famous one of them on the beach after they'd recovered *La Venganza*. Smoothing my thumb between their faces, I thought about how brave they'd been. How brave Priscilla had been.

How brave my own mother had been—an artist who never feared trying something new, even when she failed. A romantic bookworm, who'd stay up all night reading when a story inspired her. Who encouraged me and Daphne to stay curious, to stay hopeful, to say *no* to every box and binary society presented to us.

She reminded me of Monty and Ruby and Priscilla, too.
And Eve.

I sniffled, shoving my wild hair back from my face. Daphne was right—I *was* stressed and overworked and uninspired. But that had been my perpetual state ever since Mom died. Indulging in joyful whimsy sounded great and all, but someone needed to stay on top of the bills and school lunches and birthday party invitations.

Someone needed to be the responsible one.

Now, here I was, with no story, a pissed-off editor, and no clue of what to do next. I'd flung myself out here the way my dad flung himself into everything that he did, with no planning but all purpose. I'd eaten at strange rest stops, and slept in my car, and perfected the art of eating french fries while driving.

And Monty Montana was going to stay hidden.

I wasn't even that upset about it anymore, not with Eve's very obvious anguish about what happened to her aunt still floating through my thoughts. Would those same paparazzi and tabloids come out of the woodwork if I put Monty back in the spotlight again...regardless of how well-intentioned my story might be?

My subconscious certainly thought so. I'd managed to write a single paragraph last night that I knew, as soon as I finished, could *never* be published: *"I'm currently chasing a woman who refuses to be captured—and prefers it that way. She's a mystery on purpose, and why does every mystery need to be solved? Why do I need Monty to tie up her magnificent life for me in a neat and tidy bow to be consumed by readers who will forget about her hours later?"*

My phone buzzed in my lap, and I half expected to see one of Greg's unhinged text messages. But it wasn't Greg—it was Kristi, my fact checker.

"You're calling early," I said when I answered. "Everything okay?"

"I had a little breakthrough this morning and just sent something extremely interesting to your email. Can you go check it?"

I rose from the balcony and walked back into the room, waking up my laptop and reading my messages.

"Priscilla Blackburn was involved in an auxiliary club," Kristi was saying. "One of those sewing circles where wealthy white women discussed charity projects, garden parties, that kind of thing. Though recent history has shown that, given the opportunity, many of these groups were used to shield some fairly radical activism for the time period."

I clicked on the image Kristi had sent, a grainy photo of two women dressed in clothing from the time period: voluminous skirts, restrictive corsets, lace-covered sleeves. They sat, stern-faced, in a drawing room. Beneath it read: *Priscilla Blackburn and Adeline Grant, 1898.*

That sweeping wildflower feeling returned.

"Who was Adeline Grant?" I asked softly.

"They ran that auxiliary club together and were known to be very close friends, from school age onward. It's a bit of a bizarre tragedy, though. Adeline vanished from New York City on the very same day as Priscilla. And like Priscilla, she never appears again in any historical records."

Monty and Ruby. Harry and Eugene. Priscilla…and Adeline. Adeline Grant.

The missing piece.

Chapter Twelve

Eve

Priscilla and Adeline

The storm rolling in was going to be a problem—but I no longer had the luxury to wait it out.

With one eye on the clouds, I tossed my duffel bag into the backseat of my car, along with my treasure-hunting gear, and secured Monty's absurdly large pile of notes on the Blackburn Diamonds.

It was too early in the morning for Cleo to be here, but we'd finally sat down last night and crafted a plan for me to be gone from The Wreckage—briefly—while I went after the diamonds. She understood both my fears and the urgency surrounding it all, but leaving her without extra help didn't feel right.

Cleo had informed me, quite adamantly, that we had tons of friends who were more than willing to assist her in my absence. Her actual demand, in all of this, was that I "stop staring off into space like a lovelorn romance novel hero" and make a move already on Hotter Lois Lane.

As if Harper Hendrix were just some gorgeous stranger I'd met at a bar—and not a complicated force of nature who'd upended my life from the moment she'd swept into our store.

Not that it mattered anymore. She knew how Monty felt, knew there was no way she'd intersect with my aunt while out searching for Priscilla's diamonds. For all I knew, she was halfway home to New York by now, back to climbing the many rungs of her career ladder.

I was much too familiar with that kind of preoccupation. I'd been raised in that kind of life, brainwashed into believing my value came from the kind of accomplishments you could brag about at dinner parties.

And if I'd had an especially erotic dream about Harper being in my bed last night—naked and flushed, her skin warm and soft, her body arching up to meet mine—it was only because of what happened at the diner with Waylon. Receiving the news together about Harry's partner, Eugene, followed by Waylon's own furtive hope that Priscilla had survived her ordeal.

I'd *felt* her visceral reaction to this new information. Had seen the brightness in her eyes, the soft smile on her lips, the way she seemed to blush from pure joy alone. It was an eagerness that I recognized—the eagerness of the thrill, the chase, all the puzzle pieces suddenly locking into place.

All these hours later and I hadn't been able to shake free of that shared moment.

A burst of cool wind sent dust and dirt flying down the street in front of me, reminding me of every second I wasted, ruminating on a woman I was never gonna see again.

What I *did* need to do was get to Kept King, one of the ghost towns close to Haven's Bluff. For a while, Monty and Ruby believed the diamonds were buried out there by the old mine.

While nothing of note had been found recently, a small cluster of diamonds were recovered in the early 1980s by a local who'd since passed away.

There was no way of knowing if they were Priscilla's. But it was enough for Monty to throw a whole lot of time and resources into seeing what she could dig up.

And late last night, surrounded by Monty's old maps and scrawled notes—many on wrinkled envelopes and takeout menus—I finally realized the likely route Jensen's team was taking. They were circling closer and closer to Haven's Bluff by eliminating every nearby spot already known to be a bust through gossip and word of mouth.

If Monty was right, and Jensen had been planning this for years, part of his strategy seemed to be revisiting every place where a clue could have been missed.

The abandoned Kept King mine still bothered Monty, too. Based on her notes and the corresponding dates in her journals, this was right around the time she and Ruby had begun the process of separating.

And right after I'd realized Jensen's route, I'd come across journal entries I'd never read before, from Monty and Ruby's time digging at Kept King. Her emotional state was more obvious here, her handwriting a little shaky and thoughts left unfinished. A piece of notebook paper had fallen out from these pages, and scrawled across it were the words: THE DIAMONDS FOUND BY THAT LOCAL IN THE EIGHTIES HAS TO BE IMPORTANT, RIGHT?? NO TREASURE HUNTER'S DUG UP JEWELS IN NEW MEXICO BEFORE THAT OR SINCE...

RUBY SAYS I'VE BEEN DISTRACTED OUT HERE AT THE MINE. HELL, MAYBE I HAVE BEEN... SHE'S BEEN DISTRACTED TOO, NOT THAT SHE'LL ADMIT IT.

After that, a paragraph crossed out, then in different-colored pen: *WHAT IF THOSE FEW DIAMONDS WERE IT? WHAT IF THAT'S ALL WE EVER GET OF PRISCILLA—A CLUSTER OF DUSTY JEWELS THAT SOME GUY ALREADY PAWNED DECADES AGO? HER WHOLE LIFE, REDUCED DOWN TO A TRANSACTION?*

And on the very bottom, in thick black marker, she'd scribbled: *FEELS LIKE WE MISSED SOMETHING OUT HERE THAT'S RIGHT IN FRONT OF US.*

The grief and distress seared into my aunt's words had brought tears to my eyes. Made me wanna travel back in time and hold her close. Tell her what she'd always told me during my darkest moments—that no failure was ever truly the end. That she was doing her best as her marriage fell apart around her.

Except Monty was hiding from me right now and clearly keeping her own secrets. So all I could do was take that same urgency and see if I could find something out there that they'd missed.

I rounded the back of my car and opened the driver's side door. Just as I was about to hop in, another car squealed into the parking lot, braking to a hard stop right next to me.

The last person I expected to see was Harper, jumping out with a relieved look on her face and her beautiful hair, free from its bun, wild and windblown. It was almost too much for me to take in—how gorgeous she looked, makeup-less, in yoga pants and an oversize, faded T-shirt. The kind of outfit she might wear while lounging around on my couch, reading a book, with her feet on my lap.

Then I remembered our last conversation. How pissed I still was to realize that Harper was willing to trade in my aunt's hard-won privacy to advance her career. How *fucking* typical of every reporter I'd ever—

"I can see you getting mad at me, Eve," Harper said breathlessly. "But before you say anything, and before you leave, I need you to know...I'm here to make amends. And propose a truce. If you'll have me, that is."

I cocked an eyebrow in her direction. "There's nothing you can say to change my mind. We've said all that needs to be said, haven't we?"

Harper beamed then—there was no other way to describe it, and no other way to describe the cozy warmth that flooded my body at the sight of it.

"We haven't, though, that's the thing," she said, coming around to stand next to me. "Because I found the missing piece. The piece that changes everything. And if I'm right, it ties *all of it* together."

"But Monty's still a hard *no*," I pointed out. "There's no missing piece there."

She shook her head. "I'm not going to write a story about your aunt. Technically my editor doesn't know this yet, and there's a *teeny-tiny* chance I could get in major trouble, but you were right, Eve."

I was having a hard time keeping up. "Right about what?"

Harper stepped closer, still smiling as strands of her hair whipped around her face. "I've been thinking a lot about what you said, about the implications of disrupting her privacy. Of what could happen afterward, the harm and the hatred. It was wrong of me to try and force my way in when everything you've told me about your aunt makes it clear that she's a woman who knows herself well and doesn't change her mind easily."

I shifted against the door, studying the purple circles under her eyes, the marks on her bottom lip from where she'd been biting it. Of the many things Harper could have said, the *last thing* I'd ever expect to hear were the words "you were right."

"Thank you...for listening," I managed to say. "And for... And for respecting her. I know what you're giving up to do so." I raked a hand through my curls. "For the record, I don't think you're a bad person for needing stability in your life. Famous or not, your dad sounds like he was an asshole."

"Oh...it's whatever," she said, looking embarrassed.

"It's more than *whatever*," I said firmly. "It sounds like it was pretty bad for you at home."

Yet another thing that had rattled around my frazzled brain in between lusty fantasies and treasure-hunting drama: cringing every time I remembered Harper's burst of vulnerability about her dad and the way I'd sidestepped it like it was radioactive.

Her throat worked as she swallowed. "It was bad. Really bad. Thank you, I uh... Well, listen, I didn't break the speed limit to rehash Bruce Sullivan's worst traits as a father. Trust me, we'd be here all day." Harper laughed nervously while my stomach twisted in sympathy. "I broke the speed limit because I figured out what was missing from the article I'm *actually* writing. About Priscilla Blackburn...and Adeline Grant."

My heart froze in my chest. Before I could say a word, Harper was holding out her phone, where a blurry, black-and-white picture filled up the screen. I'd know those women anywhere, the mystery that had dominated most of Monty's life and so much of mine.

The secretly queer relationship we'd always believed was our family legacy.

But I'd never seen whatever this picture was, the two of them in some drawing room. This further proof of their existence—no matter how banal—sent a surge of adrenaline through me.

We could have uncovered the rarest jewels from that Spanish warship we found and none of it would ever matter as much as this does to me.

"Hendrix...where did you get this?" I asked shakily.

"My fact checker, Kristi," she said. "I told you...I've got resources. She's one of them."

Nodding, I cocked my head at the car. "I need to tell you something. Hop in. I'm on my way to look for the diamonds out at the Kept King mine, and I'm trying to stay ahead of the storm. And Jensen."

But Harper remained still, eyes wary behind her glasses, chewing on her lip again.

I cracked a smile. "You've been begging me to partner up on this all week. And now you're skittish?"

"I'm suspicious, not skittish," she said flatly. "You're keeping secrets, I can tell. I just dropped what should have been a total *bombshell* about Adeline Grant, and you didn't even blink. What aren't you telling me?"

I held her gaze as the wind rushed around us, tugging on my clothing and the strands of Harper's hair. There was no going back after this. I'd be divulging a secret Monty had entrusted to me and me alone. But if Harper was telling the truth about the story she *actually* wanted to tell, that meant she had the power to change the narrative around Priscilla—who we'd always believed was the hero. Not the villain.

I turned around and dug back through Monty's pile of notes, until I pulled out a manila envelope that contained some digital photos. Sifting through until I found the best one, I handed it over to Harper.

Her eyes widened immediately.

"This is the locket that Waylon Boyle pawned to Nadine, who in turn sold it to Monty. Priscilla Blackburn's locket. Though when she got home and examined it more closely, she realized that the picture of William was a decoy. Beneath it is a picture of—"

"Adeline Grant," Harper breathed. "Eve...that's *Adeline*."

"It is," I said. "And there's more."

Harper peered up at me, the reporter I was about to divulge my most precious secret to. But the hunger in her eyes didn't feel manipulative.

She looked as hungry for the truth as I felt.

"Priscilla Blackburn is my aunt," I said. "And Monty's, too. She's our great-great-times-four relative. Per my family, per Monty...the missing Blackburn Diamonds have always been ours."

Chapter Thirteen

Eve

Damsels and Distress

Harper placed her backpack in the trunk of my car, and then we were off, tearing down the empty road toward yet another ghost town.

With one hand on the stick, the other on the wheel, I sent covert glances over at Harper, who was staring down at the locket picture with an expression I couldn't read.

She'd finally scraped her hair into a messy-looking ponytail— at least, messy for Harper—and she was drumming her fingers against her lips, looking bare and even more tempting without her usual red lipstick.

"Are you okay?" I asked.

She was quiet. Then, "Priscilla Blackburn is your aunt. Which makes her Monty's aunt. And it appears as though she didn't just steal a bunch of diamonds and run off. She escaped with Adeline...the woman she loved."

"Yes," I said softly. "Yes to all of it."

"That's why this is so personal to you. This is the secret

you've been keeping from me."

"This is the secret we've been keeping from *everyone*," I clarified. "Based on the evidence that we have, our great-aunt Priscilla was a queer woman who risked it all for the woman that she loved. Monty and I have spent a lot of time hoping that they made it, that they survived. It's why we're so protective of it."

"And what about the actual diamonds?" she asked.

I glanced in the rearview mirror, noting what looked like rain off in the foothills. We'd left the city limits already, the land around us expanding into grassland prairie.

"Diamonds or not, what Monty and I are searching for is answers. Like you said the other day, we're also fervently hoping for indisputable clues as to who she really was."

Harper turned her head, and I felt her studying my profile. "You want to know if she and Adeline were their own tiny revolution."

My throat tightened. The brief look I shared with Harper felt as charged as the electricity building in the sky overhead.

"You got it, Hendrix."

Harper smiled fully at me then—what felt like her first real smile, and it was more impish and crooked than I would have expected from someone like her. It was like taking a punch to the sternum. But in a good way.

Whatever emotion she saw written across my face had her blushing.

I tore my focus away from her and back to the road.

"You said you'd been keeping this secret from everyone," she said, breaking the silence. "Does that mean...your family? Your friends? Because if I'm going to pursue this story, this all becomes public knowledge."

"I know that," I said, nodding.

"Does...Monty know that?" she asked.

Guilt curdled in my stomach. "Let me worry about Monty. She's keeping secrets from me, too, anyway. Can't say she'll be that surprised."

My tone came out more petulant than I'd intended, but Harper didn't push.

"Monty was basically disowned by my family while she was still a tabloid oddity in the nineties," I explained. "Later she told me she only ever came home to Princeton to see me, to make sure I was okay. She was the original troublemaker—loud, cocky, gay as hell. My parents are elite academics, obsessed with their image, and Monty's always been...too rough around the edges."

Harper snorted. "Does 'rough around the edges' mean 'gay in a way that makes them uncomfortable'?"

"Yeah, yeah it does. Too angry, too outspoken, too in-their-face," I said with a wry grin. "How'd you guess?"

"My dad isn't an academic necessarily, but he's part of that same crowd. I'm very familiar with that kind of surface-level support. 'Love is love' but nothing deeper than that," she said, a trace of hurt in her voice. "No curiosity in learning more about me or about how being queer shapes my view of the world. My father has no real interest in disrupting the status quo."

I followed highway signs toward Haven's Bluff and the Kept King mine. We were now the only car on the road in the midst of the growing storm.

"It's super fucking shitty," I said quietly, "when you realize they don't *really* want to know you. All of you."

"It really is," she replied. "Shitty, too, that your parents abandoned Monty at a time when she could have used the extra support."

"I don't think she ever forgave them for that," I said, then swallowed the rest: *or for what they did to me.*

"All of that is to say," I continued, "if we find anything at all in regards to Priscilla and make it public, it'll be a fight with my parents either way. If you think me and Monty are obsessed with the Blackburns, you should see my family. Dad loves being related to William Blackburn, and it's a banger of a story at their stuffy dinner parties. A turn-of-the-century American innovator and his scheming thief of a wife? Their guests eat it up."

"Of course they do," Harper muttered. "The man stripped the land of its resources, hoarded inherited wealth stolen from enslaved people, and had not a single qualm about his workers dying in unsafe factory conditions. People like your parents probably think he's a hero."

I shook my head. "Yes and it's absolutely reprehensible. It's why Priscilla and Adeline were always these symbols of courage after Monty told me the truth. Just like you said, there are people like your dad, like my parents, like William, who uphold the status quo because it benefits them. And then there's Priscilla and Adeline, Monty and Ruby, breaking the rules because they know it's all fake."

Optics were king in my parents' world. If you weren't showing up with high-profile promotions or glamorous literary awards, then you were totally fucking worthless to them. Life was about impressing others and making them desperately crave your accomplishments.

How would it change things if they knew Priscilla was just like me and Monty? Queer and radical and *free*?

Thunder rumbled ominously in the distance. I changed gears, picked up speed, trying to stay ahead of it.

"So what's the Kept King mine and why are we going there right now?" Harper asked, turning to look out the window. "And on a scale of one to ten, how haunted is it? I'm not sure I can do another *actual* ghost town again."

I hadn't forgotten her reaction back at Devil's Kiln, the way she'd trembled in my arms, her very tangible fear. *My mom died suddenly when I was fifteen.*

"No ghosts this time, though it does have a reputation for having some pretty bad vibes," I admitted. "If you want to stay in the car—"

"*God* no, being alone would be even worse," she said with a laugh. "I'll stay with my knight in shining armor, thank you."

"I'm assuming I'm the knight in this scenario?"

"Unfortunately, yes."

I gave a lopsided grin. "Always did have a thing for damsels."

Harper gazed wistfully out the window. "And I always had a thing for women who trust reporters and respect the upstanding institution that is journalism in this country. But some dreams just aren't meant to be."

I pressed my lips together, trying not to laugh. "It's a goddamn shame."

Harper sent me a sly look, flirtatious almost, before refocusing on the task at hand. "But what's the rush? Did you see something on X Marks the Spot that made you think it was time to move?"

I glanced in the rearview again and gave Harper a quick summary of my Jensen theory, what I knew about the mine and Monty's journals. "And because they were searching here around the time they were splitting up, I got the feeling she believed they'd missed something major."

"But what if the diamonds found there in the eighties *were* Priscilla's, and that's all there ever was?" Harper asked.

My muscles went taut, thinking about what Monty had written. "Let's hope not, because that would mean we've all been on a giant wild goose chase this whole time."

We drove in semi-tense silence the last few minutes, down a pothole-strewn road. The town itself was eerily still, with no sign of other cars or people. The few remaining buildings were rotting, and it didn't take long until we were pulling up to the spot on the map where Monty had circled.

The old head frame was still partially erect, rising above us like a giant wooden insect, and you could just make out the entrances of some of the tunnels. Visibility was impaired by the massive chain link fence, though, at least eighteen feet high.

I slid out of the car, then walked up to the fence with my head craned back. A square sign slapped against the metal, the only sound besides the wind, rattling the gate.

The sign had a blood-red skull-and-crossbones displayed prominently in the middle. The text surrounding it read: WARNING! DANGER! STAY OUT! STAY ALIVE!

Harper appeared next to me, saw the sign, and said, "Oh, absolutely fucking not."

Chapter Fourteen

Harper

**Five days left to find buried treasure,
write this article, and avoid imminent death**

"The dig site's behind this gate," Eve said, clearly fighting a smile. "So we're going over or under. Pick your poison."

I scowled at her. "As a rule, I generally don't do anything that requires signage begging people to *stay out and stay alive*."

She raised an eyebrow. "Where's the girl who pulled me into a dark and scary cave just so she could eavesdrop on the competition?"

"The cave didn't have a sign out front that said 'beware: imminent death ahead,'" I said, exasperated. "Even if we don't fall into a mine shaft, I have to assume we'd be breaking all kinds of laws they don't mention here. You know...because of the 'imminent death' part and all."

Reaching into her back pocket, she pulled out a pair of bolt cutters. "It's only illegal if we get caught."

"We're definitely getting caught."

Crouching down, she slid her fingers along the side of the

fence. But after a few minutes, it was obvious the tool she'd brought wasn't doing the job. Rubbing the back of her head, she stepped back and gazed up at the fence again.

"Looks like we're going over." She twisted at the waist and tossed me a wink. "Whaddya say, Hendrix? Where's your sense of adventure?"

My heart stuttered to a stop, my lips threatening to pull into a smile.

I propped my hands on my hips instead. "Oh, I don't know. Probably in the same place where I keep that stick up my ass."

This time, Eve's grin was wide and full of charm. "Come on, live a little. What would Priscilla and Adeline do?"

"You can't use Priscilla and Adeline every time you want me to break the law," I protested. "What they did doesn't apply here. Some of us like to color *inside* the lines, thank you very much. Especially when danger's involved."

Eve cocked her head. "Sounds boring."

"It sounds *safe*."

She walked to the fence and hooked her fingers through the metal. The wind was constant now, the air heavy, the hair on the back of my neck standing up with every burst of lightning in the distance. Probably sensing my nerves, her expression sobered. "Do you trust me?"

I held her gaze. "I don't know yet. Do you trust me?"

"I don't know yet, either," she echoed. "But I get why you're afraid. I'm saying this as a kid who was also scared a lot growing up and told to 'just get over it.' This place makes me uncomfortable, too. But Monty and Ruby spent months here and always felt safe. That's why I'm here. I wouldn't do anything to put you in harm's way, I promise."

She'd been teasing me before, but there was a sincerity in her eyes now that surprised me. It reminded me of how she'd been back at Devil's Kiln when a fake phantom had sent me leaping into her arms and she'd still taken me seriously.

"I can't write this article if I'm locked up in jail. Or, you know, dead," I said, smiling a little now. Completely against my will.

She gave a nod. "Then let's not get caught. Or get...dead."

I blew out a breath and reluctantly waved at the fence. "As long as we're on the same page about not getting dead, what could possibly go wrong?"

"Nothin'," Eve said, already starting to climb. She shoved the tips of her hiking boots into the fence and began hauling herself up to the top.

"Do you really not trust me, though?" I called out to her.

"Not one bit," she called back. "But you don't trust me either, right?"

"Right, but..." I wrinkled my nose. "I proposed a truce. You accepted it."

Eve stared down at me from up high, bemused. "That was like...barely an hour ago. This shit takes time."

"We don't have a lot of time," I pointed out.

"Then we don't have a lot of trust," she said. Plainly, as if stating the weather. I didn't know why it bothered me so much. This was all temporary, of course. We weren't *really* partners, even if driving out here together, chasing down Priscilla and Adeline together, made my skin buzz with something sparkly and shiny. More than excitement. Purpose, maybe.

When I poked around in my memories, I couldn't recall feeling this way for a long, long time. Maybe ever.

I watched Eve ascend the fence, noting her muscular shoulders flexing with every motion, the tattoos rippling across her skin. The easy confidence in the way she swung her leg over the top, pausing only to shove the curls from her eyes and send me a rakish grin.

"Trustworthy or not, looks like I'm winning," she said.

I narrowed my eyes. "Sure is easier to win when the other person isn't aware it's a competition."

"Everything's a competition when it comes to you, Hendrix," she replied, lowering herself down on the other side.

"That's not true." I propped my foot against the fence, sturdier than it looked, and started dragging myself up. "Our relationship is based on so many things." Up a foot, then up another. My fingers were already cramping with the effort. "Mutual respect." I was starting to pant. "Honest communication."

"You annoying me until eventually I let you come on this trip with me," Eve called up.

I sent her a knowing look through the metal. "Be for real. You would have been disappointed if I hadn't shown up today."

"I think you mean *celebrated*."

I scoffed as I reached the top, pausing for a moment to catch my breath. "You're such a liar."

"You're making a lot of claims for someone still stuck at the top of the fence," she said, and when I glared down at her, her smile was much too smug. But before I formulated a response, I peered out across the town, the flat prairie golden against gunmetal gray clouds. Lightning peeked through every few seconds, and drops of rain misted the tops of my shoulders.

My stomach hollowed, muscles rigid as I balanced myself the way I used to as a kid, climbing trees without fear. I never had to go very high to feel a playful sense of adventure, like I was flying, a hawk turning lazy circles in the sky.

I inhaled the scent of dust and rain. Felt the wind flatten my clothes against my body, my hair a mess of tangles.

"Pretty beautiful up there, isn't it?" Eve asked.

"I always did like being up high," I called back. "I never get to do stuff like this anymore."

"Feeling like a bird is pretty fucking cool," she replied.

I glanced down at her. "I was literally just thinking that."

We shared a smile. Tentative, almost hopeful. Maybe it was easier, totally alone, surrounded by so much wide-open space, to feel like genuine curiosity was within my grasp again. Imagination, even.

I'd felt this way from the first moment I'd arrived in New Mexico, looking for Monty.

I hooked my leg over the top, hoping I looked at least somewhat graceful. Then I put my weight on my left foot, felt my shoe slip off the fence, felt my right foot slide after it.

And I fell.

I didn't even have time to scream. My body lurched downward, my arms outstretched, my lungs frozen with fear. I hit something soft, and then I was on the ground. The impact knocked the air from my chest, but someone was clutching me around the middle.

It was Eve, holding me from behind, her legs sprawled out on the ground next to mine.

The shock reverberated painfully through my bones, and I winced, leaning forward.

"Holy shit…are you okay?" Eve asked, breathless.

"Yeah, yeah…I think so?" I did a little mental scan. "Just a bit banged up. Did I squash you like a bug down here?"

Her mouth was pressed to the back of my hair, hands now hovering at my hips. "Not at all. I tried to catch you but failed. Obviously."

I dropped my forehead to my knees, shuddering through another breath. "The effort was seen and appreciated, trust me."

"Any knight in shining armor would have stepped in." I heard the grin in her voice. "I'm not special, milady, just here to serve."

I chuckled, my head still spinning, her hands on my body a complete distraction. Her forehead pressed into the space between my shoulder blades. The tip of her nose dragged along my spine. Her breath was hot through the thin material of my shirt.

When her hands tightened on my hips, I swallowed a sigh, wishing I could lean back, let her nuzzle into my neck. Let those hands slip beneath my shirt, cup my breasts while I arched against her.

Eve Bardot had no right to look this good and feel this amazing mere seconds after I fell seven feet onto hard-packed dirt.

"Do you think you can stand up?" she murmured.

"Definitely," I lied. "I feel great, actually. I love being surrounded by rusted metal equipment and gaping holes in the ground that probably lead straight to hell."

Eve laughed, then pushed herself up with a wince. Brushed some of the dirt off the backs of her legs and held out a hand. "Say the word and I'll take you back. I'm serious."

I grasped it, letting her pull me up. Her eyes darted up and down my body, like she was checking for injuries, but I waved her off. "Really, I'm fine. I'll probably just be a little sore tomorrow."

She seemed reluctant to stop fussing over me. And I was reluctant to admit how much I liked her attention. It gave me a strange feeling in my belly, a warmth more affectionate than sexual.

Finally, she unfolded a worn-looking map, though the wind was making it difficult. She squinted down at some mystery location while I examined our surroundings. It was depressing and derelict, abandoned to time. There were a few raised platforms, now overtaken by weeds. Some mine openings on the hillside, leftover cart tracks.

If Jensen's team had made it here before us, there were no obvious signs—but then again, given the general state of disarray, I wasn't sure we'd know even if they had.

"I brought a bunch of equipment but wanted to stake out the area first," Eve said, shoving the map back into her pack. "Let's head to Monty's favorite dig spot here, see what we can find before it really starts to rain."

I followed Eve, stepping gingerly on a worn footpath. "And you're sure it's safe to walk all the way out here?"

"Monty and Ruby were out here for months with no problems."

I narrowed my eyes at her retreating back. "You sure are confident today."

She peered at me from over her shoulder, cracking a smile. "But that's me every day."

Our boots crunched over dried plants, gone crispy in the sun, and more tangled weeds. "You know, you're not the only person who teases me about being the rule-following, responsible one," I said. "My sister does, too. Everyone likes to hate on us until there's trouble and we're the ones who have to fix everything."

Eve halted, waiting until I was walking next to her. "Is that what you think your job is? To fix everything?"

"Well...yeah, of course." *Who else is gonna do it?* "Maybe that does make me boring, though."

Eve sent me a look that had heat crawling up the back of my neck. "You could never be boring, Hendrix. Doesn't suit you."

I swallowed, directing my gaze back to the trail. "Do you, uh... Do you talk to your family still? You mentioned they disowned Monty."

Her jaw tightened. "When I left Princeton and moved out here with Monty, I basically left for good. We're not completely no-contact, but whenever we do talk, it's shallow, at best, and still awkward."

"Your parents don't sound very...warm," I said. "Uptight workaholics, too, huh?"

Her lips tugged down into a frown. "They live a life completely devoid of joy. Everything they do has an outcome. Nothing is done purely for pleasure. They've bought into every lie that capitalism tries to sell us. Individualism, hoarding their resources, being obsessed with what others think."

She shrugged, casting a glance my way. "It's sad, really. In her own way, I think Monty always felt bad for them."

My heart ached to hear it. "My mom died when she was only forty-five. She missed out on so much of her own life. Losing her as a teenager changed me, dramatically, from the inside out. Changed how differently I viewed the singular pleasure of being alive. The gratitude I have, to wake up and be able to breathe."

I pressed my hand to my chest. Caught Eve studying me, her gaze full of curiosity.

"What I mean is..." I hesitated, nervous with her eyes on me like that. "I hope your parents start making time to enjoy the little things, even though I know that sounds so cliché. It's true, though. They should go watch a sunrise every now and then."

Eve was quiet for a moment. We passed beneath the head frame creaking eerily in the wind. The rain was still just a warm mist, but I could feel moisture seeping into my shoes.

"Are you doing that, though?" Eve asked. "Taking the time to watch sunrises every now and then?"

I bristled at that. "I mean...no, not recently. But I've been out here in New Mexico, trying to find your aunt, among other things. I haven't had a lot of time."

At Eve's answering silence, I added, "And sometimes you're just making a series of choices that get you through the worst of it. Surviving isn't *only* about sunrises."

She nodded, kicking a rock out of the way. We were now on a rotting wooden path, around which we could see several open mines, dark and dangerous-looking. The kind of pit I pictured tossing a stone into and never hearing it hit the bottom.

The wood creaked with our every step, and the rain was picking up, turning colder.

"But when does that change for you?" Eve asked. "When do you get to focus on the sunrises again?"

A sharp defensiveness was rising in me. I could feel it. "I don't know, Eve. I don't have any of this figured out. Do you?"

She smiled, but it was sad at the edges. "No one has it figured out. It's just… I hit my own rock bottom before Monty asked me to move out here with her. I was only in that place because I was trying to make other people happy. So…are you happy?"

I hesitated. Then hated that I hesitated. "Yes. Yes, of course, I am. And you already asked me this."

"Didn't think you were telling the truth then. Don't think you're telling the truth now."

I stopped in my tracks, stunned. Annoyed. The board I was standing on warped in the middle, groaning loudly with my weight. But I was too focused on the arrogant tilt to Eve's mouth to move.

"You really think you've got me figured out," I said quietly. "From the minute we met, you've made one assumption after another, and they've all been *laughably* inaccurate."

Those lips tipped into a smirk. "Is that so?"

I took a step closer, until the tips of our hiking boots touched. Rain was starting to drip down the back of my neck, but I hardly noticed. "I'm Bruce Sullivan's daughter. I'm used to people thinking they know me when they don't. It still pisses me off, though."

"At least I'm not lying to myself about what I really want in life," she muttered.

"Oh, you mean keeping every romantic relationship you have casual so you never have to be truly honest with another person?" I arched an eyebrow. "If you think your whole deal isn't *immediately* obvious, Eve, then let me be the one to tell you otherwise."

Anger flashed in her eyes, her gaze searing into mine. She ran her tongue across her teeth, sizing me up like an opponent in the ring.

"At least I'm not in relationships that sound about as exciting as watching paint dry," she said.

"Why do you care if they were exciting or not?" I leaned in as close to Eve as I dared, feeling the twin impulses of lust and irritation flood my nervous system. "As if I'd ever make the mistake of dating someone like *you*."

Eve's voice dropped to a taunting whisper. "As if you could handle me, Hendrix."

I wanted too many things at once. Her hands, tearing at my wet clothes. Her teeth, grazing my neck. Wanted to fall to my knees right here in the rain and feel her fingers clench in my hair.

But none of that happened.

Instead, the wood buckled beneath our feet with a jarring *crack*.

And this time, we both fell.

Chapter Fifteen

Eve

Hot Lady Lumberjacks

I t was a false floor.

Common at old mining sites and something Monty had *specifically* noted in her journal to watch out for. But, as always, I'd spent our time walking around feeling the usual pull of intense attraction, compelling curiosity, and mild irritation with Harper.

Which meant I hadn't been paying attention one bit.

One second, we were mid-argument, standing in the rain, the only people around for what felt like miles. The next we were tumbling down together, so quickly my head spun. I landed first, hard, on the dirt-packed ground.

And Harper landed on top of me. Again.

Dust flew up around our bodies. It felt like every bone had been jarred and shaken. Harper's head was down, curled against me, and she was coughing. Wincing, I peered up at the spot where we'd fallen, realizing we were only about four feet down, in what had probably been storage. Rain continued to fall through the body-size hole above us, and the sound of the wind sent shivers down my aching spine.

"Oh god, did we fall into hell?" Harper asked weakly, still coughing.

"Hope not," I managed. "Unless spending an eternity arguing with each other *is* hell."

She shifted on top of me, shattering whatever shock I'd been in, so I now grasped the full extent of our situation. Which was Harper, sprawled on top of me—her untamed hair against my throat, her soft hips pressed to mine, her knees squeezing my waist.

She dropped her hands to either side of my face and pushed up with a bleary groan. Her glasses were crooked. There were streaks of dust along her jaw. She was close enough that the freckles splashed across her nose were visible, even in the dim light.

The deepest craving I'd ever known clawed through me.

My hand rose without thinking, only instinct. I threaded my fingers into her thick, tangled hair and brushed it back from her forehead.

The smile that flickered across her face was much too adorable given our current situation.

"I fell on top of you," she said, voice raspy. "Again."

I let my own smile curve up. "If you wanted a date, you could have just asked. You didn't have to stage an elaborate fall into an old mine just to get close."

A haughty eyebrow rose. "It's cute that you think I have to manufacture these grand plans just to get a hot girl under me."

"Don't I know it, *heartbreaker*," I teased. "You can try and pretend you didn't leave a trail of devastated hot people back in Brooklyn, but I'm still calling your bluff."

She sighed, biting her lip. "It wasn't like that, Eve. I swear I'm not like that."

"Not like what? Worthy of being with someone who falls for you so completely that they're devastated when you leave?"

She blinked, looking stunned, then pleased, then much too pretty. Her eyes traveled down to my mouth, lingered there. "I thought my relationships had the excitement level of watching paint dry?"

"Am I wrong?" I asked.

Her face darkened at that. She shifted back, like she was about to move off me, but I stopped her. Took her by the wrist.

Tugged until she was back where she started—straddling me with her nose only inches from my own.

"I don't think *you* were the boring part," I said, my voice low. "You have been unbearably captivating from the moment we met. I should have made that clear, and I'm sorry."

Her lips parted on a shaky breath.

"What I was trying, and failing, to say…was that if you ended these relationships every time, and they were always polite and amicable, they probably weren't the right person for you. If passion is something you want…then you deserve it."

Her mouth tugged up on one side. "So you're saying you think *they* were the boring ones?"

"Am I wrong?" I repeated with a grin.

She tried to hide a smile behind her hair. "Maybe…"

I laughed. "What was that?"

"You think I'm captivating?"

"In the most infuriating way possible."

Her eyes were softening, her body relaxed where it lay atop mine. But I still sensed her walls up and knew exactly why.

"Hendrix," I said roughly. "I'm really sorry. About earlier. I wasn't explaining myself well, and I wanted…wanted you to know that I understand the choices that you had to make. Are still having to make. I've had to make them, too."

I brushed another strand behind her ear, watched her lashes flutter. Wondered how Harper Hendrix had gotten me here: flat on my back in the middle of a storm, baring slivers of myself I hadn't thought about in a long time. And doing it eagerly at that.

"When?" she asked softly.

"Before I moved out here to be with Monty, the reason why I dropped out. I was constantly sick, had this painful, unrelenting anxiety. I ended up in the hospital a few times with panic attacks. My last one was the worst. It was like…it was like I was drowning. That's when Monty showed up, asked me to move out here and be with her."

Except you hardly even see her anymore, my brain reminded me, and fuck if that didn't still hurt. The thought of Monty seeing the real me that day, crumpled in that hospital bed, as vulnerable as I'd ever been.

And she still wouldn't share all of her secrets with me. Was currently camping in the middle of nowhere, clearly going through something, and I'd barely merited a single phone call.

"Before that," I continued, pushing through, "I would have chosen the panic attacks over being honest with my family. Because the other option meant choosing my own happiness over theirs, and every single part of me wanted to run from that feeling."

Her eyes were soft and warm, searching. "That sounds terrifying."

"My brain was screaming at me that getting this PhD was all that mattered, that it would magically fix all that was wrong with my life." Emotion welled in my throat. "It was really terrifying. I was…sometimes still am…so fucking scared."

Harper nodded, her face carved open with empathy. It shone through her every pore, the way I felt seen in that moment. "I know that feeling, have lived with that feeling. *Drowning* is an accurate way to describe it. At the time, it seems permanent."

"Yes," I agreed. "It really does."

"I'm so sorry that happened to you."

"It's a part of my life, and I'm not ashamed of it," I said. "I just didn't want you to think I come to this stuff easily, because I don't and I didn't mean to sound so dismissive. I remember what it was like being in survival mode. And there's nothing for you to apologize for."

Her dark brows met in the middle. "That's not entirely true. I'm sorry about what I said, too. I...well, your whole deal isn't *entirely* obvious."

My lips twitched. "Oh, good. Glad to know my enigmatic air of mystery is still intact."

She gave a slight tip of her head. "Not by much."

A sinuous pleasure spread through my limbs. My fingers curled into her hair, a big, greedy fistful. I let my other hand tighten at the base of her spine, where I clutched the fabric of her shirt. Her breath faltered. I felt it against my lips.

"I'm sure you're more honest in your relationships than I give you credit for," she murmured.

"Maybe," I said, more to myself than to her. Those words had sent a defensive ripple through my thoughts—spiky and arrogant. I wasn't sure if it was because I believed Harper was wrong about me.

Or because, deep down, I believed she was right.

"You got any tips on how to be more honest?" I asked.

"Not really," she said, practically a whisper now. The rain was a soft mist around us, soaking our clothes, but I was only aware of Harper's delicious weight on top of me. "Do you have any tips for just...doing what you want? Enjoying the chaos?"

As she said that, she shifted her hips, pressing them down onto mine, a pressure so satisfying that I responded without thinking. I let the hand that held her shirt begin to slowly drift up, along her spine. A deliberate drag, the very edges of my nails skimming her skin.

"It's pretty simple," I whispered back. "Figure out what feels good to you. And seek that feeling any way that you can. No shame, just sensation."

There was a heavy pause—nothing but the sound of the rain, the rush of wind, my own pulse roaring in my ears. Then Harper said, "Can I smell your neck?"

A delighted smile startled across my face. "Why my neck?"

Her teeth snagged her lower lip. "Because you smell really fucking good. No shame, just sensation, right?"

"R-right," I said, a little dazed. Then I settled back, tipped my chin up, belatedly realizing how easily Harper had flipped our positions. I wondered if she could guess how I usually operated when it came to sex and dating, how much I craved being the one in control. To tempt, to seduce, to be responsible for another person's complete and utter unraveling.

In every fantasy I'd had about Harper, she'd been the one to come undone, as many times as I demanded it.

But now Harper Hendrix was lowering her gorgeous face to that spot right where my shoulder met my neck, spilling more of her hair across us both. My right hand splayed across the small of her back, now bare. The other tugged, very gently, on the hair trapped in my fist.

Harper moaned, less an actual sound and more a shiver against my throat. It felt wrenched from the very core of her, not controlled or contrived.

It struck an immediate chord deep in my body, in the filthiest

recesses of my brain. Had me aching to do something drastic—
flip her over, bury my head between her thighs. Hear that breathy
moan tumble from her lips again and again and again.

The tip of her nose traced a line up the front of my neck.
Tentative, then growing in confidence. My eyes fluttered shut, my
body adrift on a dream that this could be real, that this quiet
intimacy between us in the middle of nowhere wasn't a fluke.

"You smell like a hot lady lumberjack," she said, and I could
hear the smile in her voice. Felt her lips move. "Like *oh, here I
am chopping wood in the forest, but I'm sexy about it.*"

Laughter bubbled up from my chest. From hers, too, the
sweetest sound. Harper inhaled again, nudging her nose against
the shell of my ear. Her other hand cupped my face, thumb under
my chin, tilting it back so she could explore.

I liked being handled like this, liked being *smelled* like this.

"And what does a hot lady lumberjack smell like?" I finally
managed to ask.

She hummed. "Dry leaves on a hiking trail. Moss on river
rocks." Another heady inhale. "Sweat and sun and lying around
in the grass." Her lips hovered at my ear. This time I arched back
of my own accord, enthralled with the space between her mouth
and my skin. Barely there. *So* close. "You smell like you'd build
me a fire if I was cold. Like you'd build me a whole *house* if I
wanted it."

My hand tightened in her hair. I was breathless and blushing,
spinning out on the image she sketched for us both.

"Of course I would," I murmured. "All you'd have to do is
ask, Hendrix."

She pushed up until her nose grazed mine. Her glasses were
foggy, so I set them in her hair, let the heat and curiosity in her
eyes strip me bare.

"What do I smell like?" she asked.

Fighting a smile, I tipped my face up to press it into the crook of her soft neck. Inhaled at the spot where her pulse fluttered, let my lips ghost across the skin there. "You smell like you've been eating oranges at the beach." Another inhale, along the shell of her ear. "Citrus, sand, saltwater." Another, this one across her jaw, smudging the dust there. "You smell like vacation."

Harper laughed again, shuddering slightly when I dragged my lips—very, very lightly—across her cheekbone. "How interesting." She sighed. "I can't remember the last time I went on vacation."

"I'll take you," I said, picturing Harper in the waves, the taste of salt on her skin. "We can go anywhere you want."

She hummed beneath her breath. "Is that a promise?"

Our eyes were locked together now, lips hovering close. I wanted this kiss, wanted this woman, even as I knew there wasn't a world where we worked as a couple. I didn't even want to *be* a couple.

We didn't even fucking trust each other.

"Eve?" she whispered, doubt flickering through her gaze.

I opened my mouth to respond—to say what, I didn't really know. But then a flashlight was shone down on us both, and a big, booming voice said, "Y'all all right down there?"

Chapter Sixteen

Harper

Five days left to find buried treasure and, uh, hope that Eve forgets that I called her a hot lady lumberjack...

It was like snapping out of a trance.

I yelped in surprise, tumbling off Eve and hitting the ground for the third time that day. Wrapped up in Eve's strong, tattooed arms and woodsy scent, I hadn't noticed how steadily the rain had soaked us through. Or that the dirt coating our bodies was slowly turning to mud.

Or that everything *hurt*.

I sent a cautious glance toward Eve. She was grimacing, slowly sitting up. When our eyes met, she blushed and looked away.

Oh god oh god oh god.

I'd just pinned Eve Bardot to the ground *and smelled her.* Because I wanted to—desperately. Because I could—and she obliged. Because I'd been filled with a wild and almost feral desire to *inhale her.*

It had to be this random hole in the ground we'd fallen into.

The two of us were all alone, in an abandoned town, literally four feet below the dirt. It was like every need and craving I usually suppressed rose to the surface here. Hungrily. *Ferociously.*

No rules, no stress, no deadlines.

She was just so fucking *gorgeous*. Somehow even more so now, rain-slicked and streaked with dirt, like she'd crawled for miles to get to me. And I was straddling her hips, and her hands were tugging on my hair, and her mouth on my neck made me feel positively *starved* with lust.

Had I really told Eve that she smelled like she'd *build me a house*?

A cringe-y embarrassment scorched through me just as Eve pushed up to stand.

"Are y'all dead or what?" the voice asked again.

"Not dead," I called up, aiming for cheerful. "We are in need of rescue, though."

The flashlight traced a path up to Eve's face. She frowned, shielding her eyes. "Tammy…is that you?"

"Eve Bardot, as I live and breathe!" Tammy said. "You wouldn't happen to have your aunt with you down there, would you?"

Eve stiffened. "No, she's… She's off the grid again. Can you help us get out of here?"

Tammy unfurled an honest-to-god rope ladder. I heaved myself to stand next to Eve—gingerly rolling out my wrists and ankles to feel for sprains. My body felt bruised, but not broken, and my glasses had withstood the impact.

"I saw you two fall as I drove up," Tammy was saying. "You're lucky it wasn't worse."

Eve nodded over at the rope. "Do you need any help?"

"Not at all," I said brightly, brushing past her. "I'm all good thanks to Tammy here."

The rope was slick beneath my hands as I climbed, but I still managed to hoist myself out of the hole. Eve followed gracefully behind me, letting Tammy pull her up by the hand the last couple feet. The storm had worsened while I was down there shamelessly smelling Eve's neck—lightning crashed in the distance, and the wind whipped dregs of dirt past our ankles.

Tammy opened a large umbrella, and the three of us huddled beneath it. I couldn't quite make out her appearance beneath her many rain layers, but I caught glimpses of wiry purple hair and wrinkles around her eyes.

"It's good to see ya, Tam," Eve said, pulling the other woman in for a hug. "Not sure what we would have done if you hadn't come by. What are you doing all the way out here anyway?"

She shot Eve a devious grin. "Same thing you are, I suspect. But I checked X Marks the Spot as I pulled up and saw some chatter. Someone spotted Jensen's crew out near Haven's Bluff. So I'm thinkin' this spot might be a bust after all."

Eve's friendly smile collapsed into a scowl. "Well, shit. I'm not ruling out this site at all since it's filled with untapped potential, and we'll need to come back. In the meantime, though, we should go after Jensen. What do you think, Hendrix?"

But Tammy grabbed Eve's wrist before I could answer. "You're not working with Monty on this? Is she all right? With everything that happened with Ruby, we're all just..."

Eve shrugged. "You know how she gets. I told her my plans, but she wasn't interested."

I noted the rigid line of Eve's spine. Felt another whisper of guilt for all that the media had done to her aunt. I didn't have all the details yet, but I understood Monty to be the most important person in Eve's life. Knew that she'd saved Eve from a terrible environment with her parents, had brought her out here to heal.

The media—people like *me*—had chased Monty into the shadows, forced her into hiding.

I shifted on my feet, remembering the two missed calls I had from Greg on my phone and at least one snarky text message. I'd been feigning confidence before hopping into Eve's car this morning, boldly declaring that I'd changed the angle of my story, from Monty to Priscilla.

It was technically the truth.

Greg just wasn't *aware* of the changes. Yet. I'd never begged for forgiveness over permission before, and my nervous system couldn't decide if this was a thrilling adventure or a terrifying mistake I'd regret immediately.

"Here, take this," Tammy said, passing us the umbrella. "I've got another in my bag. And I might or might not have cut a hole in the fence back there, so if you crawl through it, please remember that I definitely *did not* do that. Another very hot and beautiful older woman did. I am gonna hang around here a bit, just to be sure, but I'm rooting for you and Monty. Always have been, always will."

Eve hugged her again. "Thank you for saying that. I miss you."

"Miss you, too, baby. Come by the show sometime and bring that stubborn pain-in-the-ass with ya."

There was a pause. I pointed a thumb at my chest and said, "Wait, is she talking about me?"

Eve shook her head with a grin. "Not you, Hendrix. Monty. But if the shoe fits…"

I yanked the umbrella from her with a glare. Tammy let out a laugh that could only be described as a *hoot*.

"Don't let Eve get too cocky now," Tammy said. "She's also about as stubborn as they come. And half the good-lookin' people in this town would call her a pain-in-the-ass."

When I gave Eve a smug, wide-eyed look, her response was to kick a rock down the path and take the umbrella back.

"Oh, is that so?" I said triumphantly. "Sounds like real *heartbreaker* behavior to me."

Tammy peered over at Eve with an expression I couldn't read. Whatever it was, Eve ducked her head with flushed cheeks. "I'll tell you about it later, Tammy. Anyway, we gotta go. We're wasting time. Come on."

She strode past me, umbrella in hand, and I managed a hasty and incredibly grateful goodbye to our surprise rescuer before rushing off to catch up to her. Our shoulders brushed together, and we quickly jumped apart.

The embarrassment came crawling back. Not only had I *smelled* this woman, but I'd also demanded she *smell me, too*.

You smell like vacation.

I'd been startled by the fantasy that had stormed through my imagination at those words. The two of us sprawled out somewhere pretty and warm. My head in her lap while I read, her fingers scratching my scalp.

"Tammy runs a dive bar in town called The Rogue Cat," Eve said, breaking the silence between us. "Once a month, she stars as a Dolly Parton impersonator in a show called *9 to 5* that Monty used to take me to when she hung around more. Tammy's big in the treasure-hunting scene, too."

I blinked. "A purple-haired Dolly Parton impersonator rescued us?"

"Sure did."

"I like her even more now."

We reached the cut part of the fence. Eve reached down, pulling the metal back until I could slip beneath it. We jogged to the car, both of us sliding inside with dripping-wet hair and mud-caked boots. Eve cranked the heat up, turning around to rustle through the bags in her backseat. She tossed me a fluffy, clean towel and grabbed one for herself.

"Where in Haven's Bluff are we heading?" I asked, rubbing my hair dry.

"A place called Diablo's Canyon," she said, drying her hair with one hand while pulling out a map with the other. She flicked on the car light, illuminating Monty's scrawled notes and tiny symbols I couldn't parse. "We'll take the metal detectors, shovels, and our head lamps to a spot right here."

Her finger tapped at the location.

I glanced out at the rivers of water pooling down the windshield. "And if the storm doesn't let up by then?"

Eve winced. "The good news is that I doubt Jensen's digging in this. The bad news is that it seems like he's still got a head start."

"And why there?" I asked, trying to ignore the anxiety thrumming beneath Eve's words.

"Diablo's Canyon is the site of the original train station in Haven's Bluff," she said. "It was torn down about fifty years ago, but back in 1900, the town was comprised of just Harry's general store, a saloon, a post office, and this station. Monty and Ruby had a working theory that Priscilla and Adeline buried the diamonds somewhere around here. And therefore lost the locket in this area, too, leading Harry to take ownership of it for reasons we still don't know."

Eve paused to scrub at her wet hair. "This is all just theorizing, but Monty thought they stashed the diamonds for safekeeping—either because they were being followed or because something scared them. They were unaccompanied, traveling through the frontier. Anything could have happened."

I chewed on my lower lip, pulling the map into my lap to study it further. Tiny *X*'s dotted the illustration, along with the word "BUST" written across a few places. The sight of Monty's notes squeezed my heart, something about the cheery hopefulness in the slant of her letters.

"Waylon didn't mention it, but Harry could have come into possession of the locket because he's the one who stole the diamonds from them in the first place," I said, feeling my stomach fall. "And just…gambled them away or spent them all. Or, thinking more optimistically, Priscilla and Adeline made it safely to their destination, diamonds in hand, and that's why they've never been found. But I'm sure they've considered every angle?"

Eve's lips pressed into a thin line. "Every angle in as many ways as possible. Both of those theories have kept me up at night before. I know it has for Monty, too, though we obviously would love it if your second theory were true." Her eyes rose, finally meeting mine and sending a *zap* of awareness through me. "Monty was never satisfied with this stage of the search. Things were bad between her and Ruby at the time. I get the impression she wasn't as focused or as diligent."

I swallowed. "Monty Montana doesn't seem like the kind of woman who takes failure lightly."

Eve tipped her head in agreement and carefully re-folded the map. Then she must have seen something in the dim light of the car. She caught my chin, tilting me toward the light with a pinched brow.

"It's just dirt, not bruises," I said gently. "I'll be sore tomorrow, but I'm running on adrenaline right now. I feel just fine."

She took the end of one of the towels and carefully brushed the dust from my cheeks. "Yeah, but I put you in harm's way.

Something I specifically promised not to do. If we're gonna trust each other..."

She trailed off, dropped her gaze. She moved the towel to my neck, cleaning a spot below my ear. My heart skipped at the thought that Eve, too, was concerned that we didn't trust each other yet.

"You couldn't have predicted us falling through a wooden floor," I said.

"I should have been more careful," was her response.

I placed my hands over hers, stilling them. Thought about what she'd admitted to me back in that room—nervously, like she didn't share it often. Her panic attacks, the anxiety, the intense urge to please parents who sounded like they demanded perfection from their daughter.

"Here," I said, tugging the towel free. "Let me dry your hair. It's still soaked."

She sighed. "The curls have a life of their own."

"Well, they're lovely. I'm sure people tell you that all the time," I said, touching her head and tipping it down. I began working the towel through the curls, letting my nails scratch against her scalp.

"I like hearing you say it," she murmured, sounding drowsy. "It's different when you say it."

You have been unbearably captivating from the moment we met.

"How so?" I asked, voice shaky.

There was a long pause. Then Eve said, "I can tell you really mean it."

The rain hammered against the top of the car. My fingers moved through Eve's short hair, until she was staring at me through soft, heavy-lidded eyes. The smile that appeared was less wicked than her usual. It was sweeter, warmer.

Hopeful.

It pierced right through my chest, so swiftly my brain could only say, *Uh-oh.*

"Did your parents care about what you went through?" I asked, needing to fill the silence. "The panic attacks, being in the hospital... What was their reaction?"

"Oh, um..." She rolled her lips together. "They thought I was being over-dramatic. Making it up to get attention."

My hands went still in her hair. "Oh, Eve. I'm...I'm so sorry. That's awful."

She took the towel from my hands, folding it and placing it in the backseat again. "Suffering is the price we pay for hard work," she said. "That's what they told me."

"Suffering isn't love," I said softly.

"No, it isn't." Her throat worked as she swallowed. "It's okay, though. I've got Monty. I've got my friends, Cleo, The Wreckage, a whole queer community out here who've shown me what true love looks like. And it's not the kind that demands I sacrifice my health and well-being. It's reciprocal, joyful, abundant."

I felt it then, this sharp yearning to be held and cared for by a community like that.

To be held and cared for by someone like Eve.

By Eve, specifically.

Thunder rolled in the distance, reminding me of the present danger sitting right in front of me. Something was happening out here, some buried thread was being yanked out into the open, unraveling everything I thought I knew about life in the process.

Eve was part of that, whether she knew it or not. Whatever was brewing between us would last only until the moment I got on that plane and flew back to my real life.

She'd already made that much clear.

Which meant it didn't matter how tempted I was to throw caution to the wind and *leap*—into sensation, into chaos, into the hot mess that would be casual sex with Eve Bardot.

I needed to avoid getting too close to her at all costs.

Chapter Seventeen

Eve

Cowgirls Welcome

Twenty minutes later, I pulled off the highway just shy of Haven's Bluff—and parked in front of the Boot + Saddle.

We'd crawled our way through a deluge of rain, going about ten miles an hour, no sound in the car except the incessant *whir* of the wipers. It was a tense silence, but instead of worrying about where Jensen was or how the hell we were gonna find anything in this storm, I was worried about Harper.

I'd never seen her this quiet. She'd stared stoically out the window, braiding and unbraiding her hair, giving monosyllabic answers to everything that I asked.

Something had happened in the space between her towel-drying my curls and the two of us floating our way down a flooded highway.

Maybe I'd gotten too comfortable, letting her tend to me like that—her fingers gentle, soothing, the real concern etched into her face. So at odds with the way she'd held me down and explored my neck, though the intensity was the same.

Harper's *specific* intensity was the same, like a hunger finally freed.

She'd hardly touched me, yet I was still devoured. It was stupid, really. Caring about a person like this when they were only going to leave.

More than that, Harper was flying back to a life that looked an *awful* lot like the life I'd escaped from: controlled and career-obsessed. An exhausted life, constructed solely of promotions and deadlines.

And it didn't really matter that I was starting to see the way the landscape of this wild and untamed place was changing her. Recognized it because the same thing had happened to me the first weekend after I'd moved out here with Monty. She'd taken me on a road trip to Moab, where we woke early to watch the sunrise. The red canyons had turned a peachy-gold, the sky like a dark plum as the first rays stretched across the horizon. At the sight of it, a knife-sharp pressure shifted and released from my chest.

It was a type of freedom I'd never experienced before. A freedom I wanted desperately for *everyone* to feel, including the woman sitting across from me.

Still—I knew Harper's type, had *been* that type of person years ago. One week back home and she'd get swept up again in the whirlwind. Whatever happened out here would become nothing but a distant memory to her.

Including however she felt about me.

Harper gazed out through the window at the blue neon sign in the shape of a cowboy boot. It blinked weakly in the rain, casting a dull glow onto the smaller sign below that said COWGIRLS WELCOME.

"Don't tell me *this* is Diablo's Canyon?" she asked, arching an eyebrow.

"Close," I said, one hand on the door. "*This* is Monty and Ruby's favorite bar in all of New Mexico. A little queer paradise tucked between canyons for rural and city folks alike. We need some place to ride out this storm for a few minutes anyway, and they happen to make the best veggie burgers around."

Her lips quirked into a tentative smile. It shouldn't have affected me so deeply, except it did.

And that was gonna be a problem.

We dashed inside, and I watched Harper's reaction as she took in the Boot + Saddle's most famous attraction: the shimmering, saddle-shaped disco ball that hung over the dance floor. People crowded the small space, moving as one in a line dance. The silvery lights were reflected in her glasses, bouncing off the twirling bodies.

Her shoulders loosened immediately, lips curving into a full, toothy smile. "I like it here."

"Hoped you would," I replied, trying not to feel so pleased about it. "Let's head to the bar and grab some food to go. And keep your eyes peeled for Jensen. A lot of local treasure hunters love this spot, queer or not, him included. I don't want him to know we're on his tail."

"Yes, sir," Harper said, giving a flirty little salute in response. She looked adorably disheveled and was smiling at me again, and I needed to *get it the fuck together* before I let messy feelings prevent Monty and me from finding Priscilla's diamonds for a second time.

At the bar, I caught Marla's eye and waved her over. She tossed a bar towel over one shoulder and scooped me in for a giant hug. "Now what in the world are *you* doing here tonight? I haven't seen you in *ages*."

I pulled back with a grin, cocking my head at Harper. "This is Harper. It's her first time here. We're, uh...doin' a bit of digging outside of Haven's Bluff tonight."

Marla's eyebrows shot up. "Interesting. *Very* interesting. Well, if anyone comes through asking, I didn't see either of you."

I pressed a finger to my lips and gave her a wink. "You're the best."

Marla was a tall woman with salt-and-pepper curls and a charming smile. She and her husband were both members of the Navajo Nation. They'd always wanted to open a bar together, but after their daughter came out as trans, they were even more dedicated to making the Boot + Saddle welcoming to all.

She shook Harper's hand and said, "And how long have you two been dating?"

Harper turned bright red while I coughed into my hand.

"We're not, absolutely not," I said quickly. "Harper and I are just...work partners." I hesitated. "Reluctantly."

"Wore her down, huh?" Marla laughed.

Harper caught my eye, but her expression was unreadable. "Something like that."

Marla flagged down a server, who took our takeout orders, then she turned back to me with a line between her brows. "You haven't seen Monty recently, have you?"

"I was gonna ask you the same thing," I admitted. "She did finally call, but she's, you know...hiding out somewhere. Haven't heard anything from Ruby, either."

Marla nodded. "Same here." Another bartender called Marla's name, dragging her attention away. "Listen, I gotta get back for the rush, but keep me in the loop, okay? I'm worried about your aunt. I'm sure you are, too."

"I am, and I will," I promised.

She pressed a kiss to my cheek. "Happy hunting, you two."

As soon as she left, the opening chords to "Boot Scootin' Boogie" came on, causing the dance-floor crowd to let out a hearty cheer. Harper angled her body toward the lively sounds, and her eyes widened with a burst of happiness.

She was already tapping her fingers against the bar and wiggling her hips *just* slightly. I knew enough about Harper thus far to understand she probably didn't get to do things just for fun these days.

We didn't have time for this—for any of it, really. But then Harper looked at me with the most delighted smile, and it felt like being gifted an entire field of sunflowers.

"Everyone out there looks so beautiful," she said dreamily. "What's this song they're dancing to?"

I was taking her by the hand before whatever common sense I had left in my body could kick in. "Come on, Hendrix. Let me show ya how to line dance."

She burst out laughing. "Eve, I'll make a fool of myself."

"I beg to differ, cowgirl. It's a watch-and-learn kinda thing. If you can ace journalism school, you can learn the Boot Scootin' Boogie. Trust me."

She flushed prettily. "Fairly presumptuous of you to assume I *aced* it."

I pulled her to the very edge of the dance floor, reluctant to let her go. "Am I wrong?"

She hesitated. "Okay, I aced it."

"I know brilliance when I see it," I said with a wink. "Just watch me, okay?"

An extremely cute woman with bright-blue hair slid right next to Harper, giving her a flirtatious smile. A second later, she dropped her cowboy hat onto Harper's head, who laughed in surprise.

"The hat looks good on you," the woman called out as she twirled.

"Thank you so much," Harper called back. She spun to face me, eyes big behind her glasses. "Guess I'm a real cowgirl, now. Jealous?"

I nudged my knuckle beneath her chin. "She's right. It does look good on you."

We shared a charged look beneath the spinning disco saddle. Then the line dancers moved into place next to us, and I started to move. I walked forward four steps, kicked up my thigh, then did the same thing going backward.

Harper yelped and grabbed my arm. "Wait, wait, wait…is this a heel-toe step?"

"It's a lot of things all at once," I said over my shoulder, giving a clap. "Don't think too hard about it."

The crowd moved, as one, four steps to the left. Four steps to the right. Spun to the side, then started all over again. I turned on my heel and slammed right into Harper.

"Oh my god, *sorry, sorry*," she squealed.

With a laugh, I gently turned her until she was facing the right direction. "You're doing great."

She executed a complicated-looking heel-toe step into a quasi-jumping jack. "I believe that description of me is"—she twirled, kicked her thigh up—"highly inaccurate."

Then she crashed into me again.

This time we both laughed. I took her hand again and didn't let go. "Watch this part," I said, shaking my hips. "One-two. One-two. Spin." We spun as one. "And then back-back-back *and* turn again."

I watched Harper watching *me*—her brow creased in concentration, cheeks pink, teeth sunk into her lower lip. With every correct step, she'd beam at me like she'd won some sort of prize.

"You know, I think"—she shimmied, stepped to the right—"I might be getting this, after all."

But when I went to agree, the pretty blue-haired woman had swept in, making Harper laugh again with a joke I couldn't hear. I released her hand and let myself melt back into the crowd, watching as Harper and the other woman moved off the dance floor, where they were now talking.

I spun. Clapped. Spun again. *Definitely* didn't care if Harper was talking to someone else. It wasn't like I had a monopoly on her time and attention.

I twirled, again, and briefly lost sight of them in the crowd. When I found them, the other woman was gazing at Harper with an expression that directly mirrored the one I'd worn the first time I'd seen her. She seemed downright fucking *enchanted*, same as I'd been, and Harper looked both shy and pleased, touching the top of her cowboy hat with a quick grin.

Every muscle in my body tensed.

The crowd shifted, and then I was near them. Near enough to hear Harper admire the other woman's outfit.

Which did not matter to me *in the slightest*. I didn't do jealousy. Ever. And even if I did, it wouldn't factor in here. Not with a woman I still spent the majority of my time arguing with. Who would be gone soon anyway, off to flirt with and date whoever she wanted to on the other side of the country.

Harper tucked a lock of hair behind her ear and gave the blue-haired woman what seemed to be a look of brazen romantic interest. My stomach clenched painfully, and I stopped mid-spin, knocking into two other people.

I apologized quickly and caught Marla flagging me down by the bar. Raking a shaking hand through my curls, I strode back through the crowd and only cared a little bit that the blue-haired woman was now teaching Harper how to dance.

And that Harper looked like she was having the time of her life.

"Your food's ready," Marla said, dragging my eyes from the crowd to her knowing smirk.

"Huh?"

She chuckled. "Thought so... You're cool with Heather dancing with your girl like that?"

I took the bag of food from her hand. "She's not my girl, not even close. And even if she was, I'm not the jealous type."

Marla eyed me with compassion. "Before I met Jim, it was hard for me to trust that kind of love, too. I'd been left a lot before, and it just got easier to keep my heart locked down and locked away. It all made me want to run in the opposite direction, anything to get away from feelings I couldn't control."

I turned at that, gripping the back of my neck. "But that makes it sound like I'm afraid."

"Aren't you?" she said with a shrug. "I mean...aren't we all?"

I shook my head. "I fought tooth and nail to get away from my family, from their harmful messages, to make it out here, with Monty, with my friends. I feel so *free* now. I feel the opposite of afraid."

Marla wrapped an arm around my shoulders and squeezed. "I don't believe the fear ever really goes away. But over time, we can change how we respond to it."

She got called away then, leaving me to watch Harper chatting excitedly with Heather. Leaving me to wonder about this pain in my chest, a yearning I didn't have a name for.

A fear I wasn't ready to name, either. Not just yet.

The back door opened, revealing a flash of sky that looked decidedly less rainy than it had before.

And Jensen, striding in with his crew, all of them wearing the biggest shit-eating grins.

Chapter Eighteen

Harper

***Five days left to remember why I'm out here
while not getting distracted by Eve***

Eve and I saw Jensen and his crew at the exact same time, moving through the room with body language that screamed *victory*.

My stomach sank, and my lungs froze. I shot a panicked look over to Eve at the bar. The second our eyes met, I felt some inner instinct yank me in her direction.

"Harper?" Heather asked. "Is everything okay?"

"Yes— Well, not exactly..." I stopped mid-stride and touched her arm with an apologetic smile. "I'm so sorry. I'll be right back, okay?"

I didn't wait for a response. Eve moved toward me, and I ducked around groups of people, trying to stay hidden from Jensen's view.

We collided beneath the disco-saddle. Before I could say a word, she had my hand in hers and was dragging me to a small, dark hallway behind the wooden stage.

"Why does he look like he just found a whole bunch of buried treasure?" I hissed.

She shook her head. "I don't know, but it's making me nervous."

Eve ducked into the hallway and pulled me close—my back pressed to the wall, both her hands braced by my head. She angled herself to block us from view, the only light coming from the disco saddle, sending a prism of sparkles along the right side of her body.

"He couldn't have found anything...right?" I asked. "For one thing, they all look dry, so they couldn't have been out in this storm."

Eve had her phone out, scrolling with a furrowed brow. "Nothing on X Marks. Knowing Jensen, he'd have posted about it the second he found it. But they could be celebrating something else. A clue. Some new insight, maybe."

A round of cheers went up. Not from the dancers, but from Jensen's team. Peering past Eve's arm, I caught sight of them doing shots at the bar.

"Goddammit," she whispered. "I always wanted it to be me and Monty. I always..." She ran her fingers through her curls. "Always wanted Priscilla to be *ours*, something we shared together. But maybe that's stupid."

She bit her lip, looking absolutely devastated—a rare crack in her armor that made my own heart ache on her behalf.

"Stories like Priscilla's and Adeline's aren't just words on a page for queer people," I murmured. "They're...they're oxygen, the air we need to breathe. A reminder of our joyful existence."

Eve caught my eye as another wave of disco light sparkled across her body.

"You wanting this isn't stupid, Eve," I said. "It's brave. It's hopeful. Cherishing this story, cherishing her life. Going after what you desire even if you fail."

My mother had raised us through the world of books, each day a new adventure. I once saw what I did as a journalist to be something similar, but now I wasn't so sure. Over the years, my father's outrageous influence and ego had crept into those dreams, stolen them away in bits and pieces.

The need to prove myself to him, to prove I was *better*, was ebbing in volume the longer I was out here, replaced by wide-open sky and dusty red canyons.

And the wild, untamed hope of two women, racing hand-in-hand across the desert toward their new life.

"You think I'm brave?" Eve asked softly.

"Of course. You chose yourself over your family's toxic behavior. That takes courage."

She swallowed. "My family would disagree with that assessment."

"Well, they're fucking idiots. You did the right thing, getting away from them."

One side of her mouth tugged up into a smile. It had me realizing where we were standing—in the dark, outside of prying eyes, her tattooed hands on either side of my head. She was so beautiful it took my breath away, all roguish curls and high cheekbones.

Not twenty minutes earlier I'd broken the rule I'd *just* set and let myself get pulled onto the dance floor by this goddess. She danced like a dream, of course, her wicked charm and sly swagger making me feel *seduced*, like we were on an *actual date*.

No part of me knew what to do with that. Not my brain, not my body, certainly not my heart, which was currently thrashing inside my rib cage like a scared rabbit.

"Heather's cute," Eve said.

I cocked my head. "Who?"

"The woman with the blue hair. You were talking to her right before Jensen came in."

I touched the center of my forehead. "Oh, right, Heather. She's super sweet. We were talking about Brooklyn a bit."

"Does she live there?" she asked.

I frowned. "I have no idea. Why?"

"Nothing, you just…" Eve cleared her throat. "I was picking up on some vibes, is all."

A heady warmth spread across my chest. "Eve…were you jealous I was talking to her?"

She scoffed. "What's there to be jealous about? Besides, even if we were together, that's never been my style. That shit's toxic."

I held her gaze, refusing to back down even as she looked like she wanted to fidget. "Then if that's the case, maybe I'll get her number before we leave. Give her a call when she's back in Brooklyn next month."

Her dark brows knit together. "So you did think she was cute?"

"Oh, extremely. Totally my type."

Eve went rigid, though she forced a smile. "You should go for it. She'd be a fool to turn you down."

That same heady warmth climbed the back of my neck. "Do you think so? I wasn't sure if she was flirting with me or just being nice."

She dipped her head closer. "Hendrix, you're absolutely stunning. She's lucky you even talked to her."

My belly swooped like a flock of birds in the sky. "Oh my god…you *were* jealous."

Eve was briefly lit by the disco ball, bright red cheeks on full display.

"You have no proof," she said, clearly trying not to smile.

"No one's ever told you they were jealous before?" I asked.

"It's never been like that," she said easily—though she was blushing even harder now. My entire body felt electrified at the knowledge that I could make this cocky, self-assured woman *blush*.

I let my eyes linger on her full lips. I was breaking all the rules now. But it was just this once. Just *one moment* of indulging in what I really wanted. Our shared moment back at the Kept King mine clearly hadn't been enough for me.

My secret fear, though, was that when it came to Eve…it would never be enough.

"Anyone you've dated who hasn't gotten at least a *little* jealous is lying through their teeth," I whispered. "You inspire desperation, Eve Bardot."

Eve shifted, boxing me in more closely. The tip of her nose hovered just an inch from mine. "What exactly are you implying?"

"You asked me how to be more honest in your relationships," I said. "You can start by being honest about how much you want *me*."

A muscle ticked in Eve's jaw. One hand came around to cup my cheek, her thumb sliding beneath my chin. Tipping my face up. The tension between us simmered with a taut, frenetic energy.

"You want to know how desperately I want you?" she whispered hoarsely. She reached down, gripped my thigh, pulling it high around her waist so she could pin my hips to the wall with her own. My lips parted on a gasp. "Do you want to hear every dream I've had of you in my bed? Every time I wanted to kiss you, mid-argument, and stopped myself?"

She dropped her face to the crook of my neck. I dug my nails into the back of her hair, holding her there, arching into her body.

"I want you so badly I *burn* with it, Harper," she murmured against my skin, the sound of my name on her lips sending a jolt of ecstasy through me. "So *yes*, I was jealous, because I've never felt like this before, and I'm losing my fucking mind about it."

Her teeth were against my ear. Then her mouth was in my hair, at my temple. I fisted my hand in her shirt, our breaths mingling. Shaky.

I couldn't be sure, but I thought Eve's fingers were trembling where they cupped my face.

Pressing up onto my toes, I hovered my lips close to hers. "Then do something about it."

Chapter Nineteen

Harper

Don't! Get! Distracted! By! Eve!

E ve kissed me, and the world stopped.

Her mouth on mine was as fraught and feverish as the arguments we'd fallen into again and again. She demanded everything, and I gave it eagerly, yanking her hard against me. She gripped my face with both hands, kissing me harder, deeper. Kissing like she knew tomorrow would never come and she only cared about this very moment.

Only cared about *me*.

I want you so badly I burn with it, Harper.

I knew exactly how she felt. Knew, in one searing moment, that every other kiss I'd shared before had been some lukewarm facsimile of the real thing. This would have scared the hell out of me if my brain was able to comprehend anything other than the words *more, yes, please.*

Eve was moaning with every slide of her tongue against mine—throaty and husky, curling my toes in my boots and sending my hands around her back to grip her ass. Drag her close, grinding against her like I could will the clothes on her body to disappear through my desire alone.

She dove a hand into my hair and twisted, tipping my head to the side. Exposing my throat to her clever mouth. She pressed kiss after deliberate kiss down to the ball of my shoulder while I whimpered. My shirt was still on, but it didn't stop Eve from pressing her mouth to my breast through the fabric. Palming, squeezing, one hand skating beneath my shirt to find my nipple through my sports bra.

My spine arched off the wall. My nails dug into her scalp as I held her in place, practically climbing her body from the onslaught of pure sensation.

"I can't stop thinking about you, Harper," she groaned against my throat. Her tongue traced a path up to my jaw. She nipped it lightly, with her teeth. Caught my mouth again for another passionate kiss. "I haven't had a moment's fucking *peace* from the second you stepped into my store."

I flipped our positions with a soft growl. Her back hit the wall, and my palms slapped down on either side of her face. Our chests were heaving. Eve's lips were already swollen. She wasn't wearing a bra, so I hooked a finger in her tank top and gently tugged down. Her breasts were small and perfect, and I already couldn't get enough. Rolling her tight nipples against my palm, nuzzling the skin between them. I sucked her left nipple between my lips with a greedy sound I didn't even bother to hide.

"Fuck, I love that," she whispered, hands fisted in my hair. "Please don't stop."

"Never," I murmured and meant it. I sucked and pulled on her taut flesh, unbearably turned on by her reaction. "I could do this all night, Eve. You're so beautiful I have to remind myself to *breathe* around you. I just—"

Eve tugged me up and crashed our mouths together. I closed my teeth around her bottom lip and tugged. "I could just *devour* you."

She hissed in a breath. "I want that." Tipped my head back and scraped her teeth along the side of my neck. "So fucking badly."

Eve flipped us again. I breathed out a laugh, up for the challenge. Then we were kissing again, hands grasping at clothes, our lips in constant motion. She hooked my knee around her waist again and pressed her thigh between my legs. The pressure was so right, so specifically perfect, I would have moaned loud enough to startle the dancers if Eve hadn't pressed her hand to my mouth.

"God, you're sexy like this," Eve whispered against my ear as my eyes fluttered shut. "I should get down on my knees right in this hallway and devour *you*, Hendrix."

I groaned into her palm, rubbing myself against her thigh.

"Let everyone watch," she said. "Let everyone see how goddamn lucky I am."

We were starved for each other. We gasped, we trembled, we burned like a wildfire. Eve Bardot was about to make me come in this random hallway—and I wanted that more than anything else in the world. Would happily grind against her leg in the dark, the heavy bass of the music pulsing between us, while she kissed me senseless.

I'd avoided this attraction for so long because deep down I knew it would be like this between us, a lit match tossed into a dry field. A passion that scorched and destroyed if it wasn't controlled.

"Oh my goodness...*sorry*."

We froze in place, panting and wide-eyed, our hands tangled

in each other. Marla was standing just a few feet away with her eyes covered, trying hard not to laugh.

"I didn't see anything, I swear," she said, backing away. "And I don't think anyone else in the restaurant did, either. Though you wouldn't be the first people to use this space for...lascivious reasons."

"Oh my god, I'm so embarrassed," I groaned, dropping my face to Eve's chest. Her shoulders were shaking with quiet laughter. She held the back of my head, keeping me close, her lips in my hair. The sweet protectiveness of the gesture was almost as overwhelming as our electrifying kiss. I felt frazzled, flushed.

Completely overwhelmed.

"You okay?" she murmured.

"Yeah, yeah, of course." Rearing back, I tucked all of my clothing back into place and straightened my glasses. Pulled my hair up with a tie and secretly longed for a handful of pencils to stab into it.

"Sorry about that, Marla," Eve said, managing to look adorably sheepish and incredibly hot all at the same time. "We saw our competition and didn't want him to know we were on his tail."

"That's why I came to find you." She cocked her head back toward the bar. "Is your competition an older white man, balding, cigarette behind his ear?"

Eve and I shared a look.

"That's him," she said. "Jensen. Are they still out there?"

"They ordered a bunch of shots, but then that man got a call, appeared even *more* excited, and they all ran off together."

Eve tensed in my arms.

"You wouldn't have happened to catch which way they went, did you?" she asked.

Marla's brow rose. "Haven's Bluff, of course."

Eve was already on the move, pulling me along by the hand. She paused to wrap Marla in a hug. "Thank you for that. It really helps."

"And I never saw you here," she said, glancing between the two of us. "Certainly never saw you back *here*, either."

My cheeks burned. I mouthed *I'm so sorry* as Eve hustled us past, but Marla only grinned and waved.

"Happy hunting," she called back.

We were on the move, weaving through the glittery crowd and back out into the parking lot. The rain had stopped, and the clouds were clearing, leaving the air cool and clean. The foothills glowed a soft pink in the afternoon light, the road ahead long and empty.

Eve hopped into the car, and I joined her, rolling down the windows. For a moment we just sat there stunned—still breathing hard, our hair mussed and clothes wrinkled. We'd been interrupted, but I was still clenched and aching between my legs, every nerve ending wide awake.

Eve and I made shy eye contact across the console. The part of me that craved order and routine wanted to say, *Tell me what just happened and what it means for us exactly.*

And I already knew that was the worst possible thing to say. It *couldn't* mean anything. Not to Eve, who kept things light and casual. And not to me, either, who had no desire to uproot my carefully constructed life for a woman who didn't even trust me.

So I buried this urge down deep and went for a joke instead.

"Just to circle back for a moment," I said, "it seems like you *were* jealous back there, correct? I was right all along?"

Eve's answering grin was cute and crooked. I actually felt my heart wobbling in my chest—and not in a good way.

"You're a real pain in the ass, Hendrix," she said.

"Only around you."

She chuckled, but I could sense tension in the way her hands gripped the steering wheel. She peered out down the road as the car hummed beneath our feet.

"What if that call Jensen got was about them finding it?" she said, barely more than a whisper. "What if it's already gone? What if we never find out what *really* happened to Priscilla and Adeline?"

Heart still wobbling, I hooked my pinkie finger around hers. Eve stared down at where our hands met, a soft smile playing on her lips.

"Well, you know what they say... A bust is a bust 'til it ain't." I squeezed my finger against hers. "I don't want to assume we've lost when we've only just started."

Eve was nodding. She bent down, pressed a sweet kiss to the knuckle of my pinkie finger. "Thank you, Harper."

My wobbly heart toppled over, and I felt the crash inside my rib cage.

She reached over and turned up the volume of the music— some upbeat and jangly garage rock that filled the small space. Then she tossed me a wink before sliding her aviators back on.

"Let's hit the road then, shall we?"

Chapter Twenty

Eve

Feels Like Flying

Pulling off the highway, we coasted along the dirt road that led to Diablo Canyon, on the outskirts of Haven's Bluff. It was a short drive from the Boot + Saddle, but we still hadn't spoken much.

I'd cranked up the music and rolled down the windows, trying to wrench my harried, lust-filled thoughts back into some semblance of order.

That order was: *Monty's still missing. Jensen's nearby and possibly found something. You need to stay focused and find these fucking diamonds and stop, for the love of god, thinking about Harper every three seconds.*

I felt her peeking over at me. I sent her a quick glance and was immediately stunned by her pretty smile aimed at me like a bow and arrow.

"It's so beautiful here," she said.

My heart skipped a beat. "You're so beautiful here."

Her smile widened, cheeks rosy. She peered back out the window, still grinning, the wind tugging at her hair.

I'd lost the battle not to think about her...*again.*

We were coming up on the canyon walls. They soared into the sky, grandiose and awe-inspiring, and Harper tipped her head back to take it all in. The cliffs were almost too tall to fully perceive, dramatic and powerful. I often wondered what Priscilla and Adeline had thought when they'd first seen them from the train station.

If they'd seen them. If they'd ever even made it out here.

Please tell me they made it out here.

"If you want to hang out the window while I drive, you totally should," I said. "Promise I won't tell on you for not wearing your seat belt."

She bit the tip of her thumb. "I always wanted to do that."

"Go on, cowgirl," I said with a grin. "No one's around. Break some more rules."

I turned the music up just a bit louder. Watched Harper in my periphery as she unbuckled her seat belt and tentatively pulled herself up, until she was leaning halfway out the window, her hair like dark flames flickering around her. She flung an arm out wide as we drove toward the canyon. Let out a *whoop* that echoed off the walls, something sharp and ravenous at the edges of the sound.

I knew what this was now, knew exactly the kind of intensity that was Harper's spirit. Had been inexplicably drawn to it from the beginning, though it was still a mystery to me then. But I'd just been on the receiving end of it in a dark hallway at Boot + Saddle.

I could just devour you.

It was her hunger.

For life, for pleasure, for joy. Whatever she'd been keeping locked up was trying to claw its way free. And that kind of hunger always fueled my own, turning me greedy, needy, desperate. It was a craving that couldn't be placated. Every last ounce of my willpower was being used not to stop the car and drag her into my lap.

Kissing Harper Hendrix had been pure devastation.

I wasn't a stranger to hot makeouts in public places. Wasn't a stranger to hot make-outs period. This had been more. This had been an endless loop of need and desire, just the feel of Harper's soft skin, her teasing mouth, every gasp and moan.

The reminder that she was leaving in five days hovered over my head. It was usually a relief, knowing I wouldn't see the other person again. Knowing it was way less likely for feelings to get involved, for things to get uncomfortably messy.

Now I felt itchy and restless and didn't know what the hell to do about it.

I pulled to a stop near the front of the trailhead. Harper was still hanging out the window, letting her hair dangle in the breeze. She tilted her head and caught my eye, laughing a little self-consciously.

"How did it feel?" I asked, draping my arm against the steering wheel.

She wrinkled her nose. "Like flying. Is that silly to say?"

"On the rare occasion that my parents allowed me to come visit Monty out here when I was young, she let me do that exact thing on back roads like this. *Very* safely, though I thought it was super edgy and dangerous at the time."

I traced my lower lip with my thumb. "That day in the hospital, when she asked me to move out here, that's one of the things she'd said to me." I grinned fully at the memory, even as it made my heart hurt. *"I promise it'll feel like flying."*

Harper pulled herself back inside, flushed and bright-eyed. "Did it?"

"Yep," I said. "Still does."

Her cell phone rang, shattering the moment. She dug through her bag and pulled out her phone. Chewed nervously on her bottom lip for a second, then shut it off.

"Was it your editor?" I asked.

Harper began pulling her hair back into a bun. We were both sweaty and dust-streaked, but Harper still managed to look professional even with wrinkled clothing.

"Greg? No, though I do need to call him soon and tell him about the article's angle changing," she said. "It was my dad. But I sent him to voicemail."

I hadn't gotten used to the idea that Harper's dad was the most recognizable name in the news industry, trusted and well-liked by the public.

From what she'd told me so far, Bruce Sullivan was kind of a dick.

"Is everything okay?" I asked, noting her tight shoulders, the lines around her mouth.

"Probably." She mustered up a smile that seemed more tired than anything else. "These days he only calls when he wants to brag about something. He had a new book come out last week. I'm sure it's hit the *New York Times*."

I shifted in my seat. "Is he ever interested in what you and your sister are doing?"

"God no." She laughed bitterly. "He wants to know what we're doing so he can be critical, but not out of true curiosity. He reads all of my articles and only ever sends me notes for improvement."

At the shocked look on my face, she shrugged. "Passive-aggressive edits are his love language."

"So, like, your dad is definitely a dick."

Harper laughed, sounding surprised. "My friends always wondered why I wouldn't let him get me the best reporting jobs around after I graduated. But they never fully understood. I changed my last name for a reason, and that reason is that I don't want to be associated with him professionally. I barely want to be associated with him *personally*."

"Because he was always off being a fake hero?" I asked. At her quizzical look, I said, "It's how you described him the other day."

She blew out a breath. "It's...accurate. It was always easier for him to jump on a plane and head to the most dangerous conflict zone rather than interact with his grieving daughters."

"So who took care of you?"

"No one. Well...technically I did, though I'm not sure I was very good at it." Her smile was sheepish, a little sad. "Though Daphne always said the sandwiches I made her for school lunch were the talk of the cafeteria. All the other kids were jealous."

I could see it clearly in my mind's eye—teenage Harper trying her best to keep it together for her little sister. Moving alone through a house overflowing with grief.

"But it's so infuriating, the way it still hurts," she continued. "Do you ever...get stuck in a loop of hoping your parents will change? Maybe it's because I lost my mom, but some days it doesn't matter how badly my dad behaves. I keep thinking it'll be different with him one day. That he'll be different."

I thought about how desperately she wanted this story, the promotion she'd been promised for finding Monty. "Like if you do all the right things, in the exact right order, they'll finally love you the way you need to be loved?"

Harper's eyes were shining. "Yes." She swallowed. "It's stupid, right?"

"Not stupid," I said firmly. "It's totally normal and totally human. I left my parents on *purpose*, and I still hope for that exact thing."

She reached forward and touched my hand. Gave my fingers a squeeze. "I guess I'm glad to know I'm not the only one."

I squeezed back. "Right there with you."

The sun broke free of a remaining storm cloud, sending a cone of light through the windshield. We both winced, but it startled me back into action. I cocked my head toward the trail as I opened the car door.

"Let's grab gear and get out there. It's a bit of a climb, and I don't wanna be out there when it gets dark."

Moving toward the back, I grabbed my pack, compass, and two metal detectors. I unfolded the map and double checked the coordinates of the location Monty felt hadn't been searched enough.

"Any sign of Jensen?" Harper asked. "It looks like we're the only ones out here."

I squinted through the canyon walls, where I knew the Rio Grande flowed just a few miles away. "Not yet, but this isn't the only entrance. If this is where they were headed, they could already be out there. Unless they're currently digging up diamonds somewhere else."

Harper reached forward for one of the metal detectors, hoisting it over her shoulder with a cocky smile. "I'd like to see them try."

My eyes lingered as they traveled up her body. "Treasure hunting looks good on you, Hendrix."

"I learned from the best," she said, giving me her own saucy wink.

I chuckled, scooping up my pack and slamming the trunk shut before I did something *really* stupid. Like abandon this lifelong dream of mine in favor of fucking Harper on the hood of my car.

She's leaving, she's leaving, she's leaving, I reminded myself. Not because New York was some impossible journey from here.

But because I'd learned it got easier when I anticipated it. And I was always the one being left behind. First my family. And now Monty, who'd promised to never treat me the way my parents had.

So why the hell would some smart and ambitious reporter give up her hard-earned life for someone like *me*?

Chapter Twenty-One

Eve

Hot Damn

We set off along the trail, hiking down the dried riverbed that ran through the canyon. It was cooler in the shadow of the rock formations. The scrubby brush became loose and sandy, and hawks circled high above our heads.

I adjusted the straps of my pack and hefted the metal detector over my shoulder. I kept the compass in one hand while Harper stared up at the canyon walls with sheer wonder on her face.

"The spot we're going to is less than a half mile in, though we need to hike a trail up into a smaller cliff to do it," I explained. "We'll climb up, scope out the site with the detectors, then head back for the shovels if it looks like we're a go."

"How did Monty and Ruby narrow these places down in the first place?" Harper waved her arm at the expanse of open space surrounding us. "Talk about a literal needle in a haystack."

"It's tedious and time consuming and very expensive." I took a swig of water and passed it to Harper to share. "It's why it took them two years and a whole team. Once they narrowed down potential spots through research, they'd go out and sweep areas like this one for hours at a time. And it's not an exact science. Something can be buried deep but shift around while digging, so you'll still lose it. Whatever you've found could have broken due to the elements, or it's deeper than you can get to."

I jerked my thumb back at the detector. "The only reason these have ever been used to find the diamonds is because it was reported that they were stolen and encased in a large metal box that William had made specifically for storage and transport."

Harper's excited smile slid off her face. "What if Priscilla didn't bury them in a metal box?"

"That's just one of the many anxieties that used to keep Monty and Ruby up late at night."

She winced. "And false positives?"

"That's another issue," I said with a shrug. "It's common. Frustratingly common, to hear the real die-hard treasure hunters talk about it. Buried power lines can set them off. You can even swing them too low to the ground and have it issue a false positive."

Harper and I rounded a turn, coming to the spot where I was pretty sure we needed to hike up to the top. The trail had been washed away, leaving nothing but gnarled tree roots and a few rocks marking the path. I re-checked the map and the compass before turning to Harper.

"Looks like we're going up again," I said. "Though I'm hoping with significantly less falling than we did at the Kept King mine."

"It could end up in my favor if we do. You haven't been the damsel yet."

My lips twitched into a grin. "Are you trying to rescue me?"

"Everyone needs a little rescuing now and then," she said, nudging her hip against mine. "Given the opportunity, I can be quite heroic, you know."

She laid the metal detector on the ground and began to scramble up. It was a sharp incline, but doable. Small rocks scattered around her as she half climbed, half crawled forward.

"No reservations this time?" I called up.

"There's no sign here that says *caution: you're definitely going to die* so, yeah…I'm feeling a bit more comfortable."

Smiling to myself, I scrambled up after her, inhaling the smell of rain still lingering in the air. I used my knees to push myself forward, keeping pace with Harper.

"It's not a competition this time," she said, eyes playful.

"Like hell it is." I wiggled past her, but not before leaning in to plant a kiss on her cheek. "See ya at the top."

She was quiet for a second, then laughing as she neared me again. We were both out of breath now, and sweat rolled down the back of my neck. The adrenaline from earlier was finally wearing off, and I wondered if Harper's body was starting to ache like mine.

"You love this, don't you?" Harper said. "Hunting for buried treasure?"

"I love being outside and climbing around in the dirt," I said easily. "But it was always just a hobby for me. I don't even usually do it unless I'm with Monty. It's not as enjoyable without her yelling *hot damn* at every small coin we find."

"We should all be so excited at the little things," she panted. "I can see how she made it fun for you."

I propped my upper body near Harper's. "When she and Ruby used to visit me back east, they'd take me treasure hunting to get me outside and out of my head. Monty was the only one who saw what my parents were doing to me. Saw how they never believed me whenever I was open and honest about the pain I was in."

There was a small, scraggly patch of dandelions near our heads. Harper picked a single flower and gave it to me with a sweet smile on her lips. "They should have believed you. You knew your own body, your own mind, better than they did. Better than they ever *will*."

I brought the dandelion to my nose and inhaled. "Monty and Ruby always believed me. Gave me a safe space while doing something like this to talk about my parents' expectations. Their perfectionism, their rigidity, their obsession with what other people might think."

I leaned forward, tucking the dandelion into Harper's hair. "It's how I got into architectural salvage when I moved out here. A way to love history while letting go of the need to be perfect. Salvage is about loving the mistakes. Imperfections are treasured, studied as ways to learn more about the people who'd last owned them. I've never been interested in antiques in pristine condition. Objects in pristine condition are boring. They have no stories. They give up no secrets."

Harper was next to me, pulling herself up with a root that collapsed the second her hand clamped around it. She slid down just a foot, but I caught her before she fell farther. She immediately grabbed my wrist, pressing my palm to the center of her chest. I could feel her heart racing beneath my fingertips.

"You okay?"

"Yep. Just easily startled now that I've fallen off a fence *and* into an abandoned storage space." She cocked her head and studied me. "I'm thinking I've got a few cracks and chips of my own. I'm not pristine, either."

"Exactly." I flashed her a smile. "It's why you could never be boring."

"I'm glad to hear it," she murmured. "Until now, I'd never done any treasure hunting, but I'd always wanted to. As a kid, before my mom died, I loved all the adventure stories. The real swashbuckling ones, you know?" She smiled at whatever memory was coming to mind. "Can you imagine finding an *actual* treasure map, a big 'X marks the spot' and everything?"

Goose bumps shivered across my skin. "Sounds like a hell of a good time."

"Right? That's what I always thought." She kept scrambling toward the top, and I followed her. "Are we almost there?"

"Almost. Now we just gotta... What the fuck?"

Harper was there a second later, looking out. "Oh my god, what the *fuck*, indeed."

My chest seized up, like all the air had been stolen from my lungs. The location we'd been climbing toward was down in a shallow valley, but instead of packed dirt, the entire area had been torn to pieces. Giant, deep holes in varying sizes dotted the landscape. Rocks and debris were strewn about. A rusted-up shovel was propped against a short tree, clearly left behind by whoever had done this.

"Eve," Harper said breathlessly. "What does this... What is..."

"Someone got here first." My shoulders sagged with bitter resignation. "And I bet I know who it was."

"Jensen."

I pinched the bridge of my nose. "But how? We saw them, what, half an hour ago? There's no way they could have done this before we got here."

Harper pushed to stand, gazing out like she was trying to get a better view. "You're right, especially not in the storm."

A grim theory was dawning. "Back at the Boot + Saddle, we assumed they were on their way out here, getting ready to dig. What if we were wrong? What if they were on their way *home* and only stopping in to celebrate a victory?" I scrubbed my hands through my hair. "They could have...I don't know, done this the last few days when it was dry? Found something and...?"

"No, no, no, I refuse to believe they found anything of substance," Harper said firmly. "Marla said they were driving out to Haven's Bluff."

"She could have been mistaken. *We've* clearly been mistaken. He's held a grudge against my aunt for years, and he knows how much Monty wanted this. He's obviously more organized than I originally gave him credit for. Jensen's been one step ahead of us this entire time." I took out my phone to check X Marks the Spot, but I wasn't getting service out here. "So I'd be devastated if his crew did find something here before we did. But if he tore this place apart and it was still a bust?"

I glanced up at Harper, who looked about as devastated as I felt. "Then we're back to square one. No leads, no new clues, nothing to go on."

Harper winced. "Needle in a haystack."

I pressed my hand to my mouth, trying to think like Monty. Wishing like hell that she was here. She would have laughed and said, *Told ya it was a bust the first time.* Then, following some magical inner instinct, would have known exactly what to do next.

Instead, I was this-close to panicking. This-close to giving in to everything my family used to say about me. And hadn't I done exactly what they always suspected? So far I'd taken off on a whim without a real plan, gotten endlessly distracted by a gorgeous woman, and made the same mistakes Monty had five years ago.

"We should go back. Review Monty's notes again. Hope like hell the diamonds haven't been found," I said bitterly, tugging at my curls. "It's not doing us any good just staring at a bunch of holes in the ground."

Harper ducked her head, catching my eye. "What's our next step?"

I hid a grimace. "I, uh…I'm not sure. I don't have one."

I started to retrace our steps back down to the trail, needing to put my body in motion. Dislodged rocks went sliding, and mud from the rain sprayed up onto my legs. Harper was right beside me but didn't say a word. Giant waves of disappointment radiated from her body language, and I didn't have to ask the culprit.

Being back in the position of disappointing others—a position I was extremely familiar with—made me want to curl in on myself and disappear.

Once we reached the bottom, I took off at a brisk pace toward the car, carrying our gear. Harper followed, and I felt her eyes on my profile, studying me as we walked. I bit my tongue as a slew of apologies threatened to burst forth—the standards my parents had set every time I let them down.

Sometimes it felt like I spent elementary through grad school apologizing to them, endlessly angling for a brief flash of approval that still left me feeling dismissed and lonely.

Endlessly angling for a brief flash of unconditional love that never really came.

"What are you thinking?" Harper finally asked.

I swallowed past the lump in my throat. "That I'm sorry I failed again. That I'm sorry you hitched yourself to the wrong treasure hunter, Hendrix, because I have no idea what to do next."

A second later, her fingers closed around my wrist, gently halting my movement. "Hey...can you stop for a sec?"

I glanced up, surprised at the compassion etched into her face.

"You just told me that architectural salvage is about loving the mistakes," she said. "I know this analogy is going to sound so incredibly corny, but if this treasure hunt was some valued antique you discovered, you'd love it *because* of all the chips and cracks. You'd love it because it was well-handled and had clearly been through some shit."

My lips twitched despite the panic threatening to overtake my body.

"And, to be clear, I haven't hitched myself to the wrong treasure hunter." She cocked an eyebrow. "I constantly annoyed you to let me come along for a reason."

I rubbed the back of my head. "Oh yeah? What reason was that?"

"*Because*...as much as this would have pained me to admit a week ago, I do believe you know what you're doing, Eve."

A tiny—but not insignificant—amount of peace settled over my panic.

"You're right," I said, grinning broadly now. "That analogy was really fucking corny."

Her eyes brightened. "It was accurate, though, right?"

I sighed, letting my head fall back. "I thought this might have been the day we found out what really happened to Priscilla and Adeline. And I know that's foolish of me, and I don't have nearly enough evidence. I'm just out here chasing random instincts that probably won't lead to anything, but..."

Harper hooked her pinkie finger around mine and squeezed. "If it's any consolation, I got my hopes up, too."

This sliver of affection from Harper, so freely given, yanked so hard on the center of my chest I almost fell forward. "I can't stop thinking about them, about this part of their journey," I said, indicating the canyon we stood in the middle of. "Were they... scared? Were they attacked? Did they muster up all that courage to leave their situation only to be killed?"

Harper bit her lip. "Priscilla and Adeline were never heard from again, at least not through formal channels. We know it's a possibility. As is the possibility that you'll never *really* know. But it doesn't mean you and Monty can't finally tell your parents the truth of who you believe her to be. You can share what Priscilla's story means to you whether you find these diamonds or not."

"You're right," I admitted. "I guess I always wanted to be the one to find the diamonds so that I could..."

"Prove yourself to your parents?" Harper suggested softly.

I looked away, embarrassed. "Am I that obvious?"

"You're that human," she said, repeating my words from earlier. "And trust me, I get that urge more than you know."

I glanced down at our hands, tangling the rest of my fingers with hers. "I don't want them to treat Priscilla the way they treated me and Monty. My queerness was this useful oddity to them, proof to their fellow academics that they were open-minded. I felt like a helpful statistic for their reputation. On display at dinner parties to be perceived and judged by their friends."

"You're not a statistic. And you're certainly not some doll that can be trotted out and displayed to make your parents feel good about themselves," Harper said firmly. "They really missed out on knowing the real you, Eve. But it's their loss in the end."

My brows knit together at the ferocity in Harper's voice. It felt protective in a way I normally associated with friends and Monty, *never* the people I casually hooked up with. It sent heat to my cheeks, a fluttering in my chest that was as pleasing as it was confusing.

"I don't want you to go back to New York just yet," I blurted out, regretting it as soon as the words left my mouth. I pressed a palm over my eyes and winced. "Sorry, that was—"

"Me neither," she replied.

The smile we shared felt like a tentative beginning, even as every part of me knew this wouldn't last, *couldn't* last. But if we hadn't been quiet in that moment, I wouldn't have heard the scrape of rocks bouncing down the trail.

The soft sound drew my focus past Harper's shoulder to what I first thought was a strange-looking log. But then it moved, sliding across the ground, too thick and fuzzy to be a snake.

I fucking *knew* what it was, yet my brain refused to accept what was crouching low near the rock behind us. Perfectly blended in with its surroundings.

Golden eyes. Twitching tail. Huge paws.

A fear like I'd never known before slammed into me.

"Harper," I whispered. "Don't move."

Chapter Twenty-Two

Harper

Five days left to—
Who cares, a fucking cougar is stalking us!

The look of terror on Eve's face had me disobeying her orders out of sheer, primal instinct. But I couldn't have predicted the sight in front of me when I spun around.

A cougar, gliding forward on near-silent paws.

Eve hooked an arm around my waist and shoved me behind her. Then fisted my T-shirt and said: "Do not run. That'll make it chase you."

"Eve," I sputtered, already crying, already digging my heels in to do the *exact opposite* of what she'd said. She must have felt my body rebel and dragged me closer. "Eve, Eve, Eve, what the fuck, what the fuck?"

She was very slowly moving us backward. But the cougar was very slowly following. Clearly interested in us, its head tilted.

Too interested.

"Okay, okay," she panted. "Monty... She taught me what to do if this ever happened."

We took another step back. The big cat took a step forward. With each movement, its body rippled with coiled muscle, and its golden eyes never left us. Its tail twitched along the ground, sending alarm bells ringing through my body.

"So...so don't run, got that," I croaked over her shoulder. "What else?"

"Um..." Eve reached down and held up one of the heavy metal detectors. The cat's ears flattened, and it took a step back. "We need to get big. Yell. Throw rocks at it."

"So it won't try and eat our faces off?"

Eve hurled a rock, and the cat hissed its annoyance, batting its paw.

"Uh-huh. Yep. You got it, Hendrix." My fingers dug into her hips, pulling her backward. Then my foot collided with one of the shovels we brought. I scooped it up and hoisted it forward like a sword.

The cougar moved closer, then paused, its eyes assessing the shovel's movement.

I didn't trust its hesitation one bit.

Eve hurled another large stone. This time, it dodged it more easily—and didn't look very pleased with us.

It lunged.

We screamed, stumbling backward down the trail. We swung our metal detectors in arcs in front of us, forcing the animal back, who was snarling its anger. Eve got a little too close, and the cat tried to swipe at her leg. So I pulled her behind me and threw my shovel like a javelin. The cat let out a short yelp and slunk back up the side of the canyon with a deadly grace, growling the whole time.

It never took its eyes from us.

"Did it hurt you?" I asked Eve, my arms out wide to protect her.

"No, but...holy shit, I can see the car. It's close."

The cougar shifted where it lay, back to standing again. I was shaking with fear and adrenaline now, absolutely trembling from head to toe, my face streaked with tears. The only sounds were the crunching of our shoes on the dirt and the utter roar of my own heart in my ears.

"Close enough to run to?" I asked.

Her arm was like a vise around my waist, banding me tight to her. "We can't run. We can't... *Fuck*."

The cougar was on the move again. This was different—less curious hesitation and more lean, focused predator. Its speed was mind-boggling. Only Eve's arm around my waist kept me from fleeing in total terror. We moved backward, toward the car, and it began to circle us with teeth bared.

"Don't turn your back on it," Eve murmured in my ear. "We have to...have to stay calm."

It lunged again, and we tried to hit it with the detectors. Its big paw swiped so close to my ankle I felt the rush of air across my skin.

"You should go," I said. "I'll hold it off so you can get in the car. Then I'll run after you."

Eve squeezed me even tighter. "No way in hell, cowgirl. We stick together."

My chest would have warmed at the stern affection in her voice if I wasn't so preoccupied with whether or not I was about to get eaten.

The cat snarled again, hind legs primed like it was about to pounce right onto us. I covered as much of Eve's body with my own as I could, pushing us backward toward the car quickly.

"Almost there..." she whispered. "Almost, almost, almost."

We collided with the side door. One second later and I could feel Eve trying to jam her keys into the lock. It clicked open and then she was dragging me into the backseat by my shirt. With a yelp, I slammed the door shut and hit the lock.

The cougar slapped the window with a giant paw and snarled again.

It was right *there*, mere inches from us.

Eve and I scrambled as far back as we could, huddled together on the other side of the seat as we watched our tormentor grow almost comically disinterested.

Then it loped off back down the canyon, licking its lips.

I collapsed forward in sheer relief. Eve was curled around me, both of us panting and shaking. She was muttering *holy shit holy shit* into the space between my shoulder blades while I was laughing *and* crying, all at the same time.

After what could have been a minute, or an entire hour, I twisted around until we were facing each other. The sunlight filtering in through the windshield cast Eve in hues of sunset gold, bouncing off her dark curls and highlighting her flushed cheeks.

She was so heart-achingly *beautiful*, so delightfully and superbly *alive*. We were alive, *both* of us, and the euphoria that galloped through me couldn't be contained.

Still panting for breath, we stared at each other in the quiet of the backseat. Our chests rising, gazes locked, barely a foot between us.

"You saved my life," I breathed, throat tight with tears. "Eve...you saved us out there."

She speared her hands into my hair. "But you protected me, Harper... No one's ever..."

I closed the gap between us and kissed her. Desperate, breathless, grateful. There had never been a sweeter moment than this one: wrapped in Eve's strong arms, her body warm, her mouth moving hungrily. Her lips slanted over mine—hot and demanding—and the sounds we made together were barely human.

We shuddered through kiss after kiss, hands roaming, grasping. Eve snaked an arm around my waist and yanked me into her lap so I was straddling her. Off came my shirt, my bra tossed into the front seat. Eve buried her face between my breasts with a sound of pure animal satisfaction.

My head fell back on a long moan as Eve palmed my breasts with reverence. I was grinding down on top of her, using the headrest for leverage, working myself in frantic circles as she sucked my nipple into her mouth with a rough groan.

Desire spiked between my legs, a pulsing, relentless need that had me pulling Eve back from my breasts so I could kiss her again. We moaned together, her hand fisted in my hair, the other expertly rolling my nipple until I cried out her name.

"God, I love the sound of that," she growled, licking and kissing up my neck until I was crying out her name again. "Were you sent here to completely fucking ruin me, Harper?"

"Possibly." I sighed. "Are you sure you weren't sent here to ruin *me*?"

Her arms locked tight, and then I was flat on my back on the seat, my legs opening wide and wrapping around Eve's waist. She took my mouth again, our tongues stroking, her lips mesmerizing. She only paused to sit up and shed her own shirt, followed by her pants, leaving her half naked, covered in dirt, adorably disheveled in black Calvin Klein briefs that hugged her narrow hips.

I gripped her there, holding her still so I could take her in: the colorful tattoos, her lean muscles, that rakish grin. I pushed up halfway, using my arms, then tipped her forward and took one of her nipples into my mouth. Hushed curse words spilled from her lips, making my toes curl. I opened my eyes and lapped at her nipple, peering up at her through my lashes.

Her nostrils flared when we made eye contact. The grip on my hair tightened. Twisted.

"You're not a good girl after all, are you?" she teased.

I swirled my tongue, watched her eyes grow heavy-lidded. "Not out here in the desert, I'm not."

She shook her head, clicked her tongue. Slowly pushed me back down until she was hovering close, nudging the tip of her nose against mine. "You're desperate for it, aren't you?"

I arched beneath her. "Desperate for you."

I grabbed her ass, dragging her cunt against mine. There were still too many layers between us, but the initial friction felt so good that we moaned together. Eve caught my lower lip with her teeth, tugged. Scraped those same teeth at my jaw. Bit the spot where my throat met my shoulder, marking me. Claiming me.

Meanwhile, I was trying to shed my pants and underwear, wiggling beneath her. She laughed and pressed my hands to the seat.

"And who said you could do that?" she whispered in my ear.

"Please," I begged. "Please fuck me, Eve. It's all I ever think about."

Eve caught my chin. Held me still as I writhed beneath her, her dark eyes burning into mine. "Are you sure?"

And I knew what she was really asking. *Was I sure* I wanted to complicate things? *Was I sure* I wanted to turn a relationship that was messy from the beginning into something even messier now?

She had certainly seemed sincere when she blurted out that she wasn't ready for me to fly back to New York. I had no reason not to believe her, and yet every reason to believe she'd never want more than this. She'd only told me about a dozen times that sex for her was casual and temporary.

Except nothing between us had *ever* felt casual. Not our many arguments and misunderstandings, not our tentative trust, not this new and tender intimacy. And that potentially made me the same as every other person Eve had fucked in the backseat of this car.

It had *never* been like this with anyone else, this fraught and reckless passion that had my head spinning non-stop. But what if it was *always* like this for Eve?

What if I wasn't special in the least?

If she was an expert in "casual," then I was the expert in avoidance. Back home, if I'd have met Eve, I would have run for the hills. Because here I was, dangling my heart in front of her without any thought to the consequences. But in the sticky heat of this moment, Eve was promising an electric ecstasy that my brain *and* body were demanding I trust.

"Yes, I'm sure," I said. Absolutely sure about the sex. Less sure about what happened after.

But I didn't want to think about that.

Eve's next kiss was slow, lingering. She drank me in almost lazily while she slipped her hand between my legs, cupping me through my yoga pants.

I gasped, breaking our kiss. Eve's index finger trailed up the seam, stopping to lightly circle my clit. My back rose off the seat at the sudden surge in pleasure.

Eve's mouth hovered at my temple. "Can I take the rest of your clothes off?"

I was so fucking ready that I helped her, shoving at my pants and underwear like they were personally offensive. We only stopped for a moment to grab wipes from Eve's bag, hastily cleaning our fingers. Then I guided her hand back between my legs, so turned on I was practically whimpering.

Eve watched me, fascinated, before doing as I wanted and pushing two fingers deep inside of me.

"Oh *god*, I needed this," I groaned. Looking down, I watched Eve's hand working between my legs and blushed to the very tips of my ears. Amused, Eve kept her fingers moving and sucked on my nipples until I was sobbing, clenching, writhing.

"I like you like this, Hendrix," she said, nipping at my mouth again, "completely at my mercy. I could keep you on the edge for hours. Just because I wanted to."

I rolled my hips, trying to nudge her palm closer to my clit. "Don't you fucking dare, Eve Bardot. Don't you *fucking dare*."

She chuckled, kissing me, her fingers slick and skillful. She added a third, and I started babbling.

"I'll give you anything, anything, *anything*," I begged. "Please, Eve, please, please—"

"All I want is for you to come on my tongue," she said. "Twice."

Her next kiss left me with stars in my eyes, a kiss that promised certain euphoria for my good behavior. Eve shifted down the seat, draping my right leg over her shoulder and pressing my left knee wide. Leaving me completely exposed to her mouth.

A mouth that descended upon me with a deft and deliberate hunger. Keeping her fingers moving inside me, she made soft, careful circles around my clit. I cried out again at the contact, at the sight of her head between my thighs and the edges of her wicked grin.

"You taste *fucking* incredible," she groaned, giving me a long, indulgent lick. "I could eat you all night."

"Please, please do that," I panted. "Eve, I'm so...I'm so..."

I didn't need much, and she was adept at reading the cues of my body. Her fingers worked, her tongue circled and circled, and my body broke apart beneath her focused attention. My climax ripped through me, and I might have screamed or sobbed. I crested and crested, the sensations unyielding, and then Eve did something exquisitely clever with her tongue—and I came again.

Twice on her tongue.

Just like she'd demanded.

And as she crawled back up my body for a sweet, delicate kiss, my heart whispered: *You're in big trouble now, cowgirl.*

Chapter Twenty-Three

Eve

Well and Truly Ruined

Even after being stalked by a cougar, it was dawning on me that Harper Hendrix was the real danger tonight.

Splayed out like this, she was a fever dream of pink cheeks and naked curves, her brazen pleasure on full display. And with every breathy moan that fell from her lush mouth, I was losing my ability to keep my distance.

Not that I'd been doing a great job of that since meeting Harper. She'd poked and prodded at my walls from minute one. And now she was dismantling them even further.

Kiss by kiss by kiss.

She crooked her finger until I obliged another one, licking my tongue against hers. Mere seconds after her second orgasm and she was already writhing against me, raking her nails down my spine. Insatiable, absolutely fucking *insatiable*.

I'd never been so turned on by another person in my life.

And she's only going to abandon you like everyone else.

The thought vanished as quickly as my remaining willpower.

But I knew it'd be back.

While I was nuzzling beneath her ear, entranced by how soft her skin was there, she was busy shoving me backward. With only a little bit of laughter, and one bumped head, she maneuvered us until her hips landed between my thighs.

She peered down at me with swollen lips and untamed hair, freshly fucked and eager to please. Much too adorable for my brain and heart to handle. She'd carefully placed her glasses in the front seat so her blue eyes were exposed, bright and vulnerable, her septum ring winking in the light.

Swallowing, I reached up and cupped her face, completely overcome. She turned her head and caught the tip of my index finger between her teeth. Then she sucked on it, all the way down to the base.

She was equal parts sinful and innocent—wide eyes, arched brow, firm tongue. I rolled my hips, trying to get closer to her. She kissed my palm, the inside of my wrist, eyes closed now like she was just as overwhelmed as I was.

Dangerous. So very fucking dangerous.

"Harper," I gasped. "What are you gonna do to me?"

She hummed under her breath. "Whatever I want, of course."

A grin flew across my face, but she was all ferocious hunger now. She trailed her fingers along the top of my briefs, letting the material snap against my skin. I hissed between my teeth.

"Off?" she asked.

I nodded, captivated. She sent my underwear flying, then slid one, then two, then a third finger into her mouth. I watched her take those fingers until they glistened, until saliva trailed down her wrist. The ache between my legs was unbearable. I reached down to touch myself, content to watch a naked Harper just like this, but she slapped my hand away with an imperious smirk.

Then she lowered her body down onto mine, her hair spilling onto my chest, and kissed me until we shared a single breath. She moaned against my mouth like I was her favorite meal and she planned to savor every last bite. When she lightly pinched my nipples, delicious sensation shot through me. I was reduced to a boneless, melting mess of pure need.

"I want you to come on my hand," she groaned. "Need to feel how wet you are for me."

"Do it," I said, my head falling back. "I like it hard, cowgirl."

Her eyes flashed as she curled her fingers and slid inside, filling me perfectly. We both moaned at the same time, and I clenched, fluttering around her.

"*Fuck*, you're so wet," she whispered, giving an experimental thrust. "How hard do you want it?"

I surged up and kissed her. "Harder."

She grinned. Dipped her head to bite down on my neck as she thrust again, sending minor shockwaves through my core.

"*Jesus*, that's good." I sighed. Harper was watching my reactions, staring down at her fingers moving fast and rough. Then rougher, her palm glancing off my clit over and over. She didn't stop kissing me, either. Her mouth was urgent, incessant. She caught every ragged moan that fell from my lips. My nails dug into her back, my spine arched.

"You are so sexy, Eve," she murmured. "I'm serious. You should be illegal. You should be fucking *outlawed*."

I tried to laugh, but I could only gasp. There was no scrap of control for me to hold onto. Nothing to keep me steady as Harper upended my entire world.

"Don't stop, don't… *Fuck*," I cursed.

The muscles in Harper's forearm bunched as she kept thrusting, nudging my clit, stroking every hypersensitive nerve ending. She bent and took my nipple between her lips, swirling her tongue. A pending climax twisted deep in my belly. Every other word out of my mouth was her name and her name only.

The orgasm she'd so skillfully built me toward detonated with the force of a hurricane. I almost bucked Harper off the seat, but she stayed on, working me through a series of aftershocks that made my entire body tremble.

Harper let me catch my breath for a few moments before crawling up my body and nuzzling her face into my neck. "You seem well and truly ruined now."

I pressed a long kiss to the top of her head, enchanted by her sweet and cozy warmth. Enchanted by how perfectly she fit against me. "And I have you to thank for that."

I gave in to the need to hold her tight just then, with memories of the cougar filtering back in through the haze of lust and pleasure.

Harper shuddered, popping her head up to look me in the eye. I brushed the tangled hair back from her face and couldn't ignore the lightness in my chest as I did so.

"You really did save our lives back there, Eve," she said. "You were so calm. You knew *just* what to do. If it had just been me, if we hadn't been together…"

"I wouldn't underestimate your persistence, Hendrix," I said, smiling. "If that cougar had known the truth, it would have been terrified of you."

Her lips quirked up. "Yes, I'm sure I could bore it to sleep reading the in-depth reporting I did on the city of Buffalo's zoning laws last month."

I laughed softly, tucked another strand of hair behind her ear. "You protected me. Without me even having to ask."

Her brow creased. "I'd do it again in a heartbeat."

Cupping her cheek, I brought my lips to hers again, kissing her senseless in the back of my car surrounded by nothing but ancient canyon walls and wild, rushing rivers. Soon, the sun would set and the night sky would be awash with the cool shimmer of the Milky Way.

I knew, then, why Monty had been so concerned about her lack of focus when she went after the diamonds. Because Harper had me well and truly distracted. A first for me, and as terrifying as the sky-high cliffs that rose nearby. So I'd have to work even harder at making sure I didn't do anything especially foolish over the next few days.

Like think of her as mine.

Chapter Twenty-Four

Eve

A Wild Goose Chase

Morning birdsong woke me.

My eyes fluttered open, then I squinted at the bright sunshine pouring in through the car windows. It took a good five seconds for my brain to comprehend where, exactly, I was.

And who, exactly, I was with.

Harper took this moment to snuggle in closer, her nose and mouth pressed to the side of my neck. My hands had stayed tangled in her hair all night. Even now, I lightly scratched along her scalp without thinking twice about it. Felt the soft weight of her relaxing on top of me.

She was beautifully, gloriously naked, and I peered down at her in utter amazement. I'd spent much of last night mapping every inch of her with my mouth, my hands, my tongue. The round curves of her ass, the flare of her hips, the soft dips in her belly. I smelled like Harper. Tasted like Harper. Was coated in a fine dusting of dried sweat and dirt.

I'd cracked the windows last night so we wouldn't overheat

as we slept. Reclined the backseat so we had a bit more room and grabbed my bag to use as a pillow. But we were kissing again as soon as we lay down on our sides, facing each other. A kiss that began as a tease but turned relentless within seconds. Once we started, we couldn't stop, didn't *want* to stop. Sweat had glistened on Harper's chest as we moved together in one long, endless grind. Every delicious drag of skin against skin had her gasping into my mouth, had me shuddering and desperate.

It was only when Harper resorted to begging—*pleading*—that I slipped my hand between her gorgeous legs and watched her come gloriously undone.

The sight of her pleasure left me so dazed, so fucking *enthralled*, I almost didn't realize that she'd shoved me onto my back. And the wicked grin she'd flashed right before her tongue slid along my clit was all the warning I got before she devoured me.

Just like she'd promised.

We'd slept tangled together for most of the night. Something I didn't often do, *especially* with someone I was trying not to get attached to. But even if there'd been another option—even if we hadn't fallen into a deep sleep after incredible, mind-blowing sex—I wouldn't have taken it. Would have gladly chosen to spend the night with her in my arms, just like this.

And that was a scary enough realization to have me stirring awake now, searching for my phone and any scrap of clothing.

Harper groaned against my throat. "No moving. More sleeping."

"We gotta get up, Hendrix," I said, laughing. "People will be here to hike at some point, and then they'll discover our sordid sex den. Also…we're both naked."

She didn't move. "But I *love* our sordid sex den."

My lips brushed the top of her head. "What if I promised coffee?"

Harper raised her head up, pushing all the hair off her face. There were crease marks on her cheek, a bleariness to her eyes. I could see the shadow of bruises from yesterday's injuries, along with some scratches and scrapes.

"That's the first real night of sleep I've had since I arrived in New Mexico," she said through a yawn. "Though I also feel like I've been run over by at least ten trucks. And how do you still look so hot after everything that happened to us yesterday?"

I nudged a knuckle under her chin. "And how are you still the most stunning thing I've ever seen?"

Gripping the back of her neck, I pulled her down for a kiss that deepened again within seconds. Harper moaned, opening for me, letting me take what I wanted even after the intensity of last night. I cupped her face. She clung to my wrists. I considered flipping her over again, wondering if I could make her come before the first hikers arrived.

My phone went off in a shower of jingling notifications.

I froze, mid-kiss.

"What is it?" Harper murmured.

Shit, shit, shit.

"I, uh…" She sat up so I could roll over, root around in my bag. "I set Google alerts for the Blackburn Diamonds. That's what the notifications sound like. Which means I must be getting a sliver of cell service again."

Grabbing my phone, I swiped to see what the messages were. Harper pulled her T-shirt up from off the floor and draped it over her head, curling up next to me on the seat.

My heart slammed inside my rib cage and a growing dread had my throat tightening with emotion.

"What does it say?" Harper whispered.

I followed the notification links to the X Marks the Spot community messaging board. A few locals had spotted Jensen's crew in Haven's Bluff.

Had spotted me and Harper, too.

Then I finally found the message in question. From Jensen, posted late last night, well after we'd escaped from the cougar into the backseat. For those asking, Diablo Canyon's still a bust. We're going dark for a bit, pursuing a new lead on the diamonds.

I heaved a massive sigh of relief. "Okay, so the good news— they didn't find the diamonds here. Bad news—they've gone dark, pursuing something new, so we can't even tail them to see what they learned."

I stretched my neck from side to side, wincing at the pain there. Wincing as the feelings of inadequacy came crashing back into my body, kept successfully at bay by our near-death experience and the night of incredibly hot sex.

"But none of this really changes the position we were in before the cougar attack," I continued. "I have no clue where to go from here. No clue if there's even somewhere for us *to* go."

Harper leaned over and kissed me on the cheek. "Well, I'm still in this if you are."

"Are you sure?" I asked softly.

"Extremely sure. I believe in Priscilla and Adeline, and I don't think they'd want us to give up." She bumped her forehead to my cheek. "I believe in this story, Eve. And I believe... I believe in our ability to figure it out."

I turned, our lips meeting for a kiss. "Looks like I really did underestimate how persistent you can be."

Harper grinned. "That, and it's easy to feel defeated when you haven't had coffee or eaten a real meal in eighteen hours.

Which we haven't. Oh, also, some pain meds and a hot shower might help."

I matched her smile with my own. "Seventy-two hours ago, I would have hated saying this...but you might be right."

"I know I am," she said, giving me another kiss.

I tipped my head back toward the window, trying to assess the best place to find a free shower and coffee out here near Haven's Bluff.

Then I remembered. Dialing my phone, I said to Harper, "Don't worry. An old friend of Monty's has an airstream RV park, just outside town. She'll hook us up."

And half an hour later, she did. Faith's Paradise RV Park glimmered like an oasis in the desert. Thirty-plus vintage airstream trailers were arranged in a spiral, with a turquoise pool in the middle, surrounded by kitschy string lights, lawn flamingos, and inflatable palm trees.

Before she owned the park, Faith used to salvage with us out in Santa Fe, using her incredible eye for detail and an almost unnerving ability to unearth valuable objects from piles of trash. Her silvery-gray hair was so long she could sit on it, and when we found her, she was sitting in a lawn chair, smoking a joint and tapping away on an old typewriter.

"It gets a bit boring out here some days," she said, by way of a greeting, "so I'm trying my hand at writing a science fiction novel. Erotic, of course."

Harper brightened. "Spicy aliens? I love it."

Faith took a long drag on her joint. "Yeah, and that's just chapter three, sweetheart. Anyway, you two look about ten different kinds of fucked up. What was it you said you needed, Evie?"

I pushed my sunglasses onto the top of my head. "Access to the camp showers, if you'll have us. Some food and coffee if there's anything fresh at the camp store."

Faith nodded, rummaged around in the pockets of her robe, then handed me a few tokens. "Coins, for the shower. I'll grill up some egg-and-cheese bagels and get the coffee going. Maybe some ice packs and ibuprofen, too. What the hell happened?"

I arched an eyebrow. "Fell down a mine shaft, then we were chased by a cougar."

Faith cocked a finger gun in my direction. "That'll do it." She set her typewriter down and stood, tightening the belt of her robe. "An old lady hears rumors about these things, you know. About those missing diamonds everyone's been a fool over for as long as I can remember."

I arranged my face into the picture of innocence. Harper was staring up at a bird in the sky so intently it was like she'd never seen one before. Faith looked between us and snorted.

"I knew it," she said. "Those diamonds ain't real, Evie. You know that, right?"

"*Faith*," I chided, "I'm not having this argument with you again."

"Told your aunt she was a damned fool when she did it," she called over her shoulder, walking toward the camp store. "Telling you the same thing now!"

"Where's your sense of adventure?" I called back. "Where's your enterprising spirit?"

Her response was a raised middle finger.

Turning to Harper, I said, "You don't know her, but that actually means she likes us."

Harper stole a shower token with a sly smile. "Arguing as a charm tactic? Sounds like someone else I know."

Then she danced away before I could tug her back and kiss that adorable smirk right off her face. And distract myself from the way Faith's words spun up every secret fear I had about what was feeling more and more like a wild goose chase. And the nagging worry I couldn't shake that I'd already failed, yet again.

Chapter Twenty-Five

Eve

A Hobby Carried on the Shoulders of Good Luck

After the best shower of my entire life, I walked back toward Harper, toweling my hair dry and sipping from a giant Styrofoam cup of coffee. I'd parked the car near the pool, and that was where she was now, curled up on a lounge chair, surrounded by a pile of Monty's notes.

Kids splashed nearby. Families were already grilling by their trailers. Dogs barked, music blared. The RV park was slowly filling with the sounds and smells of vacation, but I only had eyes for Harper, biting the tip of her thumb as she read, completely unaware that I was watching her.

She wore a peachy-orange sundress that rode high on her soft thighs, thighs that still sported a few of the bite marks I'd given her last night. Her wet hair was piled high in its usual bun, with just one pencil jammed through this time. Her cheeks were pink from the shower, face scrubbed of makeup, and her freckles stood out dark against the bridge of her nose. The tops of her shoulders sported a light sunburn, the straps of her dress already slipping down.

I could have devoured her on the spot.

Harper glanced up as I approached and immediately caught me staring. A wide, toothy grin spread across her face, as if she couldn't contain herself.

I couldn't contain myself. And needed to. Badly.

It was only gonna hurt worse in the end if I didn't.

"This is an amazing resource, Eve," she said, pointing to the stack of notes with the journal she was flipping through. "I can't believe Monty just left this with you."

I crouched on the end of the chair, squeezing the last bit of excess moisture from my curls. Harper reached forward and finger-combed them into what felt like some semblance of order.

"After she and Ruby didn't find the diamonds, she got even more paranoid, asked me to hold onto all of her treasure hunting notes, maps, and research," I said, leaning into Harper's touch. "It's not all of it. She's got a storage unit nearby with more of her detailed research, but these are some of the more important pieces to her."

"Paranoid about what?" Harper asked.

"Someone breaking in and stealing all of her hard work," I explained. "Not that my place is that much safer, but I couldn't talk her out of it."

Harper chewed on her lower lip, her brow creased. "Did you ever read this passage in her journal? If I'm doing the math right, this was, like...two weeks before they uncovered *La Venganza*? And she's talking about your dad here, right?"

She handed it over to me, and seeing Monty's blocky handwriting sent a spike of pain through my chest.

I LIE AWAKE AT NIGHT AND WORRY ABOUT WHAT CLUES I MISSED. WORRY IF RUBY'S MAD AT ME, FOR TRYING SO HARD AT SOMETHING I'M OBVIOUSLY NOT VERY GOOD AT. IT'S NOT LIKE THIS IS A JOB OR A SCIENCE. IT'S NOTHING BUT A HOBBY CARRIED ON THE SHOULDERS OF GOOD FUCKING LUCK.

IT FEELS LIKE WE'RE NEVER GONNA BE LUCKY. FEELS LIKE EVERY NAYSAYER IS GONNA BE RIGHT IN THE END. I HATE FEELING THIS WAY, HATE KNOWING SOME PEOPLE MIGHT HAVE BEEN RIGHT ABOUT ME.

IT'S NOT LIKE MY FAMILY EVER THOUGHT I'D AMOUNT TO ANYTHING SPECIAL. BUT EVERY NIGHT RUBY REMINDS ME TO HAVE HOPE, WHICH SHE SAYS IS SOMETHING THAT TAKES PRACTICE AND DISCIPLINE, LIKE A RUNNER, TRAINING FOR A RACE. I'M TRYING, IS WHAT I WANT TO SAY. I REALLY AM. IT'S JUST THAT HOPE DOESN'T FEEL LIKE THAT TO ME. IT NEVER HAS. FEELS LIKE SOMETHING I'VE GOTTA TRAP IN THE WOODS AND HUNT. OR CRAWL THROUGH THE DESERT ON MY HANDS AND KNEES TO FIND. BUT I'LL DO IT. FOR THIS SHIP, FOR RUBY, FOR THE THRILL OF THIS DAMN CHASE. IF I HAVE TO DIG HOPE OUT OF THE GROUND WITH MY BARE HANDS, I'LL DO IT. I'LL DIG AND DIG UNTIL MY NAILS ARE BLOODY AND MY BODY ACHES. I'LL YANK HOPE OUT BY THE ROOT AND SWALLOW IT WHOLE. CLAIM IT AS MINE.

I cleared my throat, absolutely stunned. "You're right, this was...thirteen days before they discovered it."

"They were that close to victory, and she still wanted to give up," Harper said. "I thought it was interesting, how despondent she sounded. And how desperately she fought to keep going."

My eyes rose to hers. "*Yank hope out by the root.*"

Harper inclined her head. "Yank it out, indeed."

"I...well." I paused, clearing my throat. "Monty's always seemed so confident. So self-assured. She used to come back to Princeton just to check in on me and pick fights with my parents at the dinner table. My dad made plenty of insulting comments about her, but they never seemed to stick. She'd just laugh them off and keep smoking her cigar."

I was zeroed in on that middle paragraph. *It's not like my family ever thought I'd amount to anything special.* I'd said the same thing to her, hundreds of times. She'd never gotten along with my parents. Never pretended to harbor friendly feelings toward them.

But I didn't know it was secretly worse than that. Didn't know how many of my inner jagged edges were so similar to hers.

Feels like something I've gotta trap in the woods and hunt.

"The worst thing is," I said, swallowing hard. "The worst thing is...she already felt this way, and then the media harassment started. Followed by her failing to find the Blackburn Diamonds. If she thought hope was that hard to grasp onto then..."

We sat in silence for a moment. Harper reached forward, holding my hand. "She'll come back to you, Eve. She will."

I wasn't sure how to respond to that, especially as an old bitterness crowded the back of my throat. *Your industry did this*, I almost said. *She was different before.* And it must have shown on my face, because I caught a guilty flicker in her gaze when our eyes met.

An alert went off on her phone. She paled slightly at whatever she saw there, then slipped it back into her bag. Seeing my quizzical look, she said, "It was a reminder of my flight back home. The office sent the tickets through."

"When is that again?" I asked, as nonchalantly as I was able.

"Sunday. Four more days." Her expression was relaxed, but there was a tension in the way she held her shoulders. "It's not really a lot of time to find diamonds that have been missing for more than a century, then write a story about them that's so compelling my boss promotes me instead of firing me. I'll take what I can get, though."

My stomach pitched to the ground, and now *I* felt guilty. I wasn't the boss who'd given her the directive to find Monty. But I might end up being the reason she got fired.

"That's...fast," I said, suddenly nervous. "And, listen, we didn't get a chance to talk about it, what with being attacked by a cougar, but what I said earlier, about not wanting you to leave—"

Harper's eyes widened slightly. Then she dropped her eyes to the ground, tugging on her earlobe. Two things I'd done when I'd been on the other side of the conversation I had with every person who'd ever wanted to get closer to me than I ever allowed. And even though I'd *just told* Harper that I was working on being more honest, I shrugged and said, "It came out more seriously than I intended it to. I know you're leaving, and I'm...I'm fine with it."

I thought she looked briefly—brutally—disappointed for half a second. But that disappeared from her face, replaced with a perky brightness I wasn't sure was entirely real. "No shame, just sensation, right? That's how you enjoy the chaos? Keeping things casual?"

She was throwing my own words back at me, the ones I'd shared when we'd fallen into that mine.

"You got it," I managed. "It's how I do things out here."

"I've never, ever done anything like that," she admitted. "Never done anything like we did..." She looked around, made sure we had privacy. "Like we did last night. Out in the open, with no outcome in mind, just pleasure for pleasure's sake."

"Did you like it?"

She sent me a bashful look. "You know I did."

I hid a smile behind my hand, an image from last night burning through my brain: Harper on her back, naked and disheveled. Begging.

"You were insatiable, cowgirl," I said with a wink.

Harper flicked an eyebrow up. "Yes, well, in a surprise to no one, it turns out I can handle you after all."

No shame, just sensation. I took my own advice and stole a kiss, nipping her lower lip with my teeth. "What am I gonna do with you, Harper Hendrix?"

"I've got a few ideas," she murmured. "Keep having fun with me is my first recommendation. Casual, right? I've got ninety-six hours left."

My breath caught in my throat. A week ago, I would have happily signed on for mind-blowing, no-strings-attached sex with the gorgeous woman in front of me—before sending her back home to her stress and deadlines with a satisfied smile on her face.

Now I felt hollow at the thought.

What the hell was *happening* to me?

"Sounds like a perfect idea," I managed, lying again.

She offered up a warm smile, reaching to brush back a curl from my forehead. "There wasn't a lot of room in my life to...to fuck around and make mistakes. I had too much responsibility, way too young, and I haven't shaken the habit of having complete control over everything. But maybe you're right, Eve. Maybe I do need to go out and watch the sunrise again. Remember all the things my mom loved to do when she was lucky enough to be here."

"Like what?" I asked—hurting for her, enchanted by her.

She pinned me in place with a gaze that seared. "Appreciate what's right in front of me and enjoy every bit of it while I can. As many times as she'll have me."

I rubbed at my flushed cheeks, raked both hands through my hair, suddenly antsy with an emotion I couldn't name.

"Are you okay, Eve?" she asked—teasing.

I leaned in again, this time aiming for that spot beneath her ear that drove her wild. Dragged my nose along the shell of her ear, breathing in the smell of flowery shampoo and her clean skin. "I'm just appreciating what's right in front of me."

When I pulled back, she was slightly out of breath, fussing with her messy bun with trembling fingers. "Not to be all 'I'm just a nerdy reporter who lives for research,' but I do have *some* ideas for our next steps, if you're open to them."

I grinned in response. "We should focus, you're right. What were you thinking?"

"I've been piecing through some of Monty's notes, and I think we need a new angle. So far, the only bit of information we have, that your aunt didn't, was what Waylon revealed to us about Harry Boyle and his presumed lover, Eugene. It feels safe to assume that we should start there."

"It does feel important," I said with a nod. "We've also got Waylon's genealogy report and the Haven's Bluff Historical Society, which just opened up a small research library next to the general store."

Her eyebrows shot up. "There's a *library* nearby?"

I grinned again, starting to shuffle Monty's notes back into some semblance of order. "Yes, ma'am, there is. What do you say we head out there and try again?"

Harper pressed Monty's journal to her chest and smiled. "Let's try again."

As she rose to get us more coffee, I took my phone and opened my text chat with Monty, tapping my fingers against the screen. My messages had been read but unanswered. But Priscilla and Adeline still felt tantalizingly close, shimmering just out of reach.

We didn't just need a new angle. We needed Monty Montana.

Don't get mad, but I'm searching for the diamonds again, I sent. *I know you asked me not to, but the timing felt right, and Jensen's getting too close. I'm afraid he'll take what's rightfully ours.*

I sent it, watched the little green bubble sit, unanswered, for another minute.

I'm out here trying to dig up hope with my bare hands and coming up empty, I typed. *I really need your help, Monty. I really need some hope.*

Chapter Twenty-Six

Harper

***Four days left to find the missing diamonds,
write the best article of my career, convince Greg
to give me that promotion, impress my dad,
and keep things "casual" with Eve***

While Eve parked the car, I stood in front of the Haven's Bluff Historical Society and contemplated continuing to ignore the voicemail I'd received from my father yesterday.

The red notification glared at me each time I peeked at my phone. An act I was doing every few minutes, hoping that Greg had answered my email about dropping Monty and pursuing the story of Priscilla and Adeline instead with a giant thumbs-up and an *atta girl*.

I was more likely to see unicorns flying in the sky, but a stressed-out reporter could dream, couldn't she?

Though at this rate, all I had to show for the article I *wanted* to be writing was a picture of an old locket, a few eyewitness accounts from 125 years ago, and sunburned shoulders.

Oh, and Eve Bardot, my new obsession.

Ignoring the voicemail again, I shot off a quick message to Daphne: *Help! I had very messy and extremely hot sex with my Beautiful and Heavily Tattooed Hot Lead and we're just keeping it casual, which is fine, I guess, but what if I'm already fucking it up?*

My phone began buzzing with what I assumed was Daphne sending me a slew of reaction gifs. Eve strolled up the sidewalk and was making her way toward me, swinging her car keys around her finger, the very picture of ease and confidence. She'd teased me about being insatiable with her, and I had been. Felt starved for her now even after she'd made me come *three times.* But I'd never felt so in touch with my body, so attuned to my real desires.

Call it a side effect of our near-death experience, but last night was the most vivid, the most fervent, the most *passionate* night of my life.

Fun. Casual. No shame, just sensation.

I'd repeat it like a mantra if I had to. Eve had been clear earlier—this was casual and fun for her, too. And what had I really expected? I'd known her for all of a *week*, and besides, this was good practice for reminding myself how to live in the moment again.

Though there was one person I knew who lived the way Eve lived—my father. And he'd abandoned me and my sister as soon as we were inconvenient to his lifestyle.

Perhaps that was why she looked so relieved when I told her I didn't want anything serious, either.

The notification glared at me again. This time I pulled my phone to my ear and pressed play, with all the enthusiasm of a person about to undergo dental surgery without anesthesia. *"Harper, it's Dad,"* he said, sounding like he stood in a wind tunnel. *"Sorry about the noise, I'm outside the chopper, and we're about to take off. Anyway, I'm just calling because I heard through the grapevine that you're out in New Mexico, trying to get the scoop on Monty Montana."*

I scowled up at the sky, bemoaning the fact that he had eyes and ears everywhere. And that no industry was chattier or more gossipy than this one.

"She's a famous mystery for a reason, honey, and I wouldn't be surprised if you take a big swing and miss. It happens to all of us. Just didn't want you to get your hopes up... Oh, uh, shit, that's the chopper, gotta run!"

Eve appeared at my side as I was staring down at my phone, as irritated as I was embarrassed. It was the way he always made me feel: annoyed at his ego and complete lack of emotional awareness. Embarrassed by all the ways he dismissed me constantly.

Embarrassed by how badly I dreamed he'd one day become a better person.

That he'd wake up and realize he'd always *wanted* to be a dad...instead of endlessly running away from us.

"Are you okay? Who was that?" Eve asked.

"Uh...just my dad leaving a typical Bruce Sullivan-esque voicemail," I said through clenched teeth. "Nothing to worry about... Let's head in, shall we?"

Eve's brows knit together, but then she nodded and followed me up the steps to the small, Victorian-looking building.

I didn't want to lie to Eve, especially after I'd pushed her to be more honest with me. But anything about Monty held the echoes of past arguments that I didn't want to have—which would be made worse when Eve realized that her aunt wasn't a person to my dad at all. She was a trophy, something to be won and displayed.

In the very beginning, I'd thought of her in the same way, much as I hated to admit it. Except none of that mattered now. Monty could stay hidden. If I was the reporter who broke the story of the Blackburn Diamonds and proved they were *real*, not an urban legend, then my dad would be forced to admit—

What? my brain said. *Forced to admit that he actually loves you?*

I tripped and almost fell on the upper step. Eve caught me by the elbow with a slightly concerned look. But I brushed it off with a smile and opened the door, only a little shaken up.

Inside, we were greeted with a sign that read ASK US ABOUT HISTORICAL TOWN TOURS. A bright and airy first floor opened up into rooms with galleries and photographs. After introducing ourselves to a sweet woman named Cheryl, she got Eve and me set up on the second floor with, she promised, newly digitized newspaper articles and photographs.

Dropping my bag on the upstairs table, I set up my laptop and opened Waylon's genealogy report. Then I strolled the shelves, trailing my fingers along the spines.

Local history, local authors. Birth and death records, dusty almanacs. All the minor and major life events that tied this community together, that made this place a home. Its joys and tragedies, all of its hopes and sorrows. Priscilla and Adeline could even exist within the pages of one of these records, nothing but a blur of pen strokes as they passed through.

"You look happy to be back in the land of books," Eve said.

"Euphoric." I pressed onto my tiptoes to pull down a book at random. "I'm no metal salvager. I don't know how to find lost treasure. But I love a damn fine story."

Eve smiled at me, and I was ill-prepared for the intensity there. "This is what you were doing on the day we first met. When you climbed the ladder at The Wreckage. I remember gazing up at you…and thinking you were lovely."

"Oh…that's right, I'd forgotten," I said, yet *another* lie.

I thought she'd say more, but then she seemed to shake herself, pointing down at the laptops. "Let's get on the same page about what we're looking for today."

"Right, yes," I said, trying to refocus. "Our strongest lead is the new information we know about Harry Boyle. So we're searching for proof in the form of historical evidence that Priscilla or Adeline knew Harry before they came here. Or had some specific reason to stop here in the first place. The locket, the eyewitness accounts, the log book…it all takes place in this town."

Eve grabbed the laptop with the genealogy report and sank back into one of the chairs. "Let me just say how nice it is to be doing historical research for the joy of it and not to impress a bunch of my parents' friends. I'll see if I can put my *almost* PhD skills to good use."

I bit my lip. "It looks good on you. Doing things for the joy of it."

Eve pressed an extremely gallant kiss to the top of my hand. My knight in shining armor, as always. Then she dove into the research while I pulled up newspaper articles from 1900, immersing myself in the lives of people here in Haven's Bluff more than a century ago.

We passed the next hour in pleasant semi-silence, only breaking it to muse on something we'd read or to show the other person a fascinating tidbit. We moved around the room easily—I paced with the laptop while Eve ended up sprawled on the ground, back against a chair. In fact, I was so deep in reading that I was startled when Eve called out my name.

"Harper, look at this," she was saying. "I've been going through the genealogy information about Harry, which also tracked some of his movements in the country if there were ways to fact-check it. Like newspaper articles and census data."

I leaned over her shoulder, scanning the article. "Hold up... this says Harry Boyle *did* go to New York City. At least one time."

"And it was two years before Priscilla and Adeline escaped. Per the article, Harry was visiting family that lived in Manhattan. His uncle, the mayor of New York at the time, and his two adult cousins. It's why there's a newspaper write-up about the cousins visiting Coney Island."

"In...*August 1898*," I read. "Holy shit. Okay, so, we at least have proof that Harry Boyle and Priscilla Blackburn were both in New York City at the same time. That's something."

Goose bumps were starting to shiver across my skin.

"And here he is again," Eve said. "Harry's still in New York, still being photographed because he's tagging along with his famous cousins. Looks like they attended a co-ed charity fundraiser hosted by a local women's circle."

Eve turned the laptop screen around and showed it to me. A million alarm bells went off in my head, and my heart almost shot through my chest.

"What...what, do you recognize it?" Eve asked urgently. I was digging through my bag, looking for the picture Kristi had sent me of Priscilla and Adeline at that women's circle together. Clutching it, I held that image up to Eve's screen. To the left of Priscilla, in the original picture, there had been half of a suited leg and a shiny shoe.

The leg and shiny shoe belonged to Harry Boyle.

"Holy shit, holy shit," Eve breathed.

I grabbed Eve's arm. "They knew each other. At the very least *met* each other."

She was tapping at the screen. "And the man next to Harry isn't his cousin. That's *Eugene*, his partner."

In the image, Harry and Priscilla are side by side, grim-faced in their Victorian clothing. The tiniest sliver of a moment, permanently frozen in black and white, but every single one of my instincts was screaming that this *mattered*.

I paced the room with my hands on my head, totally overwhelmed. "Okay, okay…so we have historical evidence that proves they at least met each other *there*. What evidence proves they met again here in Haven's Bluff? What assumptions are we making?"

Eve tapped her chin. "We're assuming the locket proves they got off the train here, but it doesn't. Not necessarily. Monty was always iffy on those eyewitness accounts—"

"And Kristi, my fact-checker, is convinced the log book entry was forged," I added.

Eve pushed to stand, walking back toward the records section. "We need some way to prove they got off at the train station here."

She was staring up at the wall of records like a painter examining a mural she'd just completed. After a few minutes, she slid a thick binder down titled DIABLO CANYON COUNTY TRAIN STOPS AND DEPARTURES: 1890 TO 1910. Laying it reverently onto the table, she opened the pages, her eyes wide with genuine glee.

"God bless local historians and all the weird stuff they love to keep," she muttered. "Transportation records always tell a damn fine story."

I moved around the table to peer over her shoulder. Each page contained logs with faded pencil markings—lines, dashes, symbols I couldn't parse.

"I always found this especially fascinating in my studies," Eve said. "Old administrative reports paint a fairly vibrant picture of day-to-day life, as much as personal letters can. Sometimes more. Where a group of people is headed, and where they've come from, is about as socio-political as you can get."

Eve must have caught me staring. She wrinkled her nose at me. "Sorry, this stuff can be boring."

"That's not it at all. I like hearing you talk about it. I like seeing you happy."

She turned back to scan the pages, but I could tell she knew I was still admiring her. She was fighting to contain a smile, and there was a slight flush to her cheeks. Eve seemed so sure of herself now, so comfortable in the life she'd deliberately built here. It was physically painful to imagine this same Eve in college, with anxiety so severe it sent her to the hospital, and her overbearing parents telling her she was faking it for the attention.

Maybe it was possible to create the life you wanted, free from your parents' shitty expectations. Eve was doing it. Monty certainly had.

You could, too.

My phone buzzed in my pocket. It was Kristi. *Just a heads-up*, her text said. *Greg saw your email about dropping the Monty story and he seems pissed. He's been stomping around all morning.*

The reality of my situation came crashing back down around me. If he was pissed, then I was probably back to square one: no Monty story, therefore no promotion, therefore no higher salary for me and my sister and no tangible achievements I could parade around my father. And where did that leave me?

My blood ran cold, all the panic clashing with my newfound inspiration and hope. I'd never felt this strongly before, at least not as an adult.

Before my mom died, she cultivated these kinds of feelings for me and Daphne. Always told us to hold tight to our freedom and curiosity for as long as we were able.

Having them finally return felt so powerful I was light-headed. But Priscilla and Adeline's story was unfolding so beautifully, with so many different layers, the question of whether or not I'd be telling this story became one of *need* and not *want*.

At the same time, even the pitch I'd sent to Greg felt shallow at best. This couldn't be distilled down into a handful of paragraphs, heavily edited with every vivid detail squeezed out of it. Historical moments of queer community—of joy and defiance, resistance and resilience—were always erased from the record. Or only dragged back into the spotlight for the sake of tragedy.

Or worse, ignored completely. Made invisible to perpetrate the lie that we'd never existed before and didn't deserve to.

Priscilla and Adeline's story was the exact opposite. It *demanded* to exist.

I coughed into my hand, refocused on the pages Eve was looking at.

"As far as I can tell, these documents tell the comings and goings of people passing through Haven's Bluff via the railroad." She ran her finger down. Tapped at the bottom. "Here's April 1900...I think?" She squinted. "What day did the diamonds go missing again?"

"April seventh," I said. "I looked this up earlier. Back then, it would have taken about three days to reach New Mexico via train. Assuming they hopped on right away and didn't make any other stops."

Eve scratched the top of her head. "Huh. The whole month of April, it just says 'DT-Forks.' What do you think that means?"

There was a knock at the door. Cheryl, the woman from earlier, was standing in the doorway with a kind smile. "My, you've been busy up here, haven't you?" Then she brightened even further. "Good thinking. Trains always tell a story."

"That's what we were hoping, but I keep hitting a code that I don't recognize," Eve said. "We're looking at the train schedule for April 1900. It just says 'DT-Forks' on every line."

Cheryl pulled on her glasses and came to stand next to Eve. "Oh, yes. That was an infamous month in the county. Torrential rains caused mudslides that took out a section of the track leading into Haven's Bluff. All trains were rerouted to the town next to us, about twenty miles away. That stands for 'Detour to Forks,' which is the name of the town."

Eve's gaze shot to mine.

"So you're saying that in the month of April in 1900, anyone passing through New Mexico would have stopped in Forks, not Haven's Bluff?" I asked.

"Yes, absolutely."

"What about for people who lived here at the time?" Eve asked. "Did they travel to Forks when the train came in?"

Cheryl nodded, wiping her glasses with the end of her sweater. "Via stagecoach, yes. They'd pretty much have to. It was the only way people were importing goods and supplies at the time."

Eve looked like someone had whispered the winning lottery ticket number into her ear.

"Harper," she said, her grin a million miles wide, "we have to go to *Forks*."

Chapter Twenty-Seven

Harper

Four days left and—whoops—I'm officially obsessed with Eve

We were standing in the middle of the prairie land that surrounded the tiny town of Forks, New Mexico—fully exhausted and rapidly losing motivation.

Necks aching, we'd taken a quick break from using the metal detectors, sweeping them back and forth in painstaking increments. So Eve had suggested a game, trying to perk us back up. A game describing our childhood versions of *watching the sunrise again.* The goal that I'd declared I'd now be working toward, inspired by the newfound looseness I'd discovered out here.

The only problem was how heavy it made my heart feel when we compared these tiny joys with the realities of our childhoods. All that I'd missed. All that Eve had missed.

The only difference being that Eve was out here making up for lost time.

"Seeing the first fireflies in your backyard and knowing that meant summer was coming," she said, leaning back against a tree with headphones draped around her neck.

I used my wrist to brush back strands of sweaty hair. "That's a good one. I'll also include the first Popsicle of summer, the way it would melt down your hand if you didn't eat it fast enough."

"*Ooh*, nice. How about...staying up past your bedtime to watch a movie you weren't supposed to?"

I grinned. "Finding the book you wanted at the library and reading it on the grass."

Eve crooked a finger, beckoning me closer. I came without hesitation, eliminating the distance between us so she could loop an arm around my waist and drag me close.

"I asked you to list the best parts of being a kid...and you say *the library*?" she teased.

I raised my chin. "My reputation shall not be maligned, Eve Bardot. Finding the exact book you want at the library is like having your favorite song randomly come on the radio. It's serendipity at its best."

Her dark eyes sparkled in the dim light. "I see your point, Hendrix. There was this old oak tree near our house growing up that I used to run to when hiding from my parents. This one patch of grass I used to sneak off to and read books. Not books for school or for studying but the ones I chose *on my own*."

I dropped a kiss on her cheek. "Reading a book you love in a sunny patch of grass is one of the best parts of being a kid. A part I miss very, very much. It was also one of my mom's favorite things to do with us when we were little. We'd have spontaneous picnics, read books to each other. It was..." My throat tightened. "Simple. Joyful. I...I took it all for granted."

Eve smoothed the hair away from my face. "That's something you can start doing more of if you want. Something of the *appreciating what's in front of me* variety."

"I'd like that very much," I admitted—then swallowed the rest.

I'd like to do that with you.

A large *snap* cut through the air. We sprang apart, sending the yellow lights of our headlamps in search of whatever creature had followed us out here. We were rapidly losing the light now. Which, given that I now feared cougars as deeply as I feared ghosts, had me painstakingly attuned to every crackling twig and rustle of leaves. And with my ears covered by the headphones of the metal detector I was carrying, it was far too easy to lose sight of our immediate surroundings.

There was water nearby—a river or a stream. Some jagged red bluffs, a smattering of scrubby brush. Other than that, the land was flat as far as the eye could see.

The town of Forks didn't have much in the way of infrastructure. A gas station with a sign that said NEXT SERVICES ARE FIFTY MILES AWAY. There was a motel called The Red Roadrunner, a few family homes scattered in the distance.

A single stoplight swayed like a squeaky dandelion in the breeze.

We'd arrived here in a cheerful mood and with our hopes dialed *all* the way up. That had potentially been a mistake, but we'd had a *breakthrough*. An honest-to-god *real clue* that put us ahead of Jensen's crew and back on track.

Eve had driven us here along a long, empty road with the windows down and her music loud, singing along with a relaxed grin. Every so often she'd direct that crooked smile my way, bathing me in a different kind of hope.

But three hours of exhausting and mind-numbing metal detecting in the growing dark had considerably dampened our victorious mood.

"Okay, so, getting back to it. We've already covered most of the land in the immediate vicinity of the old train station," Eve said, sliding the headphones back on. "With no luck, though we'll go back over this same spot tomorrow in case we missed anything."

With what my body had gone through in the past forty-eight hours, I wasn't sure I'd be able to even *stand*, let alone traverse this area again. But I smiled weakly and nodded. Peered out past the trees toward the bluffs.

"We haven't searched over there. Not sure if Priscilla and Adeline would bury the diamonds so close to the cliff's edge, but it's worth a shot," I said. "My only worry is how dark it's getting. And, you know...the probability that we'll be eaten by a cougar again."

"Statistically, it's practically impossible that we'd see another one, let alone be attacked."

I bunched my mouth up to the side. "Famous last words, Eve Bardot. Now we're *definitely* going to get eaten."

"Why would I be scared?" Eve propped the metal detector against her shoulder, looking all the world like that sexy lady lumberjack I'd claimed her to be. "I've got you to protect me, remember?"

I started to laugh. "Your confidence in me is charming, but I'm not sure I've got the requisite bravery needed to fight off *another* apex predator."

She was silent, studying me. Then she said, "In all seriousness...you are brave, Harper."

My eyes slid to the pool of lamplight at my feet. Eve stepped close, using a single finger beneath my chin to tip my face up.

"I don't always feel that way," I admitted.

"Back at the Boot + Saddle, you called me the same thing," she said. "Told me I was brave and hopeful. Did you mean that?"

"Of course I meant it." I waved my arm between us. "Look at you. Look at all that you've *done*."

She didn't respond at first. It was quiet for so long that heat flared across my cheeks, making me want to fidget beneath the intensity of her expression as she studied me.

Finally, in a hushed voice, she said, "Someone should have taken care of you after you lost your mom. Given you a soft place to rest, to be a teenager. To fuck around and make mistakes. To grieve. But even without all of that, you stayed and managed it all without any help. Built a life where you don't have to rely on your dad. *That's* bravery, Harper. And I wanted you to know...I see bravery in you, too."

I blinked, utterly stunned. "Thank you...thank you for saying that. It means a lot to me." It was a paltry response, but all that I could manage in the moment. Eve didn't seem to notice, though, planting a soft kiss on my cheek before striding away into the growing dark to keep searching for the diamonds.

Meanwhile, I stood in the quiet with a hand above my heart, wondering if anyone—besides my sister—had ever seen me so clearly.

I spun on my heel to follow her, but then a surprised shriek pierced the air. It was Eve, there one minute and gone the next. My metal detector clattered to the ground as I sprinted after her, terrified at what I'd find. I ran so fast that the cliff ledge where Eve had fallen appeared out of the blue. It had me skidding to a stop at the very last second, so dramatically that my arms spun in circles over the open air.

"Harper...Harper, be *careful*," Eve called up. "Back up... back up from the ledge. That's where it collapsed."

She was clinging to a tree root, legs dangling. Below her was another fifty feet of sheer rock face, ending in a river.

"Eve, *oh my god.*" I dropped to my knees and extended a hand. "Can you reach me? I'll pull you up."

She grimaced. "I'll pull myself up. You just get back from the ledge. If you fall down here, too, we're both screwed."

Rolling my eyes, I grabbed her metal detector and extended it forward. It was sturdy and just long enough. "Don't be stubborn and ridiculous. We stick together, remember?"

"*Hendrix,*" she warned.

"*Eve,*" I shot back. "I won't fall."

"That's what I thought, and now look at me."

My lips twitched. "Don't make me laugh in the middle of a rescue mission. Now grab on. I'll haul you up."

Her eyes flew to mine, and I could see the understandable fear there. Knew she was asking me to keep her safe despite her protests.

I angled out farther to get a better view but had to fight back the panic at just how high up we were. "If you keep one hand on the root, and use your feet for leverage, you can grab hold of the handle without falling, okay? Just be like that kitten in the poster everyone loves."

Eve breathed out a nervous laugh. "The *hang in there* kitten?"

I brightened. "Yes, that one. Exactly."

"A little grim considering my situation."

"Or *inspiring.*" I wiggled the metal detector. "Come on, Eve. You can do it. Eyes on me, beautiful."

After a few more seconds of contemplation, she finally grabbed hold and slowly began pulling herself up. Her muscles strained where her fingers gripped around the metal. My shoulders burned, locked in place, holding her steady.

But she was doing it.

"The faster you get up here, the faster I can take you out on a date," I promised.

"You wanna…" Eve was panting. "Take me out on a date?"

"Yes, ma'am. How else can the knight in shining armor show her damsel in distress that she has a crush on her?"

Eve reached the top—finally—and pulled herself all the way out. I grabbed her by the shirt and yanked her forward with my last remaining strength. We fell backward into the dirt, laughing, breathless, and so very relieved, with Eve on top of me.

She cupped my face, her thumb stroking along my cheekbone. "So you're the damsel *and* the knight now?"

I grinned up at her in the waning light. "I contain multitudes, Eve. And someone once told me—like, five minutes ago—that I was brave. Therefore, I'm both. Though I'm not quite sure what that makes you. A scoundrel, perhaps."

"I *have* had scoundrel-like thoughts about you." She nudged her nose against mine.

"Oh, yeah? Like what?"

"They're not-safe-for-work, cowgirl. You'll just have to be patient." She slanted her lips over mine, finally giving in to our kiss. "It does make me lucky to be rescued by you. Very, very lucky."

Our kiss deepened quickly, both of us desperate after yet another near-brush with danger. I arched up into her. Gasped. Her hands roamed my body. I dug my nails into her short curls. She swiped her tongue along mine and groaned. My legs rose high around her waist as she tipped my head back so she could kiss along my throat, sucking the tender skin between her teeth.

Stars were starting to appear above us, already twinkling and dazzling in their brilliance. And the only coherent thought I could manage was, *I could do this with Eve forever.*

Except then I noticed the small, dark, *furry* creature right next to Eve's foot. I went rigid so fast that she felt it.

"What is it?" she whispered. "And please, for the love of god, do not say the word *cougar*."

"Um...tarantula?" I sputtered.

"Oh, cool, a spider. My absolute worst nightmare from childhood."

I wrapped my arms tight around her as she started to tremble. "Let me think. It's standing still now... Maybe it's scared, too? Do they bite? Are they poison—"

The sound of a shotgun blast cracked through the air like a bolt of heat lightning. A pellet landed six inches from the spider, who didn't hesitate to skitter away into the darkness.

Our headlamps were still rolling on the ground, so they cast strange shadows on the figure that stepped forward—tall, wearing boots, faded jeans, and a low-brim cowboy hat.

I gulped, frozen in shock, and stared at the spot where the tarantula had been. "Either you have horrible aim, or you just saved us from being bitten by a venomous spider."

The person shrugged. "Nah, I've got perfect aim. That spider was minding her damn business until you two came along. Ain't no reason to hurt a creature who's just living their life."

With a single finger, they raised the brim of their hat, revealing a tanned, weathered face and a lopsided grin.

Eve looked like she'd just seen a ghost.

"Hiya, kid," the stranger said cheerfully. "Funny runnin' into you out here, isn't it?"

Eve's jaw dropped. *"Monty?"*

Chapter Twenty-Eight

Eve

Monty!!!!

Harper and I followed Monty back to our campsite, just outside of Forks, in a state of total bewilderment.

Every minute or so, Harper would mutter, "Your aunt shot at a tarantula and intentionally *missed*?"

And I would reply, "That's not even the first time she's done that."

Or I'd mumble, "How in the hell did she find us?"

To which Harper would say, "Monty Montana is *really here*?"

My thoughts and feelings were a jumbled mess. There was no way Monty was out in the random town of Forks "fishing and camping" or whatever the lie was that she'd told me. She had to be searching for the diamonds. *Had* to be.

That meant she'd lied to me multiple times, including on the phone just a few days ago when she'd begged me not to make a move.

She hadn't even addressed being completely MIA this entire time. Instead, Monty had happily tossed our gear into the back of her truck, yelled out, "Just follow me, gals!" then tore off down the road.

She hadn't changed much since I'd last seen her. Her silver hair was in its usual braid, and the same beat-up cowboy hat sat atop her head. Her plaid work shirt was tucked neatly into worn Wranglers, dusty at the knees.

Her craggy face was still all smile, except now I couldn't stop thinking about the journal entries I'd read this week. Especially the one Harper had shown me, about her fears.

I LIE AWAKE AT NIGHT AND WORRY ABOUT WHAT CLUES I MISSED. WORRY IF RUBY'S MAD AT ME FOR TRYING SO HARD AT SOMETHING I'M PROBABLY NOT VERY GOOD AT... IT'S NOT LIKE MY FAMILY EVER THOUGHT I'D AMOUNT TO ANYTHING SPECIAL.

It made me want to grab her hand and say, "But how are you *really*?"

The sight of Monty's simple campsite as we pulled up tugged hard on my heart. The metallic chrome of her old Airstream trailer and the cluster of sun-faded bumper stickers crowding around the license plate. The crackling campfire, the shabby lawn chairs, the deck of cards on the picnic table. Some of my first truly happy memories were spent doing things like this with Monty and Ruby—it had my shoulders sagging with the weight of missing her.

But then the door of the trailer opened wide and out stepped a person I hadn't seen in years.

Ruby.

Monty's estranged wife.

My heart stopped. She opened her arms wide and said, "Evie Bardot, just *look* at you. You're as gorgeous as ever."

I stepped into her embrace, completely fucking mystified.

The smell of her sandalwood lotion brought so many memories roaring back—like the time in high school when I was going through a goth phase. And she showed up that Christmas with lipsticks for me to try in shades of black and purple, and my parents almost had a joint heart attack.

"What are you doing here?" I said softly. "Are you... Is Monty... I have so many questions."

She rubbed my back. "We've got answers, we promise." She pulled back to examine me, notching up an eyebrow at my tattoos. "Still decorating ourselves, I see?"

"Always."

Like Monty, she hadn't changed much. Maybe a few more lines around her eyes, some extra gray in her curly black hair. Ruby was a decade younger than Monty, in her early fifties. Her red wrap dress was bright against her dark tan skin, the color matching her lipstick perfectly.

"I never thought I'd see you again," I admitted.

Monty came out of the trailer, carrying four bottles of beer, a half-lit cigar in her mouth. "Not givin' me a whole lot of credit here, kid."

Ruby sent her an exasperated look. "Can you blame her? You never tell anyone *anything*."

I propped my hands on my hips. "For example: what the hell is going on here and how long have you been lying to me?"

Monty sprawled out in a chair and kicked her foot up on the edge of the fire ring. "Plenty to say. But first, you gonna tell me why you're hanging around with that reporter you told me about?"

Harper and I exchanged a worried glance.

"I *can* google things, Evie. I'm not that old," Monty muttered. "I looked her up after you told me about her. Which is kinda awkward for me, since I haven't spoken to any member of the press in twenty-odd years."

"*Eve,*" Ruby said. "Tell me you didn't bring a reporter with you."

"I know what it looks like."

Monty huffed out a breath. "It looks like what it *is*. You know I'm not sayin' shit if she's here."

Harper stepped into the circle of light cast by the fire. Her throat worked nervously as she waved, wearing a small—but sincere—smile. She looked nothing at all like the impeccably made-up woman who'd walked into The Wreckage all of eight days ago. Her bun was loose and hanging off to one side. There was dirt smeared on her face, across her peach sundress.

Even her glasses were slightly smudged.

I hadn't been able to take my eyes off her then. *Couldn't* take my eyes off her now. Something Monty must have noticed, because she cleared her throat loudly to get my attention.

"My name is Harper Hendrix, and it is true that I was originally sent here to try and find you, Monty, and convince you to give your first real interview since *La Venganza,*" Harper said. "No one gave you up, by the way. The whole town protected you like you were a national secret."

Monty's response was to blow a series of smoke rings—but I could tell she was pleased by this.

"And I should say, before anything else, that just being here in your presence, with Ruby, well…it's an honor." Harper seemed to notice her disheveled appearance at that exact moment and quickly went into repair mode—bun fixed, dress straightened, a quick swipe of the dirt on her cheeks. "I wasn't expecting to meet you looking like this. Or meet you at all, really. Eve had convinced me it would never happen."

Monty cocked an eyebrow at me, and I shrugged.

"Before I came out here, I saw a picture of you two together. The famous one, on the beach, the day you found the ship."

Ruby came to stand behind Monty, placing a hand on her shoulder. Monty squeezed it, and— Holy shit, were Monty and Ruby *back together*?

"I know the one," Monty said.

Harper's gaze met mine. "I'm sure you've gotten this before, but...I saw that picture, and it changed something for me. I don't know in exactly what way yet. I'm still figuring that part out. But I genuinely admire you both, and I understand if you want nothing to do with me. And I fully understand your anger because of what happened."

Harper hadn't shared this with me yet, but I could see it. Could see it in the small ways she was expanding since she'd arrived here. Loosening up, taking up space.

I shoved my hands in my pockets. "Harper figured out the real story of Priscilla and Adeline before I even told her."

That got Monty's attention. "How?"

"My colleague at the paper I work for, she found a picture of Priscilla and Adeline at an auxiliary club together and told me that they'd disappeared on the same day," Harper said. "Once I knew that, I knew that the real story, the story I *wanted* to tell, was their love story."

"Harper wants to change the public's perception of Priscilla," I said. "That's why I asked her to join me when I decided to go search for the diamonds."

Harper grinned. "From scandalous villain to queer hero."

Now Ruby and Monty shared a glance.

"That is interesting," Ruby said. "And you trust her intentions, Eve?"

"I really do," I said firmly. I caught Harper smiling out of the corner of my eye, but wariness unfurled in my stomach. Just yesterday, when Harper asked me point blank about trust, I wasn't so sure. And only a week ago, she was barreling through my life with no thought to the consequences.

I'm not here seeking permission. I'm here seeking information. This is my job, and nothing's going to stop me from doing it.

Harper's brow furrowed as if she sensed my hesitation. But then Monty gave a short nod and stubbed out her cigar. "If Evie says you're fine, I believe her. But I'd like it clear that Ruby and I were never here. And you and I never met. No recorder. No notepad. This is off the record until I say it's back on."

Harper nodded eagerly. "Yes, ma'am, I can do that."

Monty kicked out the two chairs next to her. "All right, then. Sit down, and I'll tell ya what I've been up to."

I sank down into the chair next to her and took the beer she offered. "And no more fucking lies. I'm serious, Monty."

"Scout's honor," she said with a wink.

Harper took the other beer and sank down gracefully in the final chair, legs crossed and upper body leaned forward. The sun had finally set, bathing us in darkness lit only by constellations, the fluttering of a bat's wings like a symphony overhead.

Ruby held her hands over the fire and cast a sideways glance at Monty. "When your aunt and I mounted the campaign for the diamonds five years ago, things were tense from the start. We didn't expect it to remind us so much of what happened with the press after *La Venganza*. Or for so many others in our community to be so jealous and spiteful. It brought up a *lot* of ugly insecurities that we hadn't worked through."

"Hell, we thought getting back out there was the right thing to do," Monty added. "Saying *fuck 'em* to the people who believed we'd cheated our way into finding that ship. But Blackburn's different. It's *personal*. And I"—she coughed into her fist—"I let my ego do the talking, and there's no excusing it. Was so public about it—"

"Then we publicly didn't find anything," Ruby said. "We were so embarrassed. That's when we separated."

Monty raised the brim of her hat to send Ruby a look of total, all-consuming affection. The kind I always remembered flourishing between them.

"Those were the worst years of my life," Monty admitted.

"Mine, too," Ruby said. "I needed time and space to process everything. So I went back to Guadalajara to be with family, mostly my abuelita, who was sick at the time. When she passed, I took on all the work of dealing with her estate, the house. I didn't step foot back in New Mexico until a year ago."

"Where we reconnected," Monty said with a grin. "Off and on for a bit, feeling each other out. Then in couple's therapy for a long time. And finally…officially together about six months ago."

My body felt frozen between sheer joy and total disappointment. "Six months? You've been back together this whole time?"

Monty winced, rubbing a hand across her jaw. "It's nothin' personal, kid. We didn't tell a single soul. It all just felt so… fragile. And I didn't want to tell you then have things go south again."

I huffed out a breath, exasperated. "No, I get it. It's just…"

I trailed off, unsure of what I was really trying to say. That it hurt my feelings when she didn't open up to me? That I'd trusted her to be with me through so much, including moving here, and yet she didn't trust me enough to share this?

Monty sniffed. "Wasn't personal. I swear."

But before I could react again, Harper said, "It was you, wasn't it?"

Monty and Ruby turned toward her voice.

"Pardon?" Monty said.

Harper tapped her chin. "Eve and I, we thought Jensen was one step ahead of us in Haven's Bluff this whole time. But it's been you and Ruby. Right?"

Stunned, I said, "Did you dig up Diablo Canyon before the rainstorm hit?"

Ruby's lips curved. "Jensen's crew is still a major threat, and we've been keeping a close eye on his movements. But yes...it was us, Harper. We still need to put all the dirt back, fill everything in. It was just one of the places we couldn't shake."

"And we were at the Historical Society yesterday," Monty said. "Where we learned about—"

"The train detour to Forks," Harper said. "That's why you were out there tonight."

"Yes, ma'am."

My stomach lurched as I finally caught up to the barrage of new information. "You and Ruby getting back together in secret I understand. But just a few days ago, you told me to stand down, that the timing wasn't right to go after the diamonds. But you were out here all along?" I paused, swallowing past a lump in my throat. "We always said we'd do this together."

The lines around Monty's mouth softened, and she rolled her beer bottle between her hands. "I know, Evie. I wanted to tell you soon, was planning on it actually. But I guess I got superstitious, picturing this black cloud following us the whole time, because of how we failed last time. It made me protective, but not because I didn't want you there. I've been stuck in my head about it, is all."

Another piece of her journal entry came back to me: **HOPE DOESN'T FEEL LIKE THAT TO ME. IT NEVER HAS. FEELS LIKE SOMETHING I'VE GOTTA TRAP IN THE WOODS AND HUNT. OR CRAWL THROUGH THE DESERT ON MY HANDS AND KNEES TO FIND.**

I was still incredibly hurt by what she'd done, and knew we'd have to sort through it eventually, but in the moment, I was able to nod my head and squeeze her hand.

"I'm sorry," she said, "and I'm so glad you're here. I swear I thought it was a sign from the universe when I drove past your Mustang, because I *do* want to do this with you. I promise."

I flashed a grin, gave her hand another squeeze. "Then let's do it this time, for real. 'Cause Harper and I uncovered something wild just this afternoon."

Monty and Ruby leaned forward in their seats, intrigued.

Harper, meanwhile, brightened into a smile. "Waylon Boyle told us that his uncle, Harry Boyle, was believed to be queer, possibly in a relationship with his business partner, Eugene," she explained. "They lived together in the apartment above the general store where the locket had been stored."

"You're joking," Monty swore. "He's *never* said anything about that to me or anyone."

I raised an eyebrow. "Just wait. It gets better."

"Waylon gave us all this genealogical research that his mom had done," Harper continued. "In it, we found a picture of Harry Boyle *with* Priscilla and Adeline in New York City. It seems like they knew each other."

Monty scrubbed a hand down her face while Ruby clapped.

"I fucking knew it," Monty said. "We fucking *knew it*, Evie."

She stood and pulled me in for a hug, kissing the top of my head. I was briefly, blissfully, free of my annoyance with her for the moment. The moment we'd been waiting on for years—when our long-held gut instincts finally collided with actual proof.

"Then I guess this is as good a time as any for us to share *our* good news," Ruby said.

I pulled back to glimpse Monty's wide smile, followed by the sly look she shared with her wife.

"What is it?" I asked, hardly daring to hope.

"We have a lead, the strongest one yet, and when I tell you I've got *such* a different feeling about this one..." Monty said. "This could be it, kid. I'm serious."

Shocked, my eyes found Harper's over the campfire. Hers were bright, brimming over with possibility.

"Then let's go find ourselves a treasure," I said, and Monty threw her hat in the air with a victorious *whoop.*

Chapter Twenty-Nine

Eve

A Bunch of Hope, Foolish or Otherwise

Minutes later and we were piling into Monty's truck, gear tossed in the back. She tore down the road so quickly that she fishtailed, sending up a spray of dust.

"You two were on the right track, looking around where the train station used to be," Monty said to us over her shoulder. "We got here a day before you, so we were able to search in a larger area. Ruby had the smart idea to search *away* from the water source, thinking that they might have chosen a spot with less foot traffic."

"We covered at least a ten-mile radius near the station," Ruby added. "With almost nothing getting picked up by the detectors. But then we hit this spot, about a mile from where you were, and my detector just lit up like a Christmas tree."

Goose bumps shivered across my skin. Harper and I shared another look of total surprise. "Holy shit," I murmured. "This is really happening."

"Our thoughts exactly," Monty said, rolling down the

windows. The wind sent Ruby's curls flying as they laughed the sound of their combined delight stirring up an ache in my chest.

They were back together. And *happy*.

And had been out here without my knowledge, trying to find the diamonds. I was holding two legitimate and vastly different emotions at once: a prickly hurt from feeling abandoned by my aunt…and the total ecstasy of potentially solving a mystery that had fascinated us for years.

The emotions were so big and unwieldy, it was almost too much to take in. It must have been obvious, because Harper found my hand and interlaced our fingers. I pulled her wrist to my mouth and kissed it, felt her pulse leap beneath her skin.

My brain didn't trust Harper fully yet. My body clearly did, though. Dangling from that tree branch earlier, fifty feet off the ground, some part of me knew I was safe with her. That she'd protect me, no matter what.

"If someone had told you a week ago that we'd be doing this together, would you have believed them?" she asked.

"Maybe under duress," I said with a grin. "You've proven your tenacity, Hendrix. Really wouldn't put kidnapping someone to get your way past you."

"Hmmm." She cocked her head. "I would be an organized and extremely efficient kidnapper. You, however, would be a very annoying captive."

I dropped my jaw in shock. "In what fucking way?"

"Your constant flirting, obviously. You'd try and charm me into freeing you."

I cocked an eyebrow. "Would it work?"

"Not in the least."

I leaned in close. "Don't lie."

She crossed her arms over her chest. "I'm not lying. *Some* people can resist you. It's not like it's hard."

"And how many days did you last? Like...three?"

"It was way longer than that," she said, fighting a smile. "It was six days at least."

I leaned all the way across so I could brush my lips across her cheek. The sultry hitch in her breathing whenever I was near was a sound I now lived for.

"Your bravery is admirable," I whispered.

"There should be a national holiday dedicated to my courageous acts."

Monty let out another *whoop*, taking a hard right turn onto the road that ran alongside where we'd just been—a mile past the single, swaying streetlight. Past the Red Roadrunner Motel. Just a bit farther, toward a copse of giant trees, and then the GPS alerted us that we'd arrived.

Outside, we snapped on headlamps, grabbed shovels, lanterns, and detectors, and began trekking out toward the spot they'd located. It was impossible not to get our hopes up as our boots crunched over dry prairie grass. The universe shimmered above us, starlight guiding our way. Once at the spot, we set our gear down, and Monty handed Ruby one of the metal detectors.

"Whaddya say, Rue? Wanna give it one last go before we dig?"

Ruby gave a coy nod in response. Headphones in, she began methodically swiping around the designated area. Almost immediately, the machine spit out a series of staccato tones, growing louder with each pass.

"Now isn't that my favorite sound in the world," Ruby said.

My stomach hollowed out. Harper sucked in a noisy breath. "Does that mean what I think it means?"

"We've struck gold," I said. "So to speak."

Harper crashed into me a second later, wrapping her arms around my waist. Laughing, I kissed the crown of her head. "Don't celebrate too much, cowgirl."

"Yeah, 'cause it could just be some camper's leftover fork," Monty said.

"Or old pennies," Ruby added.

I squeezed the back of Harper's neck. "Maybe a big, rusty pipe."

She stepped away from me with a scowl, looking too adorable to be legitimately mad. "This is my first treasure hunt. I reserve the right to be naively optimistic for a few minutes before my spirit's crushed."

Laughing a little, Monty stabbed the ground with the point of her shovel. Leaned her boot at the edge and officially broke ground. "You're right, Harper. This is my favorite part, too. Before we really know. When all we are is a bunch of hope, foolish or otherwise."

Harper swallowed hard, watching me.

"*And* it wouldn't be a real dig if we didn't say a few words for good luck," Ruby said.

My aunt looked at me with a mischievous smile, yanking me back to that day in the hospital. The way she'd held my hand like she'd never let go. How choked up she'd been when she said, *"This has been such a scary time for you, kid. Such a scary, god-awful time."*

No one in my family had ever acknowledged how scared I'd been. No one had ever acknowledged how my anxiety symptoms made me *feel*: panicked, out of breath, terrified, overwhelmed. The chronic insomnia, the chest pain, the bouts of sobbing.

Monty knew, though. She always did.

"How about it, Evie?" she said. "Wanna do the honors?"

I grinned in response, rubbing the back of my head as I thought about what to say. Then I looked at Harper. "You know what they say. A bust is a bust 'til it ain't."

"Well, hot damn," Monty hollered. She tossed Ruby a shovel. Harper and I grabbed ours.

And then we started digging together: dirt flying free, our coordinated, repetitive movements. Strike, lift, toss.

We shifted when the metal detector told us to, pausing only to catch our breath or drink some water.

We made decent headway with all of us working together. Piles of dirt were scattered around, and we were about four feet down into the ground already. The last couple days had not been kind to my body, but pure adrenaline was powering me through.

Monty let out a low whistle and raised a dirt-covered rock into the sphere of her headlamp. "Look at that. A little bit of turquoise for good luck."

Harper brightened, and Monty placed it in her palm with pride.

"I've never seen it like this," Harper admitted. "Just a splash of blue in the middle of this ditch, huh?"

"Yep. Just a splash of blue, a secret just for us." Monty removed her hat to scratch the top of her head. "The Earth likes to keep her secrets. On the floor of the ocean, buried in some canyon, hidden high on a mountain somewhere. And I'm not talking about just buried treasure. I'm talkin' about every blade of grass and petal on a flower being as much a mystery as that old ship we found trapped in the reef."

She dropped her hat back on her head and continued

shoveling. "People like to say that everything's been discovered now. The world's too connected, there's not enough mystery anymore. But why would you ever stop searching for beauty when there's so much to see, right in front of our eyes? Not letting yourself celebrate that seems like a real silly way to live if you ask me."

Ruby gazed fondly at my aunt. "Now you see how she charmed me into our reckless life of adventure."

"I'm real convincing when I want to be."

A few minutes passed as we switched out, with Harper and I taking over digging while Monty and Ruby rested. I nudged her hip against mine with a sly grin and caught her biting her lip in response, trying not to smile.

"I always did want to ask you, Eve," she said, lifting a shovel full of dirt. "What was the first thing you and Monty ever found together?"

Delighted, I glanced up at Monty, who was already smiling. "A soda bottle. Very old and very sea-green colored. I still have it, use it for bouquets of flowers."

"Where was this?"

"Somewhere out in Jersey," I said. "A quarry, I think. Monty and Ruby were in town for a quick visit the summer before tenth grade, and I'd never been happier to see them. My parents always enrolled me in these hellish, pre-college camps that made my anxiety skyrocket."

Ruby's eyes softened at the memory. "Eve's parents had difficulty noticing how exhausted she was. Well, that, or they just ignored it. Though it seemed impossible to ignore to us. Your nails were chewed down to the quick. The bags under your eyes were so dark they were like bruises. You were just...*listless*. It was devastating."

I stopped shoveling and cocked my head affectionately toward Ruby, let her scratch through my curls for a moment the way she used to. "Monty and Ruby, they never ignored it, never ignored me or minimized it. It's why we were out in the quarry that day."

"Fresh air always made you happier," Monty said with a grin. "And that quarry really wasn't that pretty to look at, but anything's pretty if you spend all day with it. We had a good time together. You found that bottle all on your own, too."

"It was just a Coke bottle," I said, almost bashful.

"Well, it could have ended up in a landfill, but now it's holding wildflowers." Monty took a swig of water and set the bottle down. "Seems like it all turned out okay in the end."

I caught Harper's eye. "I remember feeling extremely chic and grown up that day, using all of their cool tools. And then later that night, I was just…" I paused, my throat going tight with emotion even all these years later. "I was just *despondent*. Monty pulled me aside before their flight and gave me this long hug and told me to remember that no one else got to dictate the truth of who I really was."

Behind me, Monty huffed out a surprised breath. I spun on my heel, quirked an eyebrow. "Do you remember saying that?"

"Sure I do, but I never thought you did."

"And do you remember what you said after that?" I asked.

My aunt shared a quick look with Ruby, looking almost shy. She cleared her throat. "I said…I said that people throughout your life would try to get you to do or say or believe all manner of things because it made *them* happy. But only you got to decide if it made you happy. Only you got to decide if it was your truth."

"Only I got to decide if it was the truth of who I really was,"

I repeated. "Those words carried me through quite a bit, you know."

Monty cleared her throat. "Glad to hear it, Evie."

And when I turned back around, it didn't escape my notice that tears were silently tracking down Harper's cheeks. But she swiped them away immediately and was avoiding looking at me. I hooked my pinkie finger around hers and squeezed.

She squeezed back.

...

The first hour after that passed pleasantly enough, with Monty and Ruby trading stories back and forth, making Harper laugh as each one grew zanier than the last. After relaying our close call with the cougar, we launched into similar close calls and mishaps on the trail. It kept our spirits and energy up.

Especially as we slid into the second hour of digging.

Concerned, Monty re-did the scans, shifted our positions around, then had our shovels striking out farther and deeper. The exhaustion of the last few days finally slammed into me full force.

At the start of hour three, a creeping dread began seeping through my body. We grew quieter, began avoiding eye contact as we rested in between shifts. Ruby kept holding Monty's hand with a pained expression.

Harper, meanwhile, grew increasingly pale beneath her head lamp. But then Monty's detector sent up a chorus of chirps just as Harper's shovel struck something metallic.

With a low curse, Monty jumped into the pit and rummaged through the dirt, sending it flying up against Harper's legs. She sent me a look that was half hope, half agony.

Monty held up a handful of rusted, metal cutlery.

"God*dammit*," she swore.

I swayed on my feet, almost too tired to realize the crushing weight of my own disappointment.

"No," Harper whispered frantically. "No, no, that can't be right. Where are the diamonds?"

I squeezed my eyes shut. "It was a false read."

Just like the floor we'd fallen through at the Kept King mine, nothing but a trick to send you tumbling into darkness.

"So what...it really *was* just some camper's old fork?" Harper was shaking her head. "I refuse to accept this. Monty, you said you had a different feeling about this one. You were so sure. This just...can't *be*."

My aunt removed her hat and set it on the ground above her with a weary sigh. Ruby jumped down into the pit next to her, pulling her in for a hug. Harper was blinking rapidly, eyes shining, and every time her gaze found mine, it felt like my chest was being cracked wide open.

"Harper," I started, but Monty interrupted.

"I don't know what to tell ya," Monty said. "Our gut feelings can still be wrong. Very wrong. And frankly, being *sure* doesn't mean jack shit. At least when I say it."

Ruby reared back to chide her before I could. "How could you have possibly known differently? We know what this business is. It's digging a hundred empty holes just to get *here*. But we have a strong lead on this new location, a location no one else knows about yet. There's always tomorrow. You understand that better than most."

I could hear the echoes of Monty's journal entry in the conversation in front of me and guessed it'd been had in various iterations throughout their marriage. To her credit, Monty seemed to accept Ruby's wisdom with less stubbornness than usual.

Maybe the past six months, learning alongside Ruby in therapy, *were* having a positive impact on my aunt. But now that I was standing here—shivering, starving, zombie-like with exhaustion—all I wanted to say was, *You still had me worried sick, you still lied to me, you still decided to do this on your own without asking how I felt about it.*

And, to make things worse, we *still* hadn't found the fucking diamonds.

Chapter Thirty

Eve

It's Complicated

B ack at the campsite, Monty and Ruby turned in early, claiming exhaustion from the intensity of the dig. But even after they promised me and Harper that this first fail was just the beginning—that Forks held so much promise, that we'd be back at it again in no time—they couldn't hide the severely defeated slump to their shoulders as they climbed into the trailer.

I knew the feeling. We'd ridden back here in a morose silence, so markedly different from the cheery lightness of earlier. The windows stayed up, and the music was off. Monty wasn't even whistling under her breath.

She'd offered to set up the tent and air mattress for us outside the trailer, but I told her not to worry about it. That if Harper and I couldn't find a motel, Faith usually had at least one RV open for last-minute walk-ups. Not that I could say what Harper's plan was or if she even wanted to stay with me. We'd stumbled upon another sliver of cell service on the drive over, and whatever message she'd seen on her phone had her looking absolutely panicked.

And when I reached across the seat to grasp her hand in comfort, she pulled away.

As soon as Monty shut the door to the trailer, I turned to see if Harper was okay. Except she was already stalking off toward the empty road ahead of us, phone to her ear. Her voice carried in the night breeze—nothing fully audible, though her tone was high-pitched and nervous.

A sick feeling stirred in the pit of my stomach, a sick feeling that felt an awful lot like reality storming back into our lives.

When she finally walked back over, I was sprawled in one of the lawn chairs in front of the small campfire I'd just started, my right knee bouncing with nerves.

"What's happened?" I asked.

She hesitated, her eyes shining with unshed tears, and I felt my heart stop. "That was Greg, my boss, and he was...he was livid with me. I was supposed to have three more days with you— *out here*, three more days out here. But he said since I broke the rules and used the paper's time and money to pursue a story he hadn't signed off on, they rebooked my flight, and it leaves in three hours."

That sick feeling became an icy despair, seizing me by the throat. I pushed to stand on shaky legs. "Can I... Shit, let me drive you—"

"It's fine, really, Eve. You should stay here with your aunts, commiserate together, be with each other tomorrow and... continue searching without me." She opened the trunk of my car and pulled out her suitcase, avoiding looking at me. "My rental is still in The Wreckage parking lot. I called a car to pick me up here, then I'll head to the airport."

Total distress surged through me, but I forced it back down through brute strength. We'd known each other for all of a week—what did I think Harper was going to do? Never go home? I'd been the one who'd bragged about keeping things casual anyway.

Except it hadn't been casual between us for even a *second...* and I knew that. Knew that she'd always leave me in the end.

"What does...what does this mean for the Priscilla and Adeline story?" I managed to ask.

"I don't know," she said. "I was already starting to think that they deserved something longer than whatever the paper would let me have. But if I decide to go that route, it means I need to pitch it around to other news outlets, which will take time. To be blunt, finding the diamonds tonight would have made things easier from an editorial standpoint. Until then...I don't have any answers yet."

I held out my hand, indicated the trailer behind me. "You heard what they said, though. This is just the beginning. We know they're out there."

Harper's entire body sagged. "There are so many potential explanations for what happened that it makes my head hurt just thinking about it. How probable do you think it is that they'll actually be *found* at this point?"

There was a caginess to her movements that was unsettling. And she still hadn't looked me in the eye. Neither eased the crushing disappointment I still felt from earlier, or the terrifying fact that she was voicing my late-night anxieties out loud. "You know I can't answer that, Harper. It's not a science. Besides, you don't need the diamonds to do what you promised. Helping us set the record straight, proving Priscilla was the hero after all."

"That's my plan," she said. "Telling their story is all I want to do. I want it with my *whole damn heart...* But first I need to...

Fuck, Eve, I need to get back and see if I can salvage all this. I'll keep you and Monty in the loop over email, if that's okay?"

Keep you in the loop over email sounded so cold and professional coming from the woman who had absolutely turned my world upside down in a single week.

"Harper," I said, even more nervous now, "you're gonna keep it a secret that you saw Monty and Ruby, right? They asked me to vouch for you and if you do anything—"

She reared back, dropping her luggage to the ground. "*Do* anything? Like what? I thought you trusted me."

"You can't fault me for being realistic," I hedged. Her eyes narrowed. "I'm worried you'll get all the way back to New York, far away from here, and you'll be pressured to out Monty somehow. It's a huge scoop for someone vying for a promotion, right? And like you said, we didn't even find anything tonight, so all you have is finding my aunt."

Her cheeks reddened. "A promotion is so far off the table for me... Eve, I broke about a million company policies and, worse, don't even have a story to show for it. At this point, I'm being sent back to beg for my job. Any job." She pinched the bridge of her nose and released a shaky breath. "God, I screwed everything up. I should have known better."

The bitterness at the edges of *I should have known better* sounded just like the Harper Hendrix I'd met at the beginning of this journey—the career-obsessed rule-follower who never wanted to take a risk. It ratcheted up my nerves, sent my thoughts flying toward every worst-case scenario.

"Well, then...then fuck that guy," I said earnestly. "He sounds terrible. The job sounds terrible. Quit and do whatever the hell you want. If you want to start enjoying the sunrises more, living like Priscilla and Adeline...maybe this is your chance."

Harper's face crumpled, like she was about to cry. I reached for her, already so pissed at myself, already breaking on the inside. But she waved me off, which hurt even more. She pressed the palms of her hands to her eyes until she got herself under control.

"Eve…" she said, voice cracking. "I can't just leave my family and move out west with my amazing aunt like you did. Daphne and I don't have anybody. We only have each other. And if I lose this job, it's going to fuck up a career I've always wanted. It's… complicated."

I grabbed the back of my neck, gut curdling. "Leaving my family wasn't just some vacation for me, Harper. You know it was complicated, too."

"I know that." She was shaking her head. "I'm sorry, that came out the wrong way. I know how horrible they are, what you had to do to survive. That doesn't mean we can all live our lives the way you do."

"You have a famous dad who can get you any job you want in the industry without you even having to try," I shot back. "Doesn't seem that complicated to me."

Her eyes flashed. "You know why I can't do that."

"Can't or won't?" At her shocked silence, I started rebuilding the walls around my heart, brick by brick. "Listen, we had to get back to reality at some point, didn't we? It can't always be spontaneous road trips and treasure hunting. We were just having fun together. No shame, all sensation."

That lie hurt. God, I wanted to punch myself in my *own* face. I'd spent so much of this week teasing Harper about never wanting to break the rules. But here I was, breaking all of my *own rules* and somehow being surprised at the consequences.

The shitty, heartbreaking consequences.

Harper nodded slowly, placing her bag back on her shoulder. "I see," she said, almost sadly. "I'm still the enemy here, aren't I? You really don't trust me."

"Harper, we barely know each other," I said, exasperated. "Five days ago, you were still out to stop me *and* find Monty."

"That's not true." She lifted her chin. "It's...it's different between us, and you know it."

She fought to compose herself, letting me wallow in the memories I knew she was referring to. Every precious vulnerability we'd shared, every divulged secret. How fiercely we'd protected each other, saved each other. The look of her dancing beneath sparkly disco light. Her hair in the wind as she hung out the window, her smile like a beam of incandescent joy.

That quiet bravery. That fierce hunger. Her soft body under mine in the backseat of the car, every breathy plea full of honest need.

I want you so badly, I burn *with it, Harper.*

There was such a sharp pain in the center of my chest I had to press my palm there. Headlights swept down the road, slowing to a stop when Harper raised a hand and flagged them down. It was her driver, here to take her away.

When she turned back to me, her spine was straight, shoulders back.

"You were always going to do this, weren't you? This is how it is with you, how it will *always* be."

"What, being practical?" I fought to keep my voice steady. "We couldn't be more different. You want a relationship that fits neatly into some kind of outcome-shaped box, and I'd prefer to never have a relationship *again*. You have a whole entire life and career you don't want to leave in Brooklyn. *I* have a whole entire life and career in Santa Fe. Why is it so wrong that I'm cutting things off before it got serious? Before someone gets hurt?"

She swiped angrily at her cheeks. "You're not wrong. You're right. *I'm* the one who should have known better. I have rules for a reason, and I broke every single one for you. But I know now that's not an option for me. So thank you for the clarity, Eve. I'll see you around."

She turned on her heel and strode to the car with her head held high. They drove off a moment later, leaving me to collapse back onto the lawn chair with only the dying fire for company. And total, abject misery washing over me.

I lost the diamonds.

I lost Harper.

I lost all the hope I'd had left in me for a happy ending.

Chapter Thirty-One

Eve

Digging Up Hope

ONE WEEK LATER

T he afternoon sun beat down between my shoulder blades as I bent over a beat-up-looking table I'd just salvaged, sanding its edges with a fury it did *not* deserve. I'd opted for sandpaper over the shop's electric sander, needing to feel every splintered edge smoothing beneath my hand.

It wasn't helping, but at least I had something to do. Cleo had pushed me out here because I was "acting like a lovelorn romance novel hero" again, and it was annoying the hell out of her.

There was nothing I could say in my defense. I was annoying the hell out of *myself*, so I could only imagine what it was like for those around me.

Sitting back on my heels, I used my forearm to wipe the sweat dotting my forehead. I was weary down to my bones. Eating and sleeping were an impossibility, so I was grumpy and irritable. My chest ached. My head swam with constant memories of Harper.

I couldn't see the rolling ladder near the bookshelves without yearning for her to be back there, smiling down at me from up high.

I'd said all the wrong things to her, shitty things that I didn't even *mean*. She'd accused me of avoiding honesty and vulnerability in my relationships, and she'd been right. At the end, when it mattered the most, I spun out a bunch of lies and then promptly boarded up the shop around my heart. Locks on the door, bars over the windows, a big sign that said CLOSED UNTIL FURTHER NOTICE.

She really was the heartbreaker all along. Because I was well and truly devastated.

I heard the telltale sound of Monty's boots on the concrete and saw her shadow gliding up behind me. I picked up the sandpaper again and bent back over the table, working away at a stubborn part in the wood. I knew what this was probably about and wasn't sure I was ready to talk about it yet.

My aunt dragged over a lawn chair and sat down. Then she notched up the brim of her cowboy hat. "*I'm out here trying to dig up hope and coming up empty,*" she said, quoting the text I'd sent her. "You're like a living replica of that text right now, kid."

Sighing, I sat back on my haunches again and yanked down the bandana covering my nose and mouth.

"Monty...look, I'm kinda pissed at you and not in the mood."

"Pissed? At *me*? I haven't seen you in almost a week, not since the bust. Kinda thought we'd be spending more time together."

"Are you being serious right now?"

She spread her arms out wide. "As a fuckin' heart attack. What's got you so mad?"

"Monty...you lied to me. About Ruby, about searching for the diamonds. I know you have your reasons for keeping things from me, and I would have understood that if you hadn't gone completely radio silent these past months." I shook my head, throat tightening. "I was genuinely worried about your safety, about your well-being. Not to mention that all it did was make me feel abandoned all over again."

Monty blew out a long breath. She tore off her cowboy hat and tapped it against her knees. "Jesus, Evie, I'm sorry. I wasn't thinking, and that's one hundred percent my fault."

I reached for her hand and held it. "I don't want you to change who you are or change the things that make you feel safe. You like your privacy. You like being a bit of a mystery. I get it. But I'm your niece, and I love you." I squeezed her hand. "We always said we'd look out for each other, didn't we?"

She cleared her throat. "We sure did."

"Then you have to let me look out for you. You have to let me love you," I said firmly.

Monty huffed out a laugh. "Well, don't you sound a lot like my therapist right now? Both of them, couples *and* individual."

I grinned, and it felt good. "Is it because I'm right and you know I am?"

"It could be." She tossed me a wink. "I know we didn't find those diamonds yet, but seeing that picture of Priscilla and Adeline in New York, seeing Eugene sitting there with them... all I keep thinking is they must have been so *terrified*. And here I've been scared of my own shadow, because of something that happened to me twenty-five years ago."

"To be clear, it was a very, very bad something," I said. "Everyone in town wants to protect you for a reason. They wouldn't do it if they hadn't been there, hadn't seen how bad it was for you and Ruby. No one should have to live in fear like that."

"But that's the thing, isn't it? We can't ever be truly protected from anything, not if we wanna live any kind of life with meaning. I could have said *fuck it* and lived my life anyway, homophobes be damned. Could have even done something to make it easier for *other* queer women in this world. I did neither. I just hid from all of it. And that never used to be me."

She squinted up at the sun. "Eve…it was never fair of me to erect those barriers around myself and then ask you to guard them. Especially when all I ever do is bail on you. I've been a mess. Really, I have. Isolated myself, pushed people away. I almost lost my soul mate because of it."

When she turned to face me, she wore the smile I loved the most. "I don't wanna lose my niece because of it, either."

My shoulders sagged forward. "You won't. You could never."

"It doesn't mean I should take that for granted, either." She dropped her hat back onto her head. "It's a long, long time coming, but…I'm happy now and a lot less scared. So why am I letting just the *potential* of something going wrong have this much power over me?"

"Does Ruby make you want to get back out there again?" I asked, the tentative hope obvious in my voice.

She laughed again. "Ruby makes me want to do a lot of things again. Live a full life, most of all."

I swallowed hard past the lump in my throat.

"I've been reading some of your journal entries from around the time you found *La Venganza*. I never knew you felt that way about Dad and our family. When I was a kid, you always seemed so confident, so self-assured. I never knew that you cared that much."

She gave me a sad smile. "Oh, I cared, Evie. A whole hell of a lot. For a good portion of my life, I spent a lot of time living in *response* to their judgments. Always trying to prove my worth, even prove that I was better than them. But it was just a fantasy. It's what I'm tryin' to tell you now, what I've learned after all this time. You gotta live for yourself."

A swell of emotion caught in my throat. Monty had been there, the day I left my program, left my family, and gotten on a plane with her instead.

And it still seemed impossible to talk about.

"I know that's all true, but...Monty, they abandoned me. They didn't fight for me. They don't even fight for me now. It's like...it's like I don't matter. I even had this completely naive idea that if you and I solved the mystery of the Blackburn Diamonds that it would change their minds about us."

She nodded. "You matter, kid. More than you'll ever know. I promise you that. And you shouldn't have to do *anything* to earn their love or their respect."

My parents and I never got along before. Wouldn't get along now. Yet some childish part of me still needed to feel wanted by them.

Needed to feel like I wasn't so easy to carelessly dismiss.

Monty covered my hand with hers, drawing my attention back to her face. "I'll never forget the day you came back here with me. One of the happiest days of my life, really. But it was also the day your parents showed their true colors, and I despised what I saw. After that, it was never the same with them."

"So you just... You just let it all go?" I asked.

She chuckled. "It wasn't easy. I had to yank it out by the roots, too. It's a process is what I'm saying. A journey, not a destination. But you can make the choice at any time to choose yourself. You already did, when you came out here. It's like I said to you all those years ago, the day we found that old soda bottle. No one gets to dictate the truth of who you really are."

I nodded, scrubbing my hands down my face. "I've spent all this time framing moving out here, leaving my parents, as this great, dramatic escape. A one-and-done. I'd cracked the code, didn't need any more help because I'd already hit my rock bottom and dragged myself out. But you're right, Monty. I was still hanging on, hoping for an approval that'll never come. Which makes me just as stuck as everyone else in this world."

Monty came to my side. "All of us are at least a *little* bit stuck on something. You'd have to be perfect not to be." She pulled me against her for a hug. "And speaking of stuck...are you ever gonna tell me what happened between you and that pretty reporter of yours?"

"No," I said petulantly, blowing out a heavy breath. "Because there's nothing to tell. She went back to New York. That was always the plan."

"Sure, sure. And Cleo telling me that you've been stomping around the shop like a grumpy pain in the ass ever since Harper left is just a coincidence?"

I scowled at her. "For the record, I only date casually for this *exact fucking reason.* I actually...actually let myself *feel something* for Harper, and it was amazing and incredible and really kind of life changing, and I can't stop thinking about her or dreaming about her or wondering what she's doing or if she misses me..."

Monty was trying hard not to laugh.

I threw my arm out. "This is what I'm talking about! I've never been so miserable!"

She wiped tears from her eyes. "I knew that reporter for all of twenty-four hours, and every time she looked at you it was as if she knew that you personally hung the moon *just* for her."

My breath caught in my throat.

"And you looked at her the same exact way. I thought me and Ruby were over, too, because I was also a stubborn, hard-headed *idiot* who let fear talk me out of love."

I covered my face with my hands again, feeling raw and overly exposed, as if Monty was plucking out every scary thought in my brain.

"The risk is what makes it worth it," she said, serious this time. "The fear is what makes it worth it. Do you think Priscilla and Adeline had a crystal ball? Any number of horrible things could have happened to them on that journey, and they still went for it."

I thought of Harper perched on top of that fence at the Kept King mine—the wind in her hair, that gorgeous smile, how she peered out at the landscape like some jaunty, swashbuckling explorer.

"What's your truth, Evie?" Monty repeated.

I gathered up every last scrap of fear in my heart telling me I didn't deserve love, telling me I'd spend my life getting left and abandoned. Yanked it out and let it float away, like dandelion seeds on the breeze.

"I want to be with Harper," I said, voice cracking. "But I don't know if I can get her back."

Monty's answering smile was sly. "Well...you know what they say about that. A bust is a bust 'til it ain't."

I felt the first stirrings of hope in my chest—tender and effervescent—and then Monty reached into her bag and revealed a box I knew well.

"The dig last week sucked," she said simply. "And I know you felt it, too. But I want us to get back out there, want us to try again. For them."

Then she placed Priscilla's locket onto a piece of tissue paper before laying it in the palm of my hand. Inside was Priscilla's picture on the left, Adeline's on the right.

A tiny revolution, barely the width of my palm.

I smiled down at it, warmth flooding my chest. "If I've seen this once, I've seen it a million times. And still, something about it just makes my heart spin."

Monty cleared her throat, catching my attention. "And I should tell you...Jensen and his crew were spotted in Forks this morning, setting up a camp."

"Goddammit," I swore. "How'd he figure it out? We've been careful."

She shrugged. "Maybe he followed us. Maybe he paid for a bunch of historical research. Doesn't matter now, he's on to us either way. Which means, if there *is* something in the town of Forks, we don't have a lot of time to figure it out."

"We need another clue," I said with a sigh. "And fast."

I flipped over the locket, reacquainting myself with the jewelry—the tarnish on the gold, the nicks and scratches. It had me thinking about what I'd told Harper that day in Diablo's Canyon.

Salvage is about loving the mistakes. Imperfections are treasured, studied as ways to learn more about the people who'd last owned them. I've never been interested in antiques in pristine condition. Objects in pristine condition are boring. They have no stories. They give up no secrets.

And that was when my eyes snagged on an imperfection in the center. Minuscule, at best, but in a certain light it looked almost...round.

"Monty, can you go inside and ask Cleo to grab a sewing needle and a magnifier from our supplies?"

"What is it?" she asked.

"Probably nothing," I murmured, bringing the locket close. "Just...following an instinct."

I could feel her staring at me before she quickly jogged inside. But I stayed focused on that small dot, so small and faint it had to be nothing.

Was almost *certainly* nothing.

But there was one rule of architectural salvage we always swore by, the one thing I'd never done with the locket: *always check for secret compartments*. I'd never thought to look before, always too distracted by Priscilla and Adeline's pictures and the mystery of what happened to them. Too distracted by what it all *meant* to consider the possibility that Priscilla had hidden not just one...but two secrets inside.

Monty returned with the needle and glass. With my heart jammed in my throat, I pushed the end of the needle directly into the small circle.

It was a perfect fit.

There was some slow, grinding tension.

Then a release.

And a separate panel opened behind the photos.

Monty gasped while I'd stopped breathing all together.

"There's something in there," Monty whispered. She rummaged around in her bag and came up with tweezers, which she used to dislodge a slip of extremely old paper.

In dark ink, faded but still clear, was a long string of numbers.

Coordinates.

Chapter Thirty-Two

Harper

One week after failing to find Monty, failing to find buried treasure, fucking up the article completely, oh and—so fun—getting my heart broken in the process

I was curled up in my favorite lounge chair at the coffee shop where my sister worked, laptop in front of me, feeling broken-hearted and pathetic.

I'd only been back from New Mexico for a week yet found myself oddly protective of Priscilla and Adeline's story, even though we hadn't found the diamonds, even though they might not even exist.

But Priscilla's story deserved to be told. That same wildflower feeling told me something about them was special, that investigating them further would all be worth it, because shining a spotlight on queer and trans love throughout history was always worth it.

But I was no longer sure that the *New York Review* was the best way for it to happen. Now that I was back home, my options felt so *bleak*.

Was I really going to pitch this story to a paper that had only one openly queer person on staff—me? And whose coverage of queer and trans rights thus far had been frustratingly lukewarm?

Earlier this morning, I'd sat through a tense meeting, where Greg confirmed that I was officially being passed over for the promotion to Head Story Editor. And that given what I'd done in Santa Fe, my current job was on thin ice at best. They'd had to scramble last minute to fill the print space meant for the Monty Montana interview, and the accounting department wasn't too pleased at the amount of money I'd spent to return with nothing.

And now this, the email from Greg I'd been staring at on my screen for the past hour.

You're coming back from a high-profile visit to Santa Fe where you found neither buried treasure nor convinced Monty Montana to do an interview. I understand that she ultimately declined, but that means you must have had some contact with her when no one's been able to reach her for years. She's a famous person with a public persona—go after her again. Her claims of "privacy" don't hold any weight, in my opinion, and pulling off this story would be notable for your career. The fact that you're not pursuing her aggressively has me honestly stumped.

I'd been in the industry long enough to read between the lines.

It was Monty or I'd lose the job.

It wasn't like I hadn't considered it. On the flight back to New York, where I was alternately crying about Eve and panicking over my job, I'd had a few uncharitable whispers in my brain about the whole thing. Rent was due. We had other bills to pay. And my proximity to the city was like some kind of Dad Forcefield...the closer I got, the more I started daydreaming again of what his face might look like, the moment I said: *Guess what, I did what you couldn't do. I found her before you did.*

But sitting here in this coffee shop, utterly wrung out and exhausted, it all felt so lifeless and hollow. I couldn't seem to recapture the easy freedom I'd felt out there, being surrounded by people who seized the beauty of this world with a hunger I'd always felt but never submitted to. The sheer gravity of the foothills, the astonishing sunsets, the luminous power of cliffs and canyons.

But even more than that, it was the electrifying sensation of true creative inspiration, appearing again, that I yearned for the most. In fact, I'd tried to cobble together *something* on the flight back home, but after fretting over it for hours had only managed the first paragraph: *"I want to tell you about an incredibly brave woman. Two women, actually, with life stories as rich in texture and detail as they are shrouded in mystery. All the best life stories are. But instead of reading something inspiring, about queerness and bravery and magic, this article will be shorn in half by arbitrary word count limits and then paywalled to death."*

Was this *really* the future that I wanted?

My sister Daphne walked over, bringing me a cup of turmeric tea and wrapping me in her arms for a bear hug.

I didn't know how people handled heartbreak, because I was an actual mess. My body ached, my skin felt much too tight, and my thoughts were foggy and scattered. I'd returned from the non-stop chaos of New Mexico to a well-organized and tidy life, a mountain of neat to-do lists and color-coordinated files at the office with not a single thing out of place.

But it all gave me that same hollow feeling. I no longer saw a well-organized life built out of a genuine interest and passion. I saw instead all that I'd assembled to protect me from the kind of pain I knew—had known since I was fifteen years old—could strike at any moment.

I could have color coordinated every Post-it note in my house and my mother still would have died.

Daphne pulled up the chair next to me and plopped down into it. "You've been staring at the same thing on that screen for an hour, Harp. You're clearly not over this breakup."

I closed my laptop and turned to face her. "I'm fine, really. You don't need to fuss over me. Can you really *say* it's a breakup if we weren't even *dating*—"

She shoved up her shirtsleeves, revealing her many houseplant-inspired tattoos. "There are no rules when it comes to things like this. If it hurts, it hurts. And for what it's worth... I've never seen you like this before, which means Eve must have been different."

Memories of Eve followed me everywhere now. The tenderness in her voice when she said, *Someone should have taken care of you.* Each crooked grin and husky laugh, how fearlessly she'd carved out a new life for herself. Her lips on my throat after I'd rescued her and she declared herself *lucky.* The desperate longing in her eyes before she kissed me in that hallway, lit up in disco lights.

I want you so badly I burn *with it, Harper.*

"She was different. She was...everything. And I can't stop thinking about her," I admitted, my voice cracking. "And I miss her. *So* much. I wish I'd just told her the truth, that I'd been lying from the start and wanted to be with her with every fiber of my being. Instead, we said a lot of shitty things to each other. We started off our relationship with arguments and secrets. Maybe that's why we ended it that way."

Daphne was quiet, her eyes searching mine from across the table. "You're different, too, Harper. Since you got back."

"I wasn't even away for that long."

"You *feel* different, though, don't you?" she asked with a smile. "And I'm not just talking about the fact that you had a hot, passionate fling. I think this is just a continuation of what I've been seeing in you for a while. You're bursting at the seams, Harp. You've been secretly waiting to be captivated again by something wild and thrilling, just like when we were kids. And then Eve came along, and Monty Montana, and this daring diamond quest…"

I blew out a breath. "Eve was right, though. We had to get back to real life eventually. It's not all road trips and treasure hunts. We didn't even find the diamonds."

"She's right," Daphne said. "But that doesn't mean you have to live your life in a state of miserable drudgery. We can work our day jobs and still invite passion and wonder and curiosity into our lives. These things aren't mutually exclusive."

I dropped my head into my hands. "God, when did I get so *serious*?"

Daphne gently pulled my hand away. "When your mom died and you had to raise your annoying little sister, that's when."

"You weren't annoying. You were perfect," I said. "And I'd do it again in a heartbeat."

"I know you would. I do." Her eyes were starting to shine. "Sweetheart…I mean this with all the affection in the world, but I don't need you."

"Daphne—"

"I don't," she interjected. "You have stayed here with me, and taken care of me, and loved me like a mother *and* a sister for as long as I can remember. But you're literally one half of my heart, and I can, and will, love and support you wherever you are in the world. So I don't want you to feel tied down here when I'm more than capable of handling things on my own. Is money tight? Sure, it always is and probably always will be. I'm a barista and you're a writer."

I laughed a little, though tears were starting to spill down my cheeks.

"But I'm happy and housed, and I don't want you using me as an excuse to avoid your dreams," she said. "This life is yours for the taking. What do you want to do with it?"

The café door opened just then, and a tall white man in an expensive-looking suit walked into the coffee shop with the body language of a person who's never heard the word *no* in his life. His smile was toothpaste-commercial white, and he flashed it easily at every person who recognized him.

I narrowed my eyes in surprise. "Holy shit, is that—"

"Dad?" Daphne called out.

He spun at her voice, frowning in confusion. Then he blinked. "Oh my goodness. Harper and Daphne, what are you two doing here?"

"I've worked here for three years now," Daphne said flatly.

"You have?" he asked. "I had no idea."

"I've literally told you so many times."

He frowned, tipped his head. "Sadly, I don't recall."

"Uh...what are you doing in the city?" I asked. "Your assistant told us you were traveling through Hungary or something."

He sighed dramatically. "My publisher wanted me back for

some poorly scheduled book tour. They all want to send you to six cities in four days, but it's hit the *New York Times*, so I have to make an appearance. I'm meeting my editor here in a few minutes. It's why I'm all the way out in Brooklyn."

I arched an eyebrow. "Were you going to tell your daughters you were home or...?"

"Of course." He touched his forehead. "I just got in, you know, and the jet lag..."

"I should get back to work," Daphne said, giving her chair to Dad. "Harper, I'll come check on you in a little bit."

Are you okay? she mouthed, while he settled in.

I gave her a nod and a cringey thumbs-up. I had a slightly higher threshold for tolerating our father's unique brand of bullshit than Daphne did.

"Your sister looks well," he said. "I truly had no idea she worked here."

A memory fluttered through my brain—pulling an all-nighter to hem Daphne's prom dress while Dad was away somewhere, on deadline.

"It's nice because it's right near our apartment?" I asked, leading a little. At his quizzical expression, I pointed out the window. "We live two blocks down?"

"Is that recent?"

My smile froze in place. "Nope. We've been there a while."

"How interesting." He ducked to peer at my eyes in a rare show of paternal interest. "You look run down, honey. Did you just get in from the southwest? I told you that Monty Montana will always be a—"

"I met her," I said, something deep inside of me finally snapping. "Funny story, actually. I was trying to get away from a tarantula, and she shot at it to scare it away."

"You met…Monty Montana?"

"Yep."

"*You* did."

I nodded, his dismissive tone coming through loud and clear. He looked visibly impressed with me for the first time, maybe ever.

And I felt…nothing. Absolutely fucking *nothing*. My gut twisted into a painful knot, every revelation from the past couple weeks rising rapidly to the surface.

Oh God, Eve was right.

"So then…your boss must be pretty happy," he said. "That'll be huge for the *Review*. Huge for you, too. She's always been a sort of White Whale for a lot of journalists, myself included." He laughed, somewhat nervously. "I can't believe *you* were the one to do it."

A strange and clarifying numbness was settling over me. The kind of clarity that splits your life into a *before* and an *after*. It was intensely terrifying. It was fiercely beautiful.

"Harper?" Dad said.

"Sorry." I shook my head. "There is no story. Monty declined to be interviewed, and even the brief moment I spoke with her was off the record."

He scoffed. "You'll wear her down. Some people just need to be convinced."

"She said no, Dad. You remember what happened to her, right? It was horrible. Traumatizing. Ruined her life."

He hooked an ankle over his knee. "I sympathize, but Monty Montana forfeited her right to privacy when she chose to do something that made her a minor celebrity. A small price to pay for the cost of fame."

"Are you serious? They turned her life into a punchline."

"Well, you have to admit, she's a bit of a character. Besides, this is outside of your purview, Harper. It's not personal. A story like Monty's could help you make it to the top. Be a little more vicious." He tapped the side of my knee with a folksy smile. "Be a little more *predatory*. Stop letting your biases get in the way."

That clarifying numbness became a rare calm, quieting my nervous system. I kept the smile on my face but leaned back and straightened my spine.

"I want to prevent this woman from being harassed again by the press because she's queer, Dad. And so am I. You have a bisexual daughter whether you like it or not, and that means the world reacts differently to me, and to a person like Monty, than it does to you. That's not an internal bias. That's our lived experience."

He had the decency to go slightly red in the face. "Of course, and I would never suggest differently. But why do you... Do you always have to make it about that? About your..."

"My core humanity?"

His gaze drifted to the street view, a telltale sign he was trying to end this conversation. He'd always been this way.

Much like Eve's parents, my father's approval was impersonal and intellectual—which was surely better than no approval at all. But he lost interest whenever I talked about "my identity." And in all of his years covering every subject matter under the sun, he had never—not once—written a story about queer or trans people.

Daphne and I had a theory—that Bruce Sullivan enjoyed being the expert on every subject matter at the dinner party. But he couldn't be an expert on my own queerness, couldn't speak to the things I'd experienced.

So he feigned indifference rather than admitting his knowledge—and empathy—had actual limits.

"Harper," he said, redrawing my attention. "If you want my advice, get out there and try again. If you pull off this story, it'll be a drop in the bucket in the end. Especially when you view your career with the long view in mind. One story, and it'll help you get ahead. That's all. You have to make sacrifices if you want this career. I've made plenty, and I have no regrets."

As a matter of fact, he'd only made one sacrifice. His daughters.

I had a scar on my wrist from burning myself, learning how to make macaroni and cheese for me and Daphne when Dad was away. There was a year stretch when my sister was in fifth grade where she only slept with the lights on because her nightmares were so bad. I had my first kiss and told Daphne, both of us squealing on the couch. There was a specific brand of orange juice she drank before every soccer practice for good luck, and I couldn't see that brand in the grocery store now without smiling. We once dyed each other's hair for Halloween and stained the bathroom tile so bad we bought a rug and hoped Dad would never notice (he didn't).

"No regrets, huh?" I said.

His smile was dazzling. "None whatsoever." Someone called his name, and he turned around, lifted his hand in a wave. "Oh, that's my editor. Mind if we table this until the meeting's over?"

My phone buzzed with an incoming text, distracting me.

"Uh, sure. Yeah, that's fine," I said, but he was already halfway across the room. Sighing, I picked up my phone to find a message from a person I had never expected to hear from again.

Eve.

Priscilla's locket had a secret compartment that we just discovered, she'd sent. *Inside were map coordinates, leading to a spot in Forks.*

My stomach pitched to the floor.

"Holy fucking shit," I whispered.

It's still a long shot, but this is our biggest clue yet. I know you might not want to hear from me anymore, but if you still believe in Priscilla and Adeline, we're heading out tomorrow at first light. Jensen's crew was spotted nearby, so we're moving fast. Monty and Ruby want you to be there if you can.

I couldn't hear a thing in the café due to the blood roaring in my ears.

A few seconds passed, then: *And I want you there, too.*

Chapter Thirty-Three

Eve

The Thrill of the Chase

"We don't have a lot of time to wait, kid," Monty said, as she stuffed one last thing into her pack, then hefted it onto her shoulders. "I hate to say it, but—"

"She's coming," I said firmly. "Just a few more minutes."

I caught Monty shooting Ruby a concerned look out of the corner of my eye, but I wasn't budging on this.

"Eve," Ruby said softly. "Waylon just told me he'd spotted Jensen's crew out near the train station. They're close. And with another storm…"

Periodic drops of rain were already starting to fall, and the dark clouds gathering at the horizon appeared ominous at *best*. The air was heavy with electricity, hot and humid, and I was so nervous I was all but vibrating where I stood.

I forced a smile for my concerned aunts. "I'm not leaving without her. Have a little faith."

Monty winced. "It ain't Harper I'm worried about."

She was right. We had bigger problems, namely that Jensen

and his team had ratcheted up their efforts here in Forks over the past twenty-four hours. They were moving so quickly, and digging so fast, it was only a matter of time before they stumbled upon the coordinates we were headed to today, even if it was purely accidental.

It was impossible to know how the coordinates had come to be, but Ruby thought that Harry or Eugene might have known a local surveyor at the time who could have assisted in the matter. Regardless, all three of us had sprung into action as soon as we'd realized what we'd found. We called in a favor from Waylon and his husband, who were our cheerful lookouts out here, keeping an eye on our competition's movements. And I'd summoned up every bit of courage I imagined Priscilla and Adeline must have felt—with stolen diamonds and dreams of heading West—and I asked Harper to come with us.

She had every reason not to answer me. But I realized now the mistake I'd made the day that she'd left.

I didn't fight for her.

I'd turned around and done the *same thing* my family had, all those years ago, letting me walk out the door to a new life like they couldn't have cared less. And I'd probably never know if they regretted that choice. If they wished they'd said the messy, vulnerable, honest thing instead.

I know I did. And I wished I'd done the same thing for Harper.

The piece of paper I'd spent hours working on last night was now burning a hole in my pocket. But I'd poured my own messy hopes and vulnerable dreams into it and could only hope she felt the same way.

"Evie," Monty said again, a warning in her tone. The sound of a car racing down the single road near Monty's campsite interrupted whatever she'd been about to say. It was a black

Jeep, built for off-roading, and for a few terrifying seconds we *all* thought it was Jensen. Or worse—another treasure-hunting team descending on us out here without warning.

But then it braked to a hard stop in front of the trailer, sending up a burst of dust. The driver's door opened and suddenly there was Harper Hendrix, hanging out the side with a cocky smile.

For the first time in my life, I felt my knees literally go weak.

"Hi, Eve," she said breathlessly. "Thanks for not leaving me behind."

My fingers flexed at my sides, the urge to pull her close almost overwhelming.

Monty cleared her throat. "I'm happy to see ya, Harper. But we, uh…got some company."

Harper twisted at the waist to peer behind her, and I followed her gaze. Spotted not one, but two cars, heading our way.

"It's Jensen," Ruby said. "Per Waylon. At this point, he's only going to follow us to the coordinates."

Dread pooled in my stomach. But this only seemed to boost Monty's spirits.

"Well, hot *damn*, we got ourselves a chase now," she cheered. "Harper, can you off-road in that thing?"

She arched an eyebrow. "Not sure, but I'd love to try."

Both cars were getting closer by the second.

"Then we gotta go. Now," I said, grabbing the rest of our things and jogging over to the Jeep with Ruby. All three of us tossed our things inside the back and then I was swinging myself into the passenger seat and slamming the door. I tossed Harper a wink and watched two spots of color appear high on her cheeks. I wanted to make her blush everywhere. Wanted to make her laugh, wanted to hear every single thing she'd thought about and learned during our week apart.

Because I'd thought about and learned a lot, too.

She chewed on her lower lip, her blue eyes bright and playful. In another world, at another time, I would have hooked a finger through the top of her shirt and dragged her mouth to mine. Would have replicated the night we'd spent fucking in the backseat of my car over and over, until we were one shared breath, one shared heartbeat.

But was she only here for the diamonds and Priscilla's story? Or was she here for me, too?

Harper started the Jeep and rolled down the windows. When she glanced in the rearview mirror, she said, "Shit, they're right on us."

"Go, go, go," Ruby chanted. "Monty and I mapped out three different ways to get to the coordinates just in case."

"That was smart," I said, impressed.

Ruby smirked. "Not our first time doing this."

Harper had pealed out onto the road, following Monty's directions, the engine roaring as she sped faster and faster. Behind us, I clocked Jensen's craggy face in the driver's seat of the other car. A light rain began smattering the windshield as Harper raced along the outskirts of Forks. It was nothing but flat, empty grassland on either side of us, though we were nearing a hilly, wooded area that bordered the edges of the Santa Fe National Forest.

"Turn left here," Monty said, directing us off the road. Harper sent me a questioning look.

I nodded my approval. "Let's fucking go, Hendrix."

With her lips twisted to the side in a smile, she yanked the steering wheel to the left, and the Jeep tumbled off the road, onto packed dirt. It jostled all four of us, but Harper laughed delightedly.

"Thatta girl," Monty called. "You're a natural."

I turned in my seat and spotted Jensen again. "Fuck, he's doing the same thing."

Harper hit the gas, and we jumped forward.

"To the right, to the right, to the right," Monty yelled, pointing at a second narrow trail leading into the trees. The thick forest growth forced Jensen and the second car back behind us. Branches whipped past, scraping and knocking against the windows.

"Did you think Jensen was going to be such a problem?" Harper asked, her knuckles white where she gripped the wheel. "Per his last update on X Marks the Spot, he and his team were offline, following another lead."

Monty snorted. "My guess is that he figured out me and Ruby were back and was tailing us somehow. We've been cautious since Eve found the coordinates, circling the location but never going right to it just in case he had eyes on us we didn't realize. But the man's not opposed to playing dirty. *Clearly*."

Harper glanced at me sideways. "You said he'd always held a grudge against Monty and Ruby. Because of *La Venganza*, right?"

The car dipped and jerked as we rode over rocky terrain. I winced, reaching for the grip by my head to steady myself.

"It started when he wasn't on the team we assembled," Monty said. "I've never had a problem with the guy, really. That pissed him off, though, because I brought in people who weren't local. But I wanted to find it with a community of women like me. All the outcasts doomed to live life in the margins. They made me feel like we could do anything."

Part of the trail ahead was slightly washed out. I opened my mouth to warn Harper, but she barreled through the flowing water without hesitation, smiling like she'd never been so happy.

I wanted to make her smile like that. Hoped like hell I'd get the chance to do it again.

"He wasn't the only one," Ruby added. "Everything we found was extremely high value, and we didn't keep it. We returned it to the Bahamas. Jensen was one of the treasure hunters at the time who really didn't like that. He kept running his mouth back in the day, saying it wasn't how we did things."

"They had a real finders-keepers mentality back then. But what we found wasn't ours to keep," Monty said. "It hadn't been the Spanish government's to keep, either. Theft has never been what me and Ruby are about."

Harper narrowed her eyes at the windshield. "Well, now I only wanna beat him more."

Monty chuckled. "If that's the case, hang a sharp left where you see that canyon wall."

I gulped at the sudden rise of rock ahead of us. "Monty...you sure? It looks too narrow."

"Don't ask me. Ask our driver," she chided.

But Harper couldn't be deterred. She just barely avoided scraping the side, and then the Jeep was crawling along what appeared to be an old fire road hidden behind the trees.

And as she did, she rolled down her window and raised a middle finger directly at Jensen's car.

Monty and Ruby burst into laughter. But I could only gaze at the gorgeous daredevil next to me with a deep admiration, my body filling with a riot of butterflies. Our car was surrounded by earthy-red canyon walls and wild, green forest, and yet I only had eyes for Harper.

Monty leaned forward between us, breaking my focus. "Now up here," she said, pointing, "there's a quick fork that takes us to the coordinates that were in the locket. Jensen's behind us still, so as soon as you brake, follow Ruby's instructions and get to shovelin'. I'll hold everyone else off."

Adrenaline surged through me, sending my heart rate into overdrive. Monty and I shared a quick, glorious look, just as Harper squealed to a stop. She was out of breath and grinning like a fool. Monty reached behind her and placed her cowboy hat on top of Harper's head.

"For good luck out there," she said. "Now let's get it done."

With a hearty *whoop*, she and Ruby dashed out of the car, grabbing gear and getting situated. Headlights flared behind us, meaning Jensen was right behind. We had this tiny pocket of privacy—ten seconds, maybe less—and I was surprised when Harper held out her palm.

In the center was the small piece of turquoise we'd found last time. She'd kept it, even after everything.

"I brought this for good luck, too," she said, her voice shaky with emotion. Our eyes stayed locked together as she raised the pretty stone and kissed it. I grasped her wrist, bringing the stone to my mouth and letting my lips graze her fingertips.

"For Priscilla and Adeline," I whispered.

She blinked back tears. "And tiny revolutions."

The litany of things I wanted to say to Harper in this moment was as long as my arm. Apologies, promises, gratitude. But I forced myself to pull away instead.

And then we were off, jumping out of the car and running through the rain toward Ruby. She was sweeping the metal detector back and forth at a spot near a cluster of rocks. With every pass, the clicks grew in volume, louder and stronger than I'd ever heard them.

Ruby peered up at us with a slow smile. "Sounds like treasure to me, doesn't it?"

The sound of a car pulling up and then raised voices had us spinning on our heels. Monty was facing off with Jensen, who looked pissed as he slammed his car door shut. Both were gesturing wildly, and I couldn't quite hear what they were saying, but she was holding them off like she promised.

"We gotta dig," I said, tossing Harper a shovel. "As fast as we can."

I wasn't sure how much time passed after that—twenty minutes, maybe thirty—because it was a whirlwind of feelings and sensations. The rain on the back of my neck. Harper's heavy breathing. The look of pure optimism on Ruby's face. The thick weight of dirt in my shovel and the endless, rhythmic sound of it hitting the ground next to us.

So when I finally raised my shovel and hit something solid, the shock of it affected all three of us. I froze in place, all of us staring at each other.

"Do it again," Ruby urged.

I did—and we all heard the same *thunk*.

I whirled around and yelled Monty's name. My hands were trembling so badly that Harper linked her fingers through mine and squeezed.

"Jensen finally drove off," Monty called out, racing toward us. "He wasn't happy about it, but he knew he'd gotten here two minutes too late. Did you get something?"

Before I could answer her, Monty was leaping into the ditch, her thick braid flying.

She crouched down immediately, working to gently clear the surrounding mud away.

Beneath her fingers was a rusted metal box.

I fell to my knees next to her and touched the metal, fingers still shaking.

"Careful, careful," Ruby was saying from above. "We don't want to break anything."

Monty looked at me. "We pull on three, okay?"

I nodded, lifting the heavy metal as dirt and rocks tumbled off the sides, covering us in a fine layer of dust. Monty swiped her hand across the top to clear it. In the center was a large, engraved *H* and a large, engraved *B* near a rusted-over lock.

Monty and Ruby were a blur of happy chaos, laughing and dancing around us, but Harper and I were totally still, our hands still entwined. In my utter astonishment, my eyes locked on Harper's.

And they were spilling over with tears.

Chapter Thirty-Four

Harper

Three hours after returning to New Mexico and we finally, finally, FINALLY...found buried treasure

Dazed and bewildered, I sat cross-legged on the floor of Monty's trailer while she and Ruby worked on opening the metal box.

The one with Harry Boyle's initials engraved into the top... buried at the exact coordinates Eve had found in Priscilla's locket.

Two weeks ago, I'd been bickering with Eve at The Wreckage about the location of her aunt. Now Monty stood just a few short feet away from me, and I wondered if I had the right to feel such sudden affection for her. She was brash and brave, arrogant and expansive. And though I knew she and Ruby were coming out of a rocky patch in their marriage, it was astonishing to watch Monty, a human tornado, be so deeply devoted to her wife.

What was it like, loving so boldly? Being loved so boldly?

Eve sat on the floor near me, one leg stretched out long and her back propped against a cabinet. I was practically levitating at her nearness, had been since I'd arrived. Just a couple hours back in her presence and it was impossible for me to fathom how I ever thought I could control my attraction to her or minimize my desire to be with her.

She was no tidy task on a list to mark "done." She was a whirlwind, scattering my plans and decimating my attempts to hold her at arm's length.

Eve Bardot had seduced me into recklessness, charmed me into taking risks.

And now that I was back in New Mexico, the biggest risk of all was admitting that I was falling for her already.

Her dark eyes slid to mine as if she knew I was thinking about her. She swallowed hard, then reached over and pulled a leaf from my hair. The brief graze of her fingers against my scalp was electrifying.

"You've got a little bit of treasure in your hair, cowgirl," she murmured.

I wanted to kiss her. Wanted to burst into tears. Wanted to beg forgiveness for every shitty thing I'd said. We'd just unearthed a piece of history together—but that didn't mean she was ready to forgive me yet.

A squeaky, metallic sound split the air, breaking my focus on Eve. A stale, musty scent filled the room.

"Holy hell," Monty murmured, "I can't believe we got it open."

Eve and I flew to our feet and gathered round. Ruby turned on the overhead lamp, shining light onto a large pile of letters bound in four neat piles inside the box. She lifted them up and out, revealing loose pictures lying at the bottom, along with some chewed-down pencils, a few scraps of paper.

In the corner of the box lay a small velvet bag. Ruby gently tugged the bag open, tipping out a few button-sized diamonds into her palm. A full-body shiver worked through me, and I completely forgot to breathe.

"So…there *were* diamonds," Eve said, sounding awestruck.

Astonished, I carefully untied the faded red ribbon that held together the first pile of letters. They fell sideways like a stack of dominoes, sending up another burst of musty air. They hadn't been exposed to the sun, so the ink was fairly legible, though the handwriting itself was spidery and faded.

I selected the first and opened it, my heart fluttering like a hummingbird in my chest.

"The envelope is addressed to Mr. Harry Boyle at the general store in Haven's Bluff," I said, eyes scanning. "Date is… wow, March 1905." I slid the letter out and read: *"Dear Mr. Boyle, my name is Clarence Clayton and I am writing for your help. Your name was given to me by a Eugene O'Neal, who told me he was visiting Manhattan on business."*

"Eugene O'Neal," Eve said, "the man who lived with Harry and who Waylon believes was his partner."

The hair rose on the back of my neck. *"He said that you could provide assistance for men like me and my husband, Theodore,"* I continued. *"He is, of course, my husband in my heart and in how we conduct ourselves privately. Not by the church or by the law. The police watch men like us too closely now. Two friends have already been jailed. If you are able to get us to a safe place, we would appreciate it. My family is suspicious."*

I set the letter down, brow pinched. "I'm confused. Harry and Eugene were helping people?"

Eve picked up the next letter from Clarence, dated about eight months later. "This one says... *Dear Mr. Boyle, thank you again for the... for the diamonds.*" She paused, eyes flicking to the tiny jewels still in Ruby's palm. "*The money we received after selling them lasted until we reached California and helped us get set up here. We're renting two rooms at a boardinghouse in San Francisco and are very happy to be together and feel safe. Enclosed is a picture of me and my husband. We are eternally grateful.*"

I dipped my fingers into the box and pulled up a faded picture, soft at the corners, of two men. Signed and dated: *Clarence and Theo, November 1905.*

Something was happening inside my brain, a final few missing pieces sliding into place.

I divided the remaining letters between me and Eve. Some had faded too poorly to read, others too torn and crumbled. But the ones we could had similar wording.

"**Thank you for the funds, it helped us leave...**"

"*We're mighty grateful for your generosity, Mr. Boyle...*"

"*The diamonds served us well and kept us fed and housed on our journey....*"

Beneath the letters, stacks and stacks of pictures dated up through 1930.

I selected another letter at random, almost numb with the gravity of what was being slowly revealed to us. Unfolding the piece of paper, I read quickly and gasped.

"I think...this letter is about Priscilla. It's dated August 1903."

I passed it to Eve, who read, "*Dear Mr. Boyle, I'm writing to you regarding information given to me by Miss...*" Eve hesitated.

"*Miss Priscilla Grant, who lives with her companion, Miss Adeline Blackburn, on Castro Street in San Francisco. She suggested that you might have resources to help me leave my parents' home. That you helped women like me, women who feel passionately for other women, as I do for my companion, Miss Josephine Highland. If you would see to it that we might escape our current situation, I do believe our lives would improve immeasurably.*"

Monty set her cowboy hat on the table and cleared her throat. "Am I hearing that Priscilla and Adeline...lived?"

"More than lived," Ruby said. "It sounds like they made it to San Francisco. And—"

"Took *each other's* last names," Eve finished.

"That's why there's no record of them afterward, why no one could find them," I said. "Anyone searching for them was looking for the wrong names."

"And there's a second letter below this one." Eve continued reading: "*...writing to inform you, Mr. Boyle, that Josephine and I arrived at my sister's ranch in the Montana Territories this past week. As I suspected, she welcomed us with open arms, as her husband's sister is the same way that we are. She lives openly with another woman on her own ranch, a few miles from here. We would not have made it here without your resources, Mr. Boyle, or without Miss Grant and Miss Blackburn's kind advice and wisdom.*"

I pressed my hand to my mouth, pulling together the brilliant threads of this story. The remaining diamonds. The years of letters. The gratitude after long journeys to safer horizons.

Not perfect, but hopeful.

"They were helping other queer people," I said. "Priscilla wasn't killed. And Harry wasn't a petty thief. This was...this was orchestrated."

Eve held a stack of letters in her hand. "Priscilla fled with the diamonds, then they used them to help others do the same thing. It's probably why there are only a couple diamonds left. This box must have been Harry's version of a bank. Hiding a huge fortune from local vigilantes while protecting the identities of the people who wrote to him."

I indicated the sweep of documents before us. "They go on like this for years. Do we know when Harry Boyle died?"

Ruby tilted her head. "1932? '33? Something like that. He likely died before he could move them. I doubt he'd leave any diamonds left untouched on purpose."

I kept digging through the letters until I found a final stack. All these years later and the love and care that went into keeping them safe was obvious. These were neatly folded, stacked in chronological order.

They were all addressed to Harry and Eugene.

And they were all from Priscilla and Adeline.

I scanned the first one eagerly—then, with a triumphant smile, I extended it to Monty. "This is a letter from Priscilla to Harry, referencing the 'idea they spoke about in New York' and saying she's certain she'll be with him soon. That she's bringing her best friend and their favorite jewelry."

Monty barked out a laugh. "Our girl was smart."

The third letter down was dated after the diamonds were stolen, postmarked from San Francisco. Opening it, I read, *"Harry and Eugene—Addie and I have settled in quite comfortably in our little bungalow on Castro Street. You should come visit us soon, the city is breathtaking, and there is art and music and extravagance as far as the eye can see. We are quite happy here and have both spoken to the local school about their openings for primary school teachers.*

"All is quiet on the notoriety front—if anyone has recognized us, they've not said a word, and we haven't seen any of those posters lying about. William is a proud man but fickle—he'll be married again by the end of year, and I doubt he'll search much longer. Your idea to list my name in the visitor log and flaunt around a bit in Haven's Bluff was a smart one. Do let us know how you get on with what we left you—if you're wise, that amount should last you for years, and I believe we can help a great many people. Any extra, we'll send along your way as well.

"Write soon, give our love to Gene, and remember that when you miss us, you always have my best locket—when you need it. All my love, P."

All the air left my body. I sagged, setting the letter down, absolutely fucking *amazed* at the secrets it revealed. "It was all on purpose."

Eve raked a hand through her hair. "They *did* know each other. Planned this ahead of time. And all the eyewitness stuff, the name in the log, that was all planted evidence. Red herrings to throw William off their trail."

"The coordinates of where they'd buried the diamonds in Forks were stored in the locket," Eve said. "So they'd always be able to find them. And I'm guessing Priscilla and Adeline must have gotten to California by stagecoach instead of the train."

"A century later and that same planted evidence was still throwing treasure hunters off the scent. We would never have thought to look in Forks if we hadn't seen about the detour." I shook my head, studying the spread of letters and pictures. "This is incredible. This is… This is beyond my wildest imagination. Did you ever think it would be something like this?"

Monty scoffed. "On a good day, I hoped that Priscilla and Adeline made it somewhere safe. On a bad day? I was sure they'd been killed. But I never pictured something with this kind of scope."

"And the connections they made," Eve said. "They protected each other. Kept each other's secrets. Like a whisper network, ferrying people from bad situations to safe ones. Or as safe as any queer or trans person could be in the early 1900s."

Eve was staring up at her aunt, pure joy on her face. The sight of it sent my heart spinning like an acrobat. "Monty... Priscilla and Adeline, they...they *made it*. Lived together in San Francisco and helped people get resources. And they were *happy*."

Monty's smile could have lit up the entire night sky. "Of course she made it. She's our ancestor, and she's just like you and me, kid."

"Stubborn as hell?" Eve offered.

Monty pulled her in for a side hug and kissed the top of her head. "A trailblazer. Someone who charted her own course, even when it was scary. Who did the right thing, in the end."

The heroes, all along. I watched the happy scene in front of me with a tender ache in my chest. Thinking about telling the truth of who I really was. Thinking about the life I wanted to grab hold of with both hands.

Thinking about Eve, the person I most wanted to tell that big and scary truth to.

I just hoped she'd forgive me first.

A sharp rapping at the trailer door drew Monty's attention. Frowning, she propped it open with the tip of her boot—to reveal Jensen. Alone this time, holding his rain-soaked hat in his hands.

"Is it them?" he asked eagerly—uncharacteristically so. "Did you find Priscilla's diamonds?"

Monty heaved a sigh. "We'll share more as soon as we can. But we need a minute to collect our thoughts first, Jensen. What we just found...it's un-fucking-believable."

He reached in and held the door open before she could shut it in his face. "Just tell me one thing. Adeline Grant...did she make it? Did she and Priscilla survive?"

My stomach lurched in shock, and Eve's eyebrows went skyward.

Ruby cocked her head in confusion. "How do you know who Adeline is?"

Jensen gulped and squeezed his hat. "Because we're related."

Chapter Thirty-Five

Harper

***One hour after finding the Blackburn Diamonds
and hoping like hell that Eve forgives me***

Jensen sat at the trailer's small kitchen table and dragged a heavy hand down his face. It had taken awhile, but we'd finally gotten him up to speed on all of it—the locket, the pictures, Monty and Eve's connection to Priscilla.

All of the letters buried in the ground, the incredible defiance, the absolute bravery.

Now he held a copy of the picture of Priscilla and Adeline in New York, swiping his thumb over the center of the image. "It had always been nothin' but a rumor in my family," he grunted. "A bit of lore, a story my mother claimed had been passed down through the generations. Our family hasn't always been here in Santa Fe. New York City is where we come from."

He set the picture down on the table. We were silently watching him, hanging on his every word.

"My mother's maiden name was Grant," he continued. "Adeline was her great-great-great-cousin. The family knew

Priscilla and Adeline were close, knew that she'd disappeared on the same exact day. Can't remember how they knew, now, it's mixed in with all the gossip. Old letters, I think. But honest to god, until now..." He gulped. "Monty, Ruby...I swear I thought I was chasin' a ghost story."

Monty cleared her throat. "So that's why you've been after this like a dog with a bone."

"Sounds familiar, doesn't it?" Ruby said, offering up a tentative smile.

Eve and I stood across from the three of them at the table, our backs propped against the wall. We were separated by just a few inches, her body heat a scorching distraction. Neither of us had said much so far. I couldn't speak for Eve, but I was content to watch whatever was unfolding between Monty, Ruby, and Jensen, a history of grudges and hurt feelings that hung thick in the small space.

Monty scratched the back of her head and shrugged. "Guess that's true. Eve and I always considered this our legacy. It's why failing to find it the first time was so painful."

Jensen's lips twitched. "Hell, it's probably why I've been a bit of an asshole recently. Felt like it was owed to me."

As if on cue, all of us focused on the tiny pile of diamonds, glittering in the middle of the table, easily forgotten amidst all the letters.

"Yeah," Monty said, cracking a slow smile. "You are kind of an asshole."

He huffed out a laugh, still staring at the pile of photographs. "They had so much fucking courage. Putting their lives at risk. Helping all these people. Makes me feel a little unworthy if I'm being honest."

His eyes rose to Monty and Ruby. "I owe you both an apology. I have been an asshole, about more than just this. I let the worst parts of myself lash out at you when you never deserved it."

"You didn't send those reporters to harass us," Ruby said. "You protected us as best you could."

"I was still pissed at you, though, and should have let it go. What you both did, finding that ship, was a goddamn miracle. And I was just jealous, let it get in the way of being a friend when you needed it. I hate admitting it, because it makes me feel so small. But now I'm sittin' here, surrounded by all these people's stories…"

He rubbed his head, his face growing red. "Jesus, there's more to life than being cruel to each other, chasing each other down for buried treasure that might not even be there."

Monty was quiet for a moment, studying the man across from her like she was meeting him for the first time. She sent Ruby a quick look then said, "I accept it. Your apology."

Jensen gave a short nod.

"And…and I get it, I guess. I was just telling Evie something similar, about what happened to us all those years ago. How I let it change me, but not for the better. Let it control me. Almost let it end my marriage."

Ruby rested her head on Monty's shoulder. "We found our way back to each other, though. I knew we would."

Monty kissed the top of her hair. "I haven't always had a lot of hope, but I had hope in us."

In the beat of silence that followed, I snuck a glance at Eve. I expected her to be watching her aunts. But she was watching me, wearing an expression I wished with every fiber of my being I could understand.

Monty pulled out her cigar box and passed one to Jensen. "Our relatives struck out on their own. Chose hope over despair as best they could. You and me, we could do the same, you know."

Jensen coughed into his hand. "I, uh…I'd like that."

Eve shifted against the wall. "The world deserves to see these letters and photographs. If you want, I can call the Santa Fe museum when we're back in town and set up a meeting. They might want to feature them in an exhibit."

Monty and Ruby brightened at that while my heart pulsed with a soft glow.

"Hey now, that's a smart idea," Monty said cheerfully.

"It'll probably put you both back in the spotlight," I cautioned. "Are you ready for that?"

"I'm ready," Ruby said. "No more hiding. We'll get through it together."

I eyed Monty, who was rolling a cigar between her palms. After a few seconds, she nodded. "It's time for me to start telling my story, instead of other people doing it for me."

Inspiration burst through my brain like a round of multicolored fireworks. An idea was starting to form, so quickly that my stomach went hollow.

"You okay?" Eve whispered.

I nodded, jittery and more than a little nervous.

"Whatever help you need, just ask," Jensen said. "My crew will feel the same way, and if anyone says differently, I'll show 'em the door." He tapped his finger on the picture of Priscilla and Adeline. "I never told you this, Monty, but my parents…" He coughed into his hand again. "My parents kicked my brother out of the house when he told us he was gay. We were in high school. I, well…I went with him. We took care of each other."

Monty's eyes softened. "I'm sure he appreciated that."

Jensen gave another short nod. "This is gonna mean a lot to him. To him, his husband, my nieces. We're lucky, to be related to these women."

I watched Monty's gaze slide to Eve, watched pure affection wash over her. "I couldn't have said it better myself," Monty said.

Eve's response to this was a smile so bewitching, so charming, so very *Eve-like* that pure delight swelled my heart. While everyone else went back to reading over the letters, I sidled up next to her and prayed I didn't look as nervous as I felt.

Hands clasped to keep my fingers from shaking, I said: "Can we go somewhere private to talk?"

•••

"So yeah," Faith said, whistling as she let Eve and me into the vintage trailer, "much as I hate to say it, we *are* sold out of most everything today in the park."

The narrow door opened. She ushered us inside with the tired grumpiness I now understood was just her regular personality. With the flip of a switch, the trailer filled with a pinkish glow, courtesy of the heart-shaped twinkle lights dangling from the ceiling.

The pull-down table in the kitchenette was also shaped like a heart. As was the small bed we could glimpse all the way in the back, covered in a blood-red velvet blanket and pink, lips-shaped pillows.

Champagne iced in a bucket. A neon sign above the sink read JUST MARRIED with flickering wedding bells.

"But we do have this honeymoon trailer, if you'd like," Faith grumbled. "Long as that's not too awkward for you two or anything."

Eve and I made furtive eye contact. Her cheeks blazed red, and the center of my stomach was one giant, complicated knot.

"Not, uh, awkward at all," I said to Faith, in the lie of the century. "The scattered rose petals really tie together your romantic vision."

Faith shrugged. "I like a little romance myself, now and then. That's why I've got two husbands, instead of one."

She placed the key on the counter and left with a door slam, leaving Eve and me alone in the soft coral light, surrounded by hearts of every shape and size. My muscles screamed in pain and I was so emotionally overwhelmed I wanted to collapse to the ground and cry. Mud was caked across Eve's boots and arms, and she looked hollow-eyed with weariness. When she'd agreed to come somewhere private with me to talk, Faith's Paradise RV Park had seemed like the best idea at the time, given I knew it had hot showers and breakfast sandwiches.

I obviously hadn't prepared for...all of *this*. Wincing, I touched the magenta banner above me that read *Happily Ever After*, and it released a shower of golden confetti onto my head.

"So..." Eve mumbled. "Here we are...I guess."

I chewed anxiously on my bottom lip. "Here we are, indeed."

For a long moment after that, we just stared at each other in the small space. A thousand apologies and regrets crowded the back of my throat. Because I was alone again, *finally*, with Eve Bardot—who loved the Milky Way and imperfect antiques, her queer friends and the open road. Who'd been forced to suffer in silence like I had and who seemed to understand, on a gut level, the shame that lived in my body because of it.

"I quit my job yesterday," I blurted out, my thoughts a chaotic mess. "I handed in my resignation letter, then hopped on the flight here."

Her eyebrows pinched together. "You...quit your *job*?"

I nodded, feeling an unbelievable lightness flood my body. "I'll always be a writer, but I'm done being a reporter. Storytelling's in my blood, but I don't have to follow in my dad's footsteps for it to *mean* something. It all just felt so joyless once

I got back. Everything I learned out here, everything we talked about, helped me see how much I'd been lying to myself about my own happiness."

"I'm proud of you, Hendrix," she said hoarsely, looking stunned. "I know how hard this stuff is, how hard it can be to choose yourself."

I sent her a shy smile. "I had some inspiration."

She ducked her head, looking slightly bashful. "And how do you feel about all of it?"

"Free as a fucking bird."

She laughed softly. "You know your mom would be proud of you, too."

I pictured my mom on the last night she was alive, the love on her face as she turned off my bedroom light.

"She would be," I murmured. "And to be clear, you were right, Eve. My editor wanted me to force Monty to do a story, and they had no interest whatsoever in treating her like she was anything more than a strategy to attract subscribers. So I didn't tell them a thing. I'll have to find another way to share Priscilla and Adeline's story, but at least now it can truly honor them."

Eve shut her eyes, looking relieved. "Thank you. That means more than I can say, knowing that you protected Monty and Ruby. But I knew you'd do right by them, Harper. I really did. I should have trusted you from the start. Should have been honest with you from the start, about everything. I'd just gotten so caught up in this idea that you were just like my parents, walking out on me because I was unlovable and easily tossed aside."

"Never, Eve," I said firmly. "You could never, ever be easily tossed aside."

Her lips quirked up into a half smile. "I had this secret fantasy that if Monty and I found the Blackburn Diamonds,

it could prove to my parents that I was deserving of their..."
She hesitated. "Approval? Admiration? I spent so much time
dreaming about something that would never be, let it drain away
so much of me. And then, the minute we opened that box and
saw those letters, all those stories, all that *love*...I realized the
only thing that mattered in that moment was my community."

Her smile widened. "The only thing that mattered in that
moment was doing it with you."

My heart froze in my chest.

"I want us to take our lives back, Harper," she said. "I know
it's a long process. I know it'll take time. But I don't want to give
my power away anymore to people who don't deserve it."

There was a lump in my throat, more tears threatening to
spill, but I pushed through, wanting to get this right. "I want us
to take our lives back, too. I want that...want that *so* badly. After
my mom died, it was easier for me to give in to control and rules
and perfectionism. It makes sense, my life turned to chaos at
fifteen and I needed something sturdy to cling to. But then I met
you, Eve. Your courage, your bravery. You showed me what I
used to want, the life I once dreamed about. The world just a big,
juicy peach to bite into, savoring every last drop. You reminded
me of who I'd always been, and I'll never be able to thank you
enough for that."

Her dark eyes searched mine, her hands forming into fists at
her sides as if she was just as eager to touch me as I was to touch
her. "God, you bring me to my knees every fucking time, Harper.
Being with you is an absolute privilege."

A hot blush crept up my throat at the roughness in her voice.
At the intensity of her staring at me like this.

"Do you want to know what you taught me?" she asked.
"That I should have fought for you from the beginning. And

definitely on that last day. If I could do it again, I would have spilled all my feelings for you. Would have said *fuck it*, let's be together, even if it's hard. *Especially* if it's hard, because you are so incredibly worth it."

She tugged on her short curls, sending them into disarray. "I meant what I said earlier. If you'd asked me weeks ago what this moment here would be about—the moment when Monty and I finally found the diamonds—I would have said calling my parents, bragging about what we'd done. Needing them to accept how wrong they'd been about us. Needing an approval that I'm working on letting go of."

"Are you still going to do that? Call them?" I asked, my heart hurting for Eve and Monty, how abandoned they felt.

She shook her head. "No. I couldn't care less now. I want to be here with you instead. And fully plan on being with you for as long as you'll have me, cowgirl. I'm in this for real."

Now it was my turn to duck my head and flush.

"I fled from that situation, but I was still letting my parents have power over me," she continued. "I was still so consumed with pride, with needing to *prove* they were wrong more than I needed to live the life that I wanted. A life where I'm open to all of it—to pain, to heartbreak, to taking risks." She paused, her gaze searing into mine. "To being with you."

I had to swallow three times to keep my voice from shaking. "But is that…is that really what you want? To be with me?"

The smile that flew across her face was the prettiest damn thing I'd ever seen.

"I want you more than I've ever wanted anything." But then she blinked, her eyebrows pinching together. "I still can't believe you quit your job and *flew* here. Left your sister, your apartment, a career you'd worked hard for. You didn't have to do any of that.

I'd want to be with you regardless of where you lived. We'd figure it out. I have faith in us."

The sweetest warmth was spreading through my chest. "Leaving Daphne isn't easy, but she wanted this for me just as much as I did. Told me as much, even, told me that I couldn't take care of her forever and that our bond's unbreakable regardless. And she's right."

I rolled my lips together, trying to collect myself. "I'm ready to chase my own dreams. And I'm ready to do it with someone who makes me feel like I'm flying."

Eve laughed softly, eyes briefly on the ground before rising to meet mine again. They were shining with tears, and when she blinked, she had to swipe at her cheeks. "I talked to Cleo about taking a leave of absence, bringing in some extra support so she doesn't have to do it alone. I've got a little bit of money saved up, and I want to do something for you. To show you that I'm dedicated."

I reared back, my head spinning. "But you love your job."

"I really do, and I'm not planning on quitting." She was reaching into her back pocket and unfolding a long piece of white paper. "It's also okay to stop and watch a few sunrises now and then, you know?"

Then she handed me the paper, which at first glance was an illustrated map of the west. Little X's and illustrations dotted the images, and next to each stop were paragraphs that read like... clues.

"Eve Bardot...did you make me a *treasure map*?" I asked. Squealed, really.

She cracked a giant smile. "You told me you always wanted to go on a treasure hunt. So I made you one." She traced a meandering path on the page with her thumb. "If we do this right, it should take us about a month. An adventure, just for you and me."

There was a chance I was going to faint from sheer happiness alone.

"Why did you do this?" I whispered, tears tracking down my cheeks.

She leaned in close and hovered her mouth over mine, taking my breath away. "I did it because I was serious about you from the start. And I'm extremely serious about us now."

I couldn't help the smile that burst across my face. "I'm pretty fucking serious about you, too."

She matched my smile, tracing my bottom lip with her finger. "So whaddya say? Wanna go on another treasure hunt with me?"

My response was to loop an arm around her waist and kiss her. A real kiss, a *hot* kiss, a kiss overflowing with yearning. I cupped her face in my hands as her fingers dove into my hair, holding me like she planned on never letting go.

It was every dream I'd had over the past week coming true. Kissing the woman who'd changed my life. Kissing the woman I thought I'd never see again. Our movements turned hard and greedy almost instantly. With a little shove, Eve had me against the wall, her lips moving down my throat.

"Yes, I want to go on another treasure hunt with you. I want that *so* badly," I breathed out. "And I missed you so much, even after only a week. Is that okay to say?"

She captured my mouth again with a soft groan. "I was *miserable* without you. It's never been like this for me before. Is *that* okay to say?"

I laughed into her neck. Traced the shell of her ear with my tongue until she shivered. "I'm so glad. I thought it was only me."

Eve pulled back and caught my chin, keeping me still. "Not just you, sweetheart. I'm an absolute goner, if it's not obvious."

I hooked a finger into the top of her pants and began walking us backward, toward the heart-shaped honeymoon bed. "It's maybe just...a *little* bit obvious."

"You love it, Hendrix," she teased, her lips on mine an urgent plea. I gave in immediately, falling back with her onto satin sheets and rose petals. We didn't stop kissing each other for a long, long time. And when we parted on a shaky breath, Eve gazed down at me with such grateful adoration that I knew, instantly—there was no going back for us.

Which was just how I wanted it.

Chapter Thirty-Six

Eve

A Whole Lot of Magic

Two weeks later

I leaned back against Harper, who had both arms wrapped around my waist. Her chin pressed into the top of my shoulder, and her breath tickled my ear. In front of us was the Santa Fe Museum, and draped across the front was a brand-new banner that read: *"Queer Joy is Resistance: Priscilla Blackburn, Adeline Grant, and the Missing Diamonds."*

The exhibition—which would showcase the letters, photographs, and lives of Priscilla, Adeline, Harry, and Eugene—would be debuting at the museum this coming winter. And there were already plans in place to make it a traveling exhibit.

Priscilla and Adeline's story was going to be told after all.

"I've seen the sign a dozen times at this point, and I still get a kick out of seeing it," I said, turning to kiss Harper's cheek.

"Now everyone will know they were the heroes all along," she said, giving me a squeeze. Her phone beeped with a text message, and I already knew who it was. This was confirmed when I heard her soft chuckle. "That was your aunt, leaving me another fifteen voice memos about the book. At this rate, we're gonna need to add on a sequel."

It'd been a busy couple weeks since we'd discovered the diamonds and letters. Besides working with the museum, Harper and I had visited Waylon Boyle at Devil's Kiln one night to thank him for lending a hand. When we told him the entire grand story of his uncle's heroic gestures, he'd gone pink in the cheeks from excitement and couldn't wait to get home and share the news with his husband.

Monty had asked Eve and me to make the announcement in X Marks the Spot, and she and Ruby had been flooded with callers and well-wishes at their house ever since. Monty was pretending that she didn't want any fanfare or fuss, except every time a former friend swung by for a visit, she was extra cheerful the whole next day.

As promised, Jensen had been fully involved every step of the way, stopping by Monty and Ruby's house often for a glass of whiskey, a cigar, and to reminisce about old times.

And Harper had approached Monty about helping her write a book.

Specifically, a memoir—a chance to tell her own story, on everything from finding *La Venganza* with Ruby to the legacy of Priscilla Blackburn. I'd been shocked—and then absurdly delighted—when Monty had wholeheartedly agreed.

"Did you ever think you'd be helping *the* Monty Montana write her memoir?" I asked.

She chewed on her bottom lip, trying to contain her smile. "Not in a million years. But she deserves to take her power back and for the world to finally get to know the *real* Monty. I think a lot of people are going to see themselves in those pages."

She pressed her mouth to the hair at my temple. "Nothing in my life has ever felt as right as helping Monty write this memoir. Except for when I met you, of course."

I turned in my arms and pushed her gently against the side of the Airstream trailer. Kissed her thoroughly, long and lingering in the late fall sunlight. The leaves were changing in New Mexico, all that autumnal sun turning the foothills a honey-gold.

Not that we'd be around to see it. We were taking off on our treasure hunt, and Faith had lent us the honeymoon-themed trailer for the trip. We'd be road-tripping through the West, with friends and family coming out to adventure with us along the way. Daphne and Cleo. Monty and Ruby.

One month of watching sunrises with the woman who made me want to fight for love.

And after that, Harper would be subletting a place in Santa Fe to keep working on the book with Monty—and so we could start figuring out the next steps of our life together.

Harper started laughing against my mouth as I deepened our kiss. "Stop distracting me, you *utter scoundrel*. I'm supposed to be showing you your surprise."

"And it's inside the museum?" I asked, nuzzling her ear.

"Sure is," she sang. She kissed my knuckles and tugged me forward, heading toward the front door. "One last stop before we hit the road."

Inside, the staff waved us through to the installation room, where they were putting together the research and layout for Priscilla's exhibit. All four of us had been by a few times already, and it never ceased to leave me momentarily breathless.

Spread out, all around us, were the letters and pictures that had been hidden in that box, buried underground. Arranged like this, the full gravity of what Priscilla, Adeline, Eugene, and Harry had accomplished was staggering. The happy letters, the happy couples, the intimate glimpse into their daily lives. The director had already laid out some design ideas, scribbled questions on Post-it notes. I could see it coming together in my mind, the way people would get drawn into these stories. Snapshots of a full life, a singular, beautiful moment in time.

"When you saw Monty and Ruby last night, did they give you an update on the diamonds?" Harper asked.

"They did, yeah. One will stay here, for display only, but the rest will be distributed to the community," I said. "Ruby had the diamonds appraised, the guy said they were probably worth at least twenty-five thousand dollars."

Harper was leaning over a glass case, staring at a picture of two men, kissing in a photobooth. "*Whoa*, that much?"

I nodded. "We talked about it, what Priscilla and Harry had wanted, which certainly would have been for Monty and Ruby to spread the wealth around as much as possible. Ruby's best friend runs a mutual aid fund that supports queer elders of the Navajo Nation. About half will go there. Then I suggested a place in Santa Fe that helps homeless queer and trans kids who have been kicked out of their houses. They have funds set up to directly pay rent and other bills."

"Priscilla and Harry would have loved that," Harper said. "What a legacy you inherited, Eve."

I gave her a sweet smile and pulled her against me. "More than I ever could have hoped for."

We were stopped in front of a collection of letters from Priscilla to Harry, and my eye caught one at random: *And maybe it's not just about the diamonds*, she'd written. *It's also what it says: we see you, you are one of us, we are in this together. It's about the hope.*

"Come on," Harper said softly, "your surprise is this way."

We walked past row after row of letters and photographs until we reached the very back of the exhibit. The few pieces hanging there were backlit, glowing against the wall, and finishing the space was the antique bar that Cleo and I had rescued a month earlier. We'd talked it over and felt that the big gay bar was most at home here, surrounded by the evidence that queer love could thrive, even in the harshest environments.

"I worked with some of the staff here to do some extra research, so you're the first person seeing this," Harper said, pointing at a framed picture of a house.

It looked like a tiny bluebell, surrounded on both sides by Victorian homes. The squat bungalow had a porch with white railings, red flower boxes, and ivy climbing up the right wall.

"Here's your surprise, Eve Bardot: the last known residence of Priscilla and Adeline. They both taught at the school that was down the street."

My mouth dropped open, tears immediately filling my eyes. "You…wait…you found where they *lived*?"

"And quite happily, it seems," Harper said. "Adeline died at the age of sixty, which was fairly old for the time. Priscilla followed just a month later."

I pressed a hand to my mouth. "They were truly together until the very end. I can't believe it."

Beneath the picture was a framed letter. It was my favorite, the last one that Priscilla had written.

The longer Addie and I are here, the longer I've realized that until we stepped foot in this house, I had never taken a full breath. Never fully filled my lungs with air, so concerned was I that I'd give my secret away. Be caught out as a fraud, an interloper, something to be feared. It's exhausting, as you well know, yet now I'm not sure how I survived for so long. Taking small sips of life, lest I be discovered for what I really was. There is no describing it, what it feels to live in the open like this. To appreciate the quiet moments with Addie—to hold her hand while in the garden. To plait her hair at night before bed. To peel oranges together on a warm summer morning. This, above all else, has made our arduous journey worth it.

I was fully crying by the end of it, Harper wiping my cheeks and kissing my temples. "Thank you," I finally said. "Thank you so much for showing me this."

She turned my head to kiss me properly, right there in the exhibit, surrounded by pages and pages of bold and defiant words. Brave and honest words. Revolutionary words. "I love you, Eve. You've made the arduous worth it. So very, *very* worth it."

With my thumbs, I swiped away her tears and felt my own heart bursting with hope. "I love you so much, Harper. I want to spend the rest of my life going on adventures with you."

She reached into her pocket and unfurled the treasure map I'd made her with a big, beaming smile. "I'm ready if you are."

So we did just that, tearing off down the road toward our next destination with the windows rolled down and the music turned up.

We had a whole lot of magic in this world left to see.

• • •

READ A DELETED SCENE FROM *THRILL OF THE CHASE*

More Eve. More Harper. More heat.

Acknowledgments

A singular image from this story has been with me from the very beginning, through every revision and iteration: Eve and Harper in the desert at night, sprawled out in the dirt, their flashlights sending up a miniature spotlight on the mysterious figure standing in front of them. Cowboy hat. Shotgun. Cocky smile.

The Monty Montana.

This happens for a lot of writers—a story first appears as an image like this one, created by the tiny movie-maker in our own minds. And then it sweeps you away...which is exactly how I felt writing *Thrill of the Chase*.

Harper and Eve first appeared to me on a quiet summer night in August 2020, while I was watching fireflies in a field in Vermont. They showed up in a different form then, in an entirely different story, until the spring of 2021, when I realized these two bisexual babes were desperate for a jaunty adventure tale. And they stayed with me in the background as I published other books, then re-tackled their story through many painful drafts and *then* began the querying process in 2023 before Eve and Harper finally landed with the fabulous folks at Entangled.

All of that to say—the three of us have been on our *own* arduous journey, and I thought that I was ready to let them go. But now that I'm here, writing this acknowledgment, it feels like my heart is breaking. I have *loved* these women and their joyfully messy quest for authenticity and true love. And I have loved Monty Montana—loved her brash confidence and cocky cigar smoking and stubborn ways—with a depth I didn't think was possible.

This story, like all stories, comes from community. I am so grateful to books like *When Brooklyn Was Queer* and the *Making Gay History* podcast, the various articles I read on radical queer history in the southwest, Instagram accounts like @queerloveinhistory, and TV shows like *Pose* and *Fellow Travelers*. All of them demonstrate what queer, trans, and gender nonconforming people already know: we have always been here. *And*...we have always taken care of one another by creating avenues and channels that exist outside of harmful structures and systems. Many of the themes in *Thrill of the Chase* developed from reading these stories and also through the mutual aid work I've been proud to be a part of in Philly since the pandemic.

We are in this together, always.

I need to say a huge, ecstatic *thank you* to my amazing agent, Flavia Viotti at Bookcase Literary Agency, for taking a chance on me and this story. And to Lydia Sharp, my editor at Entangled, who skillfully guided this manuscript through many revisions while teaching me so much about my own craft in the process. This book would not be what it is without her wisdom.

A huge thank you also to Elizabeth Turner Stokes for the most amazing and perfect cover art of all time!

My writing community held me through so much of this journey, many of whom have been with me since my early days of indie publishing (Joyce, Tammy, Laura, Tracey, Jodi, Julia, Lucy, Bronwyn). They inspired me to reach for this next glorious step and took care of me through so much of it. I hope I can return the favor someday.

Thank you to my family for cheering on my writing from the very beginning—that kind of lifelong encouragement means so much. And to my friend Kellan, who kindly walked me through the querying process with compassion and humor and made me believe that this was all possible. He made me feel brave when I needed it the most.

There aren't enough "thank you"s in the world for my soul-bro, Faith, who has been my steadfast cheerleader since we met during Sophie Kerr weekend before our freshman year at Washington College. *Thrill of the Chase* is here because Faith always knew it'd be here, and goddamn if she wasn't right. I'll find you in any lifetime (affectionate).

Finally, finally, finally for Rob—my actual treasure, the person who always makes our arduous journey worth it. Thank you for loving this world so boldly. Thank you for cheering me up every time I wanted to quit. Thank you for always longing for an adventure, planning for an adventure, and/or reminiscing about a past adventure. Greeting the sunrise with you every morning will always be the greatest gift.

Doubling the Trees Behind Every Book You Buy.

Because books should leave the world better than they found it—not just in hearts and minds, but in forests and futures.

Through our Read More, Breathe Easier initiative, we're helping reforest the planet, restore ecosystems, and rethink what sustainable publishing can be.

Track the impact of your read at:

CONNECT WITH US ONLINE

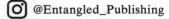 @Entangled_Publishing

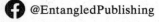 @EntangledPublishing

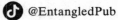 @EntangledPub

Join the Entangled Insiders for early access to ARCs, exclusive content, and insider news! Scan the QR code to become part of the ultimate reader community.